Pursuit of the Cryptics
Jacob Lake Trilogy, Book III

Gabriel Paulson

Hunters, Washington

Copyright © 2021 by Gabriel Paulson and DireWolf Publishing.

All rights reserved. No part of this publication may be reproduced, distributed, or transmitted in any form or by any means, including photocopying, recording, or other electronic or mechanical methods, without the prior written permission of the publisher, except with brief quotations embodied in critical reviews and certain other non-commercial uses permitted by copyright law. For permission requests, write to the publisher, addressed "Attention: Permissions Coordinator," at the address below.

First Edition.

ISBN: 978-1-950333-05-9 (Paperback)
ASIN: B09MJGJGKH (Kindle eBook)

Any references to historical events, real people, or real places are used fictitiously. Names, characters, and places are products of the author's imagination.

Front cover illustration by Ksenilia Denisenko

Book cover design by Jennifer L. Stoeckl. Edited by DireWolf Publishing.

Printed in the United States of America.

DireWolf Publishing, Hunters, WA USA.

For Cricket, my dog of thirteen years. She was my best friend through the diverse changes in life. She was the greatest Search and Rescue dog I ever knew. I based the character Angelou after her.

Contents

Chapter 1 Deep Well Negotiations 1
Chapter 2 Blades and Butterfly Knives 9
Chapter 3 Keepers of the Far East 15
Chapter 4 Attack of the Cryptic Creature 25
Chapter 5 The Song of Annaquinn 36
Chapter 6 Pirating the Pirates 44
Chapter 7 Friendship Hanging by a Thread 49
Chapter 8 A Role Reversal 54
Chapter 9 Fire in the Darkness 65
Chapter 10 Balladin Lights the Fire 72
Chapter 11 The Girl or the Spider? 80
Chapter 12 Lys mot Himmelen 85
Chapter 13 The Battle of the Crypts 94
Chapter 14 The Return of the Dragon 99
Chapter 15 Myra and the Masa Mabedi 103
Chapter 16 Two Keepers Too Few 109
Chapter 17 Tears of the Bowman 114
Chapter 18 Scraping the Bottom of a Shoe 120
Chapter 19 The Sangrahl Quarry 129
Chapter 20 The Wellspring Seal 136
Chapter 21 The Kulning Call 141
Chapter 22 The Surrogate Keeper 147
Chapter 23 Fire Letters 153

Chapter 24 The Wolf and the Cryptic Creature 159

Chapter 25 Kulning Cows and Wolves 165

Chapter 26 A Silence in Ghost Hollow 176

Chapter 27 A River of Lost Souls 181

Chapter 28 The Key That Opens the Crypt 186

Chapter 29 Vacancy of Home and Heart 193

Chapter 30 Broken Agreements 198

Chapter 31 The Roman Moor Bathhouse 203

Chapter 32 The Coiled Snake 212

Chapter 33 Into the Snake Pit 214

Chapter 34 Stone Channels and Broken Bones 221

Chapter 35 A Healer in the Lost City 232

Chapter 36 Where Fore Art Thou Keepers? 240

Chapter 37 The Battle of the Ghost Ships 254

Chapter 38 The Return of Jacob Lake 263

Chapter 39 The Battle of Masa Mabedi 269

Chapter 40 Gathering of the Seven 279

Chapter 41 The Immortal Mortal 286

Chapter 42 Return to the Dance 292

Chapter 1
Deep Well Negotiations

Shoebottom sat on a picket fence made of steel. Much of his life had been that way. On one side of the fence were pastures of green. He saw friendships, kindness, and the hard work that makes one feel the real purpose of being alive.

On the opposite side of the fence were pastures of gold. He saw the invigoration of the hunt, of personal gain through deception, and making the kill through agility and cunning.

At one time in Shoebottom's early life, he had walked the green pastures. He may well have been a worthy Knight of the Sangrahl, had his footsteps kept the grass stains of that venture.

Shoebottom pondered the death of his mother at a young age, the repetitive abuse of his father, and what Shoebottom had to do to survive. The pastures of gold had opened their gates and Shoebottom was too willing to enter.

Sitting on a picket fence made of steel is not a very pleasant place to be. Though he had not been there long, he did not know how he got there. A prominent question spiraled in his mind, deep in his heart. Why *are my eyes beholding the green pastures?* Worse still, *why am I thinking about HER?*

The house cat purrs and snuggles. The family dog wags a tail while it lays its head on its master's lap. Many creatures covet love and affection, but not Shoebottom.

He stood in the dark and gloomy graveyard outside the iron bars of the mausoleum, where the Gevaudan sniffed at the remaining shards of Marielle's raggedy dress. The Specter of the Well awaited word of Shoebottom's triumphant conquests, but Shoebottom hesitated to approach the well.

Shoebottom circumnavigated the cemetery as if surveying land he had just purchased and was deciding where he was to build his new house. He wanted to be out of earshot of Araqnis, whose well glowed dark and red in anticipation of him.

Seeing the Gevaudan rip into Marielle's prison attire triggered something within Shoebottom he had not felt in ages. When he reached the pathway that would take him back to the inn, he turned, casting a wary gaze back toward the misty landscape.

He walked several steps into the forest.

"Araqnis and the well. Do they represent the ultimate pasture of gold? If so, who represents the ultimate pasture of green? Was it Marielle?"

Shoebottom regarded the last skeleton guardsman, but did not linger to observe whether the skeleton guardsman regarded him back.

"Marielle had given me the key to the cheating antics of that mongrel," he said aloud, not caring if the skeleton noticed him talking to no one in particular. "Little did the Keeper girl know she was abetting a criminal mind who would work against her."

He grinned at the irony. The expression, however, did not remain long.

"In her innocent, adolescent way of thinking, she attempted to convert me towards the greener pastures. Silly, naïve woman child!"

As Shoebottom continued further into the forest pathway that wound towards the inn, he could not get the image of Marielle out of his memory. Like a hornet that pestered him without mercy, he saw Marielle sitting in the wooden chair, the rag of a dress draped loosely about her body. She had wrapped the silk blanket over her shoulders, trapping the warmth of the lantern against the North Sea chill. He could still hear the calming of her sweet voice, so much like his own mother when he himself was still a child.

"Focus, Hadrian Shoebottom, focus!" he said as the third skeleton guardsman regarded him with ominous passivity. "The Keeper girl means nothing to me."

He held his head high and, with shoulders back, turned back towards the cemetery, saluting each skeletal guardsman as he passed. "I have much to be proud of, for most of my plans have come to fruition. Tuck is dead and I have from him the two remaining Petras. I beat the cheating Arthur Schachmeister and I have here, inside this satchel, the Book of Sephus."

After Bo Eskatoll's death, Shoebottom had taken the book from Bo Eskatoll's rigor mortice grip.

Bidding farewell to the fourth guardsman and heading back toward the cemetery, Shoebottom turned the Petras in his left hand. Two Petras, as Araqnis promised, would gain Shoebottom attributes.

I could accomplish much if the blue Petra renders me invisible...

The one plan that did not pan out was Marielle. The Keeper girl had once again defied the odds against the professional criminal mind. She had eluded Dargo de Montebank four times in his pursuit of her, and now she had eluded Shoebottom twice.

But who is counting? Shoebottom staved off the annoyance that his score in capturing and keeping Marielle approached the cryptic Dargo whom Shoebottom detested and labeled both an imbecile and a fool. Should he detest the girl more, or should he congratulate her?

With Dargo, Marielle was always a step ahead of him. She ran away from home before he got there. She left Jacob's cottage just before Dargo's impending encroachment there. Her luck continued when she escaped with Jacob Lake into the vast canyon labyrinth. Her luck came from a thunderstorm and later from an imposing signal from Tuck.

What impressed Shoebottom was the likelihood that the girl must have faced Dargo inside the Wellspring cave before leaving him there to rot.

It was not Marielle's incessant luck that invaded Shoebottom's thought processes, but something far deeper.

Through the forest pathway and back into the cemetery, Marielle was all that Shoebottom could think about. It was her face that he could not erase from his memory. It was Marielle who put Shoebottom atop that steel picket fence and he had yet to slip the bottom of his shoe from it.

The presence of Araqnis deep inside the well threw no sunshine into Shoebottom's spirits. Shoebottom walked up to his familiar block of displaced stone and sat down, his knees straddling the rounded edge of the stone block well.

"Here me, O lofty Specter of the Well!" Shoebottom said with an air of mock defiance. "For I am here, Your Dragonship, and Bo Eskatoll is not!"

"You have succeeded then…" Araqnis's words were more a statement than a question.

"In more ways than expected. I fulfilled the minimum requirement by besting that neanderthal fossil you claimed could not be beat. Bo did not realize the Fire Petra was unavailable, so I brought you the other two. This surpasses our agreement and therefore, I claim what is rightfully mine."

Shoebottom took the blue and green Petras from his pouch pocket and held them in front of him. He heard a hissing sound like a leaky toilet emitted from deep inside the well.

"You know, O Specter of the Well, it is not polite to drool! Yes, I have far surpassed even your reserved expectations. Cunning and agility triumphs over wealth and power."

"*Shoebottom…*" The deep hollow sound of Araqnis's voice penetrated Shoebottom in much the same way it did when Shoebottom first heard it.

"Shoebottom, this is as I would have expected. Indeed, your cunning and agility make the very cryptic I had desired when Dargo took that honor from another. It is that genius that I desire from you now. Shoebottom! Release me and there will be no stopping me. Neither Jacob's sword nor the Sangrahl nor the forces of modern ingenuity can hold back the shadow of the immortal dragon."

"Once again, your credentials are most impressive, Your Slitherness. You have yet to send me that resume, and I expect it neatly inscribed on the finest linen parchment."

"*Ssssss*," came the sound of the hissing toilet, more irritating than before. "Shoebottom, if I should make you a cryptic to replace Dargo, what is it you desire?"

"What do you mean, *IF*? As I have fulfilled our agreement, it is now a matter of *WHEN*."

"What is it you desire?"

Shoebottom scratched the back of his head. "You know, dear boy, I had not even thought of that. Once I was a cryptic, I thought I would play it by ear, break in the new shoes, and test the waters. The only question that came to fare, kings and queens, you must beware! For Shoebottom, that's me, will rob you bare!"

"Rob them you will! Cryptic, you will become."

"I will be the most notorious villain in human history. So how does the process work then?"

"Do you see the mausoleums there ahead of you? You will send down the three Petra stones into this well and I will follow up by granting you the magic skeleton key that opens the middle crypt. Once you are inside, Dargo's immortal body turns to bones, and you emerge immortal. It is as simple as that."

"You mentioned *three* Petras. I have brought you only two."

"I have an important question to ask you, Shoebottom. You have spanned this world more than I. Prefiguring the ages that you have traveled, how would you take on the hunt for the Keepers if you were me?"

Shoebottom stuck his hand inside his satchel and took out Sephus's book. "Do you know how I found this?"

"Shoebottom, the Specter of the Well sees many things, but even I cannot place my sleepless eyes on every detail of your journey."

"I first took this book from Sephus himself. It bears all his notes and I believe some hidden messages as well. I did not kill Sephus, but his death came at the hands of Bo. Bo destroyed that which he could not see. We still could have used Sephus, for his knowledge spans beyond these pages. There is information here that not even you are privy to."

"Your plan of attack, then?"

"The Wellsprings."

The toilet bowl hissed again. "Go on…"

"As you well know, the wellsprings are the time portals to the Keepers and their agents. Sephus wrote here on page 346 that a dragon's fire can seal a wellspring which turns its waters into stone. Slippery ones, those Keepers. Therefore, I would seal every wellspring in order to corral the Keepers into one time period. Isolate them into one age with nowhere to run. Dear boy, the only way the Keepers have eluded us for four hundred years is by jumping through a portal we cannot follow them through."

"Then you will bring me the girl and the Fire Petra so that I may succeed in this task."

"You forget, Your Evilship, that I had succeeded in our agreement. I brought you…"

"Our agreement was for you to bring me the girl and yet you failed!" Araqnis's voice made the dark and gloomy cemetery darker and gloomier. Dead branches from the surrounding trees severed and fell to the misty ground. "Our agreement was for you to bring me all three Petras and yet you failed!"

Shoebottom stood up. "Those were not the full conditions by which we negotiated. Dragon or not, your word must be as gold to the prospector. There were three conditions for success. I won the match with Arthur Schachmeister, I have earned my place in the grand halls of cryptical history."

"I shall not grant you the skeleton key until you bring me the girl *and* the three Petras!" Araqnis's words boomed with a finality that would have carved its letters into the side of the nearest mausoleum.

"Bold words from one imprisoned and powerless!" Shoebottom backed away. He pocketed Sephus's book inside the satchel and placed the Petras back inside his coin pouch.

"Well then, dear boy, there are still factors by which you have overlooked. I am still a free man whilst you remain a prisoner in a dark and gloomy cemetery. You won't make good on your agreement, then I bid you adieu!"

"Shoebottom!"

"Do enjoy another three hundred years in captivity. I hope the water is pleasant down there."

At that moment, the left-side mausoleum's iron bars opened up. From the hollow depths, darker than dark, green eyes glowed, peering only at Shoebottom. The cryptic wolf, seven feet in height, emerged.

Though Shoebottom could only make out the creature's shadow, he knew that should the Gévaudan attack him by Araqnis's command, Shoebottom would be a quick meal. He stood his ground and fingered the hilts of his double swords.

Shoebottom figured if the cryptic creature consumed him, Araqnis would have no way of receiving Petras concealed inside the Gévaudan's stomach.

At the speed of a cobra strike, the creature flew out of the mausoleum and into the night. Though Shoebottom could not perceive the details of the creature in such a shadowy place, he recognized from its jowls the falling woven strands of a raggedy dress once worn by an imprisoned girl. In his rage from losing the prized Keeper, Shoebottom had given the Gévaudan that very dress—its scent forever branded in the creature's olfactory memory.

It was a rash decision. The Gévaudan was now on the world hunt for Marielle.

Chapter 2
Blades and Butterfly Knives

Shoebottom exited the cemetery with the hissing sound from the well ringing out like a leaky toilet factory during its testing phase. His feet trotted faster than his body as he ignored the skeleton guardsmen, casting their pointing bony fingers in the opposite direction of his footsteps. Shoebottom averted his eyes from the skeleton's forbidding gazes as he made his way clear of what he now labeled the Forbidden Forest.

Whistling an old tune, he found his minion, the half-witted Orface, outside the village inside an oak grove.

The simpleton was sitting on a stump, once again in the middle of consuming a leg of mutton he roasted that morning. The drippings from the mutton dribbled on the simpleton's lap.

Orface's one talent in growing up was roasting chestnuts and mutton. He focused too much on his supper to notice Shoebottom's approach.

"You've gained ten pounds since I left you this morning," Shoebottom said.

Orface swallowed a mouthful of meat, looked up, and raised one eyebrow. "You make dragon fly?" Elevating the brow on the right side of his face gave Orface the impression of having one eye larger than the other.

"No dragonflies here," replied Shoebottom.

Orface looked at his master as if his master had just canceled Christmas morning. His mutton leg slipped out of his grasp and into the oak leaf-litter carpet at his feet. "Why Chewbottom make no dragon fly?"

Shoebottom took out the book and placed his sachel into his saddle bag where his and Orface's mounts stood tied to a nearby tree. "No dragon fly, my young minion, because dragon not keep his word. You know how important keeping one's word is, don't you?"

Orface stared at his master for several seconds before the answer to his question entered his brain in full force. His expression exploded in a glow of ecstasy while he held up the fist that had earlier held the leg of mutton as Orface bit into the air.

Shoebottom ignored the mishap he had seen too many times and opened Sephus's book. "Unlike the moron that you are, Orface, I have a very detailed memory. I examined every page of this book except this last chapter on our dragon friend. Still, there is something about Sephus's writings that to me are incomplete. I believe therein lies a hidden text."

Orface searched the ground before spying his mutton leg nestled in the dry grass and leaves. He picked it up, and began consuming it again, dead leaves and all. "Yeah, yeah, Chewbottom! Orface understand. Orface never go against word!"

Shoebottom took hold of his horse and began wandering up the primitive dirt roadway. His eyes never left the pages of the book, though his rote memory took his feet just where they needed to go.

Orface followed on foot, forgetting that he too had a horse. "Orface want to see dragon fly," he said, pointing his mutton leg back towards the skeleton path.

"Someday, you will, Orface, I promise you that. For now, I have other conditions to consider. These ghost ships don't sail during the day, and only do they sail when the moon is out. We will have to wait until nightfall. Curious, these immortal blades."

Orface caught up and was walking abreast of Shoebottom and his horse. "Mordal what?"

"Immortal blades. Human hands did not forge these weapons. According to Sephus, here, there are two things that can harm a cryptic, immortal weapons and the bite of a wolf. That is the reason that fool Dargo would not enter Jacob Lake's cottage at the start of his hunt for Marielle. He thought the dog Angelou was a wolf, which he was not. You like wolves, don't you, Orface?"

Orface scrunched his face like a child taking a spoonful of medicine. "Wolfies eat Orface sheep."

"Yes, they do, and apparently they have an appetite for cryptic flesh. Here, look!" Shoebottom leaned toward Orface to show an illustrated page from Sephus's book. "There is Dargo's dagger, the one he used to kill Jacob Lake. No, Jacob Lake was not immortal, but it was Dargo's weapon of choice. See, right here, I possess the dagger's twin."

Orface scratched his head, trying to keep up with Shoebottom's words. "I do like wolfies, though, specially little wolfies."

Shoebottom turned a page in the book. "The only other immortal weapons are Jacob's sword and 'butterfly knives in the Channel of Lost Souls.' What the hell are butterfly knives?"

The half-wit scratched the back of his head with his other hand. "Orface spread butterfly on his bread! That's what butterfly knives are for."

"Useless objects," Shoebottom agreed. "No one knows their location, so we can count them out. Still…"

Orface threw away the bone of the mutton leg and let out a belch that shook the autumn leaves out of the nearby trees.

"Orface, there is something else to consider."

A smile affixed to Orface's face. Though the simpleton seldom had an idea as to the meaning of Shoebottom's meanderings, it pleased him to feel important.

"Araqnis," Shoebottom said.

"Dragon fly?"

"Yes, when the dragon flies, we may be in for more than what we bargained for. I believe perhaps we could even the score, but still keep the bargaining tools needed in order to keep our hands in the game."

Shoebottom stopped. He stared after Orface, who did not realize for five more steps that the journey had come to an abrupt halt.

Orface stopped, looking around to find out how his master disappeared. When Orface figured out that Shoebottom was five steps behind, he winced in recognition before walking back.

Shoebottom leaned on the reins to his horse. "You do indeed understand the importance of keeping your word?"

Orface nodded his ascent in such exaggerated fashion as to have blurred his own vision. "Yeah, Chewbottom, yeah, yeah!"

"Do you know that the best place to hide something is to place it where no one would think to look?"

Before Orface could answer the question with so many words, Shoebottom looked up and down the path to ensure no one was around.

"Orface, go pee."

Orface's favored brow wrinkled his forehead a second time.

"Over there, Orface, behind that tree. We don't know when we will stop again. You go pee over there and I will go pee over this way. Got it?"

As Orface obeyed by disappearing behind the burr oak, Shoebottom turned the opposite way and leapt well off the beaten path until his feet met up with the roots of an oversized ancient oak. Behind the tree, took hold of a rope he had hidden across a broken limb.

Shoebottom took hold of the rope he had earlier secured to a high limb of a different tree. Swinging, he spanned thirty feet before landing on the roots of another oak. There, at the base of the wide-trunked tree, was a hole worthy of the most finicky of ground squirrels. He dropped the leather pouch containing both Petras into the hole and placed a rock to cover it.

Returning to the pathway, Shoebottom jumped when he saw Orface's gawking stare at the wonder of Shoebottom's colossal feat.

"You did go pee, did you not?"

"Orface need paper."

"Oh, for Pete's sake! Soon, we will be back at the inn. You can hold it."

Shoebottom returned the rope to its original branch out of sight of anyone who should pass by. "Tonight, we call forth *La Constance*. You will remain at the hideout. Let me know if the knight with the dog should come along while I am gone. They have both been sniffing their way through here twice already. The innkeeper will feed you. Here is your coin."

"Where you go, Chewbottom?" Orface took the small sack of money, though his eyes remained transfixed on his master.

"I have business to attend to…" Shoebottom got up on his horse, "with a certain girl—so long as that creature doesn't kill her first." His hand fingered the lantern that represented *La Constance* while he turned and rode away.

Orface stood and watched his master disappear around the corner of the forest road. "With a certain girl," he repeated, as if digging the thought into his memory.

Turning around, Orface gazed over at the place where Shoebottom had hidden the Petras, though he did not know what took place there. He turned to walk back to the village in Brittany, whistling the same old tune Shoebottom had whistled earlier.

Then a voice entered Orface's head.

"*Orface…*"

Orface stumbled, for the voice came out of nowhere. "Who there?"

"*Orface*," came the voice again. It was deep and guttural, and echoed as if it came from the far depths of a water well.

Chapter 3
Keepers of the Far East

A Beal tree stood as the highest point of an ancient monastery that adorned a mountain hillside in northeastern India. Its wood apples and leaves shaded the tiled roof of the highest structure set into a hidden hillside nook.

The ancient builders set the tiered wooden structures into an obscure valley nestled into valleys of green. Concealed trails penetrating the woodland connected one monastery to another without access to the outside world.

The topmost chamber, the one beneath the Beal tree, was small and housed only a low, wooden table, hand-hewn and heavy as a barrel. Perpetual candlelight signified that the chamber reserved itself for something sacred.

A straw woven placemat sat atop the table. On the placemat rested the Sangrahl, the Lamp, the Holy Grail of all treasures. Though the carved stone vessel possessed no ornamentation, it shimmered with a dim light as if the gray, earthen surface progressed in its metamorphosis into pure gold.

Three Asian monks of an order long forgotten since the Fifteenth Century, sat crisscross outside the hut, and remained as still as the stone walls they guarded. Each guardian kept eyes shut in meditation while a weapon of choice rested in front of them.

Down the steep slope of the highest hut beneath the Beal tree were a series of equally small dwellings, identical in their simplistic architecture, none of them worthy of princes and kings. These were the dormitories, training rooms, kitchen and refectory to the monk's daily life.

Near to the bottom, the dwellings circled around a sandy courtyard where a young student sparred with an old master in a martial art soon to be lost in human history.

The master bore no attire or body features that would differentiate him from any other auspicious monk. His head was bald except for the tiny stubbles of hair making his tanned skin only a shade lighter than his scalp. Though his face was young, the small amount of gray hair on his eyebrows revealed a sign of his advanced years. He wore a simple Asian tunic of faded orange that he wrapped around his torso and over black leggings.

The master instructed a young student of a sort he had never encountered before—a girl. Her face was not at all typical of women from the Far East or even Indian. Her skin was milky white, and her dark blue eyes were, though captivating, unlike any that the monks had seen.

The girl wore the black costume of the student rank, not the white tunic of the disciples or the orange tunic of the masters.

While Tuck and Balladin stood leaning over a short stone wall along the fringes of the courtyard, they marveled at the progress Marielle was making in her training after spending a year there. They watched as the girl's movements became fluid, her stance light and strong, and her hands fast as lightning.

When her master projected a series of complicated attacks, the girl's movements were in perfect unison with the master's. Where the master's hand had penetrated her defenses just days prior, it found her blocking maneuvers now anticipating well ahead of the attack.

"A dance…" Tuck pondered. "It is like she has engaged herself in a perfect choreography with her teacher.

Place them onto an elaborate stage with a full orchestra and they would be a thing of beauty to behold."

"She is doing well," said Balladin. "I believe she would give me quite the challenge if we were to spar with each other. There is a talent in that girl. She may be ready for whatever may come."

"Shoebottom?"

"Perhaps—but a man like Shoebottom is battle hardened while Marielle has never hurt anything beyond a spider or a fly. What Marielle would have over Shoebottom is Shoebottom's ignorance of her new skill."

"Do not forget, my good friend, that this girl did kick an iron door into the skull of one Bouffee le Ph'art. That was before any of this training. Could she beat you in a sparring match?"

Balladin smiled. "Even a humble monk like me would not want to admit it if she could. Had I not renewed my own training in this rare and sacred setting, she might have displaced me to the ground yesterday. Look at how fast she moves her hands, relaxed and supple."

"I noticed her eyes are in constant on her opponent's middle. Wherever his body turns, she knows where the hand or foot will come."

"You are as observant with the eyes, Tuck, as you are skilled with the bow."

Marielle moved her body in constant response to her master's unpredictable movements. Her steps worked forward and backward, side right and side left, in response to each invasive maneuver by her instructor. A block with her left hand was in unison to an attack with her right. When her master took hold of her arm, she circled the hold, forcing its release so that her opponent could not control her.

The master improvised skilled attacks with both fists and feet, but for the first time, could no longer infiltrate Marielle's relaxed defenses. The dance was approaching perfection.

Tuck leaned an elbow atop the stone wall and placed a hand against his chin. "You know, it is funny, Bal. When I first met Marielle at her high school over a year ago, she was just schoolgirl. Look how her strength and prowess make her even more attractive."

"It is her athleticism, Tuck. Her strength and confidence have made it so."

Tuck nodded. "I agree. All of that mixes with a girl with the kindest heart of anyone I have ever known."

Balladin smiled. "It gladdens me, Tuck, that she has a talent for hand-to-hand self-defense. When I found Shoebottom's pirates approaching her on that Irish beach, I recognized she had no way of defending herself. Had Angelou and I not been there, she would have died."

"Or worse," said Tuck with a furrowed brow.

In a moment of pause, Marielle held her right hand forward, relaxed and ready. Her left hand mimicked the other, but protected her middle.

One last clash ensued between master and student until the master ended the fray with a loop kick behind Marielle's knee, sending her off balance. A push with a hand between her collar bones caused her to fall onto her backside.

The master smiled and hinted a bow. He offered her a hand and helped her to her feet.

"Tuck, did you see that? The master bowed."

"What does that mean?"

"In this culture, a bow represents the respect of an equal. A master bows like that to his upper-level disciples. I do not know if he intended to give her that honor, yet there it was."

Tuck placed a hand on his friend's shoulder. "We're living in the Fifth Age still, brother. How did you know about this place?"

Balladin smiled his contagious smile. "This is near to where I grew up over three centuries ago." Balladin pointed behind them toward a deep, green valley. "Right at the end of that canyon was where I met Jacob Lake and his father for the first time. Jacobi and I were just fifteen. We connected almost from the start. He too trained with me for about a year."

"Why did we not go to your home monastery to train?"

Balladin's forehead tensed with a distant memory. "It is no longer there. The regional overlord could not bear to see the monks thriving in their practices. They attacked on a day Jacobi and I took a day hike to see some ancient ruins. His father had just given Jacobi his sword, the same one Jacobi carries now.

"Did the overlord harm the monks? Did any of them die?"

Balladin regarded his brother with sadness. "None of them survived. This evil man's forces killed all of my brothers, including Jacobi's father. He burned the monastery to the ground. He did not come here, because this monastery, this place where we are standing, was secret and hidden to the rest of the world."

Tuck turned and folded his arms. Gazing into the wooded valley, he felt a sadness at what had taken place there.

Friendship… Tuck had never known friends like these. Through the winter since Jacob Lake's return, the four of them and Angelou had spent their time together. They talked of their plans and what to do next in their shared mission. They bonded into a kinship closer than family.

Tuck patted a gesture of understanding on Balladin's shoulder.

"How did I do?" Marielle approached them, wiping the sweat from her brow with a white cloth rag.

Balladin turned and regarded her. He had no words, but nodded with an approving smile.

Tuck shook his head. "I just hope I don't one day upset you. If you had this skill when living in the Grand Canyon alcove, I would never have insisted on taking Angelou from you."

Marielle grinned at the compliment. "That's right. I would have thrown you straight to the ground. Regardless, Tuck, I will never be as good as you at the bow. The master taught me the butterfly knives. I think that will be my weapon of choice."

Marielle opened a wooden box and took out a pair of identical blades. The steel of the knives was broad as a hand, and sharp as a razor. Its tip was without a point, but the edge curved to the broadside of the blade. The handle protected the hands with a curvature of white steel bands.

"The handles are part of the weapon. You can block attack as if the blades were an extension to the hands. I can move faster with these than a swordsman with blades like Balladin's."

"Very impressive!" said a voice from behind them.

Marielle knew the voice and saw that Jacob Lake and Angelou had returned from their latest quest. "Jake!" she called out, her eyes afire with affection.

Marielle returned the blades to the box. She was about to jump into his arms, to hold him tight with all her strength and kiss him as she had become accustomed to doing. Her hesitation came with the realization that there were strict rules regarding outward affection inside the walls of the monastery. Their embrace would await a later time.

Angelou, too, lopped in with a wagging tail and danced around her familiar companions.

Tuck put a hand on Jacob's shoulder. "Any luck?"

Jacob shook his head. He sat back against the same half wall Tuck and Balladin had been leaning over. His father's sword with the Fire Petra rested in a belt across his back.

"Angelou appeared to be hot on Shoebottom's trail. I don't know how he does it, but we always end up on a dead-end path."

"Where did you end up?" said Tuck.

"She guided me twice into Brittany. Our path ended in a Gaulish village inside an abandoned inn. On a table in the corner was a chessboard, still presented as if the players and the town had all vacated the place just after the checkmate. I was there twice, and the scene was identical. Nothing had changed in four months."

Marielle regarded Jacob, and all expressions washed from her face. "Jake, I believe Shoebottom played that match."

The others looked at her. "What makes you say that?"

"Was a knight at D-6 guarding the white queen at E-8? Did the white queen take the black king at checkmate at F-8?"

Jacob's eyes blinked in wonder at Marielle's perception. "How would you have come up with that?"

"Shoebottom... Jake, he described that play with precise detail by showing me the setup in the under hold prison. He must have replayed his opponent in much the same fashion but with a different result."

Jacob sighed. "What is the significance of such a match?"

Marielle shook her head. "I really do not know, but I know it was important to him."

"Angelou had taken me into Brittany before, but we could never figure out where Shoebottom went after that primitive village. Shoebottom's trail always went cold."

Balladin nodded his head in thought. "Someday, Jacobi, we will find him and from him win back the petras."

Jacob nodded in agreement. "So long as he doesn't use them to free Araqnis. That haunts my dreams when I go to sleep at night. So far, we look to the skies and find no dragon."

As Marielle took Jacob by the hand, she led him away from the courtyard. "Sorry guys, I request some alone time with my guy. We will continue this discussion come morning!"

Marielle guided Jacob out of the training arena and towards the guest dormitories. When Jacob and Marielle found themselves alone on a garden balcony, Marielle threw her arms around him. Engulfed in his embrace, she pressed the side of her face into his shoulder.

"Never leave me. I don't know if I could bear to lose you a second time." She released her hold and pressed her parted lips into his.

Angelou sat in the doorway, tilting her head and panting up at them with a look of curiosity.

When Jacob and Marielle released their embrace but still held each other, Jacob could see Marielle's eyes penetrating his with an aura of wonder. "I love you so much," he said, his own face aglow with affection.

Marielle's stance shortened as she fell from the balls of her feet back down on her heels. She held onto Jacob's broad shoulders, feeling his grip on her upper arms.

Jacob pressed his grip, feeling the rigidity of her arm muscles. "You feel very solid."

Marielle blushed. "That wasn't easy. These monks have been working me hard. I was very sore the first month and wondered if I could even move. Look!" She stepped back and pounded quick jabs into Jacob's abdomen.

Jacob let out a short laugh. "That is incredible! Look at you! Whatever happened to that seventeen-year-old who demanded we turn around and run home our second day in the wilderness?"

Marielle wrapped a powerful arm around Jacob's waist and the two of them sat on a stone bench. She gestured her fingers towards her heart. "She's still here, Jake, just as alone and vulnerable as ever."

"Not so vulnerable..."

"Believe me, I am! I may have mastered some skills in defending myself, but I still find it so daunting that our lives are at constant risk. If you died a second time, I couldn't bear it. The first time nearly destroyed me."

"Until you found your valor."

"Yes, but that was unexpected. It is inconceivable I stood up to Dargo and knew just what to do. I still wonder what got into me."

"You're a Keeper."

Marielle leaned into the crook of Jacob's arm. "Yes, and so are you. Thank God." She peered up at him. "Jake? Our future is uncertain. You lost your chance to live out your life in La Bellaroche, the most perfect place on the planet. I don't know how I could return to normal once we deliver the Sangrahl in a year, and everything returns to normal."

Jacob gazed off into the distance where the sunset painted orange splashes of clouds on the western horizon.

Marielle sat up. "What is it?"

Jacob looked at her. "It is nothing."

Marielle relaxed her shoulders. "Come on, Jake, it's me. You know you can tell me anything."

For a moment, their eyes locked, and no words came from either of them. Jacob leaned forward and rubbed his hands over his face. "I had been thinking about it the whole time Angelou and I were making our way back here."

"What were you and Angelou thinking about?"

"Marielle, how does an immortal and a mortal live out the rest of their lives together?"

Marielle took her arms away from his body and clasped her hands between her knees. She gazed towards the waning light of sunset.

Their clouded thoughts came to an abrupt halt when Angelou stood up. Both her hackles and ears were erect. Focusing towards the northwestern mountains, she let out a low growl.

Chapter 4
Attack of the Cryptic Creature

An unseen darkness enveloped the cluster of tile-roofed dwellings that made up the small monastery. The sun had set and the stars above India poured into the sky, but nothing could dispel the ominous feeling surrounding the region.

Deep into the night, the monks heard the distant howl of a wolf on the hunt far off in the distance. It was not the distant howl that would send shivers through the core of one's soul, it was far worse than that.

Brother Nightwatch paced through the cobblestone corridors, holding a long spear in one hand and a paper lamp in the other. For the first time in a decade, he set his footsteps with a foreboding trepidation. He stopped when the howling echoed off the cliffs, louder and more threatening than before.

Brother White-Crane-Teacher appeared in the hallway corridors with Brother Praying-Mantis-Teacher. They found Brother Cook at the entrance to the main courtyard. Soon all the brothers, the abbot, and the master who taught Marielle her martial art style, all congregated on the overlook bombardment. Each of them focused their eyes to the northwest, where the howling had reached a volume far above what a normal wolf would reach.

Jacob found Balladin and Tuck standing watch just outside their guest quarters.

For the second time, Angelou growled with her full focus toward the demonic creature's call. She would not join

Marielle in her quarters earlier that night, but insisted on remaining outside the door.

"What sort of devilry is this?" Tuck said.

Jake turned to his companions. "Tuck, go string up your bow and ready the Tears of the Wanderer. Balladin, ready your double swords. I will wake Marielle. Something is afoot out there and it appears to be coming this way."

No sooner had Tuck and Balladin prepared themselves for battle, all the monks of the mountain monastery appeared at the main battlements with their diverse array of weapons. For some, it was the sword, others the lance or the bow staff. There appeared no fear in their eyes. Tempering anxiety was one of many disciplines the monks had trained for since the day they entered their order.

"Jake, what is it?" Marielle sat up in her straw and pallet bed. She held her blanket tight around her shoulders.

Jacob's face glowed from the flaming light of a paper lantern. "That evil Angelou heard earlier is getting closer. Prepare for flight."

"Why? Are we no longer safe here? What about my training?"

Jacob sat next to her on her pallet. "I believe it may be a cryptic creature."

"A what?"

"Like Dargo, only in animal form. Meeshayell warned me about it. If my senses speak the truth, this is the Gévaudan."

"The Gévaudan?"

"A most hideous creature. We have to move!"

Marielle scrambled for her training outfit and her silken tunic. She stopped and turned.

"Jake?"

Jacob stopped at the doorway and looked at her. Then he knew her intended words.

The Sangrahl!

Jacob stepped up to her and kissed her. "I'll go there now and retrieve it. Remain here and make preparations for departure until I return."

As Marielle put on her Madagascar silk attire and shoes, she took pause. "If only the monks of this order had gifted me a weapon…"

The brothers, old and young, knew their posted positions, and they stood there in collective patience. Though the approach of this cryptic creature was something they had never faced before, they kept their positions without reproach.

The Gévaudan was invisible in the darkness. His position was obvious to all of those who guarded the walls of Mountain Monastery as his giant paws disturbed the once peaceful ground. Its body snapped branch and twig as it zigzagged like a dog closing into its scented target. Even though it was still a half mile distance, the quaking trees revealed its temperamental pathways.

Marielle met up with her knights just outside her and Angelou's quarters. Jacob gave her the wooden box containing the Lamp.

"Altogether once again!" said Tuck. Gripping his longbow tight in his left hand, he was both proud and apprehensive.

Balladin kept his double swords crossed at his back, but he did not draw them. Like his brothers, he measured the distance of the enemy with resilience and patience.

Marielle pressed close to Jacob Lake.

"I need to address you all about what we are facing," said Jacob. "Only my sword and Tuck's Tears of the

Wanderer will have any effect on this creature. For I believe this to be the Gévaudan, the cryptic creature. Like Dargo, this monster is immortal. The extent of what my sword can do with just the Fire Petra is unknown."

Tuck placed a Tear stone to the tip of an arrow. "Where did he come from?"

"Likely Araqnis."

"Who is Araqnis?"

Jacob's brow furrowed as the cryptic creature stopped to howl, revealing its proximity to the entire world. "Araqnis is the archenemy of Meeshayell. I know little else except that he bears the symbol of the dragon. Fellowship of the Sangrahl, we need a plan."

Balladin drew his double swords. "Maybe we should attempt to destroy it."

Tuck said, "We could test to see if the Tears of the Wanderer have power to wound this creature. After one or two Tears, Jake, you could step in with your Fire Petra sword for the kill."

"Can it swim?"

All eyes turned to Marielle.

She stepped around Jacob Lake, affirming her position as an equal now among warriors. "You speak of Tuck's Tears and Jake's sword as being the only defenses. That means the monks here are in grave danger. A cryptic creature would not hesitate to destroy them all. If we stay and fight, many could lose their lives. That creature is looking for me. When I was a prisoner on *Le Vin du Vie*, Shoebottom warned me that if I escaped, he would release the Gévaudan. It required my scent and so I thought I would be safe. Then I exchanged this tunic I am wearing now for the raggedy dress Shoebottom gave me. Shoebottom could have used that same rag to mark my scent to that cryptic wolf out there."

No one spoke in reply, but regarded Marielle with renewed interest.

"I ask you again, gentlemen, can it swim? Down that trail a mile or so is the Wellspring that brought us all here out of the Fifth Age. If the Gévaudan is truly hungry for me, he just might attempt to follow us in. If he doesn't, he'll eventually catch up. Finding *The Rising Stargazer* at the North Sea port in Holland may be a way of isolation for us. We could set sail and preserve this sacred site and all of its inhabitants who have hosted us these many months."

Jacob nodded, followed by an unspoken agreement from the others. "Balladin, can you lead us to a back door? Maybe you should take Marielle to the Wellspring while Tuck and I delay it."

"No," said Marielle. "Jake, we should all stay together. If that creature gets past you and Tuck, Balladin and I have no way to defend outselves."

Jacob nodded. "Together then. Still, we need to create a distraction to hold this place free of being its target."

Tuck shook his head. "Marielle's scent is all over this monastery. I doubt they will be free of the attack."

"Let us do what we can then," said Jacob Lake.

While Balladin relayed their plan to the abbot, Tuck, Jacob, Marielle, and Angelou made their way to the opposite side of the monastery. They went through the kitchen and the food stores. Brother Cook's service door gave them access to the outside. There, they awaited Balladin's arrival.

With Balladin leading the way towards the Wellspring, Angelou kept her keen eyes and ears alert for anything that might lie ahead on the trail through the night forest.

Walking into the darkness was akin to entering an abandoned house at night, knowing that it was haunted. Each of them carried the trepidation about not knowing what lurked ahead of them.

When the path reached a saddle between two forested hills, Jacob stopped. He and Tuck watched with horror as the sights and sounds from the valley below showed an attack, not a following.

"With Marielle's scent all over that monastery, it does not know she no longer lives there."

Tuck began whooping and calling, but the sound of battle overtook the night. "Jake, he will kill them."

"We have to go back to help them, see if we can get that creature to follow us instead."

"On foot, we will never be fast enough."

"I am the immortal here. It'll have a difficult time taking me down." Jacob drew his sword and headed back towards the monastery. He hesitated when the flash of silvery-gray fur dashed ahead of him.

Angelou had taken leave of her place with Marielle and ran headlong into the night. With her barking and howling, it became apparent the dog had gotten the attention of the cryptic creature.

Tuck walked up alongside Jacob, who listened to the night sounds, attempting to discern what was taking place.

"She'll never survive if she gets too near, Jake."

Jacob's immortal ears had become sharper than when he was still human. "My dog has the creature's attention… and she is leading him this way."

"There sure is something more about that dog than meets the eye," said Tuck. "Let's get everyone to the wellspring!"

Down into the adjacent valley, the four of them ran, the slivers of starlight illuminating hints of the pathway ahead.

In a moment, a crash of trees thundered behind them, leaving the company no doubt the Gévaudan realized Marielle's scent along the trail. It was moving towards them, leaving nothing standing along its course.

Angelou burst forth from the woods and barked her challenge to the Gévaudan. For a moment, everything became still. The dog had closed the gap and stood there, her shackles raised, her ears erect.

"Keep going," said Jacob to the others. "Keep going, Angelou knows what she's doing."

Jacob lagged with Angelou while the rest of them approached the niche at the base of a cliff where the wellspring glowed blue in anticipation of a Keeper's arrival.

Marielle waded into the Wellspring and submerged deep within.

Though the trip through the Wellspring took around seven minutes, the warm, calming effects of the underwater swim did little to quell Marielle's anxiety of what all had taken place.

At the far end, she emerged in a forest of a different sort. The Fifth Age wellspring that had transported her and the knights to Sixth Age India began and ended at the northern western coast of Holland. A September evening chill caused Marielle to shiver as she scrambled to the hidden place where Jacob and placed the provisions for their return.

Soon the others followed, and they followed the path to the port where Hothgarth had scheduled *The Rising Stargazer* for trade delivery of the spice goods. When the knights caught up with Marielle, they celebrated the fact that they had survived and hoped that the monastery they had just fled from would remain safe as well.

Marielle looked back toward the wellspring. "Where is Angelou?"

The dog emerged out of the misty forest. She stopped at Jacob's feet and stared back whence she had come. At that moment, something happened that set everyone back on their heels.

Trees snapped and fell a quarter mile away. From a clearing, the Gévaudan stood. For the first time, they could perceive its horrific, monstrous face. It stood eight feet in height at the top of its head. Corn rows of matted, charcoal gray fur covered its face. Its yellow slanted eyes wandered from one knight to the other until it rested on Marielle.

The worst part was the look of its teeth. The cryptic creature armed itself with long claws protruding from its canine feet. Its teeth resembled the long, uniform fangs of a crocodile. He became even more haunting when he grinned, revealing his dental inventory in every detail.

The Gévaudan sniffed and then growled, homing into Marielle's scent.

Tuck nocked an arrow to his bow. "What sort of creature has his own time traveling port that allows it the ability to follow us?"

Jacob stood with his sword drawn, but even he trembled at the reality of Tuck's words.

Angelou's shackles raised again, and the dog closed the distance between them. She let out a bark challenging the cryptic creature, as if to say, "If you want the girl, you must pass through me first."

The Gévaudan let out a horrifying howl that shook the needles of the timbers surrounding it. He threw the forest into a violent frenzy with the tearing down of foliage and trees to snuff the life out of the offending canine who harassed it without mercy.

It was because of Angelou's challenge to the cryptic creature that the knights of the Sangrahl made it to the Wellspring at all. Fast on her feet, the Simple-Minded One dodged this way and that, keeping the Gévaudan from making a direct chase.

Tuck recognized that the Gévaudan had emerged as a black shadow at the edge of the wood. Though he could not see the details of the creature, he could recognize its outline. He strung a Tear-tipped arrow to his longbow and took aim.

His arrow soared, and Tuck was certain it would hit its mark. As the shaft entered the chest of the gargantuan monster, the cryptic wolf convulsed and fell to the earth. It struggled and snarled, but it did not die. To everyone's dismay, it got back up on its feet, resolved more than ever to destroy the lot of them.

Balladin grabbed hold of Marielle and, breaking her of the hypnotic spell that had paralyzed her, sent her into a full run toward the port in hopes *The Rising Stargazer* would await them. Reaching the docks, Balladin spied the very ship he hoped to find and sounded the alarm.

At first, nothing stirred on *The Rising Stargazer* or any other ship in the harbor. When Balladin sounded the alarm, the crew and commander of not only the *Stargazer*, but every other ship docked there, came to life. Multiple sailors stood mesmerized and fearful at the haunting sounds that followed four figures approaching in the night.

The eight sailors of *The Rising Stargazer* emerged out onto the main deck. They had finished the unloading of cargo for the day and were looking forward to port leave when they recognized Balladin and Marielle's approach.

Hothgarth, dressed in a nightshirt and cap, recognized Balladin and Marielle and understood from their hustle and expression, this was no ordinary set of circumstances that brought them there. He barked at his crew to make ready to sail.

Annaquinn emerged from her chamber, a knitted plaid shawl wrapped around her shoulders. She looked on with confusion, for she had little knowledge of what was afoot.

With Jacob and Tuck taking up the rear guard, Marielle and Balladin boarded the ship first. Jacob and Tuck were close behind, seconds before arriving on the main deck of the ship. From their perspective, they could see the spectacle far off in the darkness.

Jacob stood with his majestic sword drawn, the fire of the Petra burning bright inside the crosspiece. Tuck stood beside him, a Tear-tipped arrow nocked and ready in his longbow.

For a moment, all became still and silent. Even the sailors watching from each of the ships were remiss to let out a breath of air from their lungs.

Angelou continued to dodge and bark as the cryptic creature reached the edge of the clearing a second time. She turned and ran up the gangplank of the ship.

In record time, *The Rising Stargazer* lifted loosed the mooring and drifted out into the bay. The well-seasoned sailors knew their post and were unfurling the sails as if their lives depended on it.

The knights stood leaning on the gunwale of the port side and stared after the cryptic creature, who continued to throw a fit on the shore.

"Were it not for Angelou, the monks of Mountain Monastery would all be dead," said Tuck. "I hit it fully with a Tear and it just made it mad."

"Your shot was not in vain, Tuck," said Balladin. "It detained it. It felt the pain of your hit. Perhaps a second hit could do it further harm."

"Let us hope." Tuck agreed, though his face was a shadow of doubt. "How did that creature jump time and place and continue the hunt?"

Marielle held onto Jake. Though she had become a warrior among warriors, it still caused her to feel the impact of the mortal danger that had accosted them and Marielle still possessed no weapon.

"So that's what a cryptic creature is like," she said. "It may be strange for me to say this, but I think I would prefer Dargo over that thing!"

Jacob Lake pointed his sword. "We're not fully out of the woods. Look!"

At that moment, the Gévaudan pressed its body into the water. Though not as fast as *The Rising Stargazer*, it swam in their direction following the scent of the ship.

Marielle was correct. The Gévaudan could indeed swim.

Chapter 5
The Song of Annaquinn

Throughout that night, *The Rising Stargazer* sailed leaving behind the threat of the cryptic creature but not its memory. The safety they felt on the decks of the frigate did little to quell their trembling.

While Tuck kept a vigilant watch on the back of the poop deck, the rest kept a steady vigil off each side of the ship.

Annaquinn, feeling the tension, began lighting lanterns all about the ship. She looked about at where each person was. Tuck, the handsome older guy with the olive skin remained at the stern, oblivious to her gaze. Balladin, the charismatic monk with the calm disposition reclined against the starboard side rail, his penetrating eyes cast far into the darkness.

Annaquinn folded her arms when she noticed Marielle talking alone with Jacob Lake in the far corner of the starboard side main deck. She knew from the start that this must be the girl Jacob had avoided talking to her about during *The Stargazer's* first voyage.

I can see why he likes her, Annaquinn thought.

Annaquinn had been longing for the affection of a male companion ever since she came of age. Her father, Hothgarth, had been overly protective of her by not allowing prospective suiters anywhere near the girl. The moment the attraction became evident, Hothgarth would send them away.

Jacob Lake had been the solitary exception to Hothgarth's guarded demeanor. Not only had Annaquinn's father approved of the swordsman who had protected her in the market square, but had not changed his position when he noticed his daughter's magnetic gaze.

Annaquinn considered Jacob Lake to be the best she had ever known.

She placed a hand up to the base of her neck when she saw the young couple kiss. It was not long and passionate, but the kiss was fraught with an undying affection.

She found Jacob's two companions, Tuck and Balladin, handsome as well, but she knew her father would not approve of either one of them.

Annaquinn berated herself for liking men at all. She was, after all, the daughter of a famous shipbuilder. Why, therefore, would a prestigious and independent Irish lass require the prospects of love and romance?

Annaquinn sat down on a spice crate at the base of the forecastle deck. Despite the fact that no one noticed her presence since their disembarkation, she took in her breath and began to sing a favorite Irish tune. Her clear, melodic voice poured out in a perfect pitch and quality penetrating into the undertones of a ship far out to sea.

Her song was solemn and the words came out slow. Whatever anyone was up to, all eyes turned to Annaquinn.

Crochfaidh mé seolta, is rachaidh mé siar
Óró mo churaichin ó!
I will hoist the sail, and journey forth
Óró mo churaichin ó!

One sailor took out a pennywhistle while another took out a lute. They walked to Annaquinn's side and played along with their respective instruments, following the melody as if they had rehearsed for months.

In the second stanza, Annaquinn allowed her voice to ring out in full volume. A sad smile appeared on her face. While singing made her happy, the lyrics were sad. She continued with words she made up as she went, integrating them with the established lyrics from the written song.

> *He sailed away to sea, despite the coming storm*
> *Óró mo churaichin ó*
> *When word came to me, that he would ne'er return*
> *Óró mo bháidín*
> *Óró my little boat*
> *Óró mo bháidín*

She looked at Jacob Lake as she sang. It would not matter if the young woman standing next to him felt a little threatened by Annaquinn's long distance gesture of affection.

Tuck and Balladin moved to where they could better listen. The ocean, being now too dark to see anything, gave them no more cause to be on watch. Other sailors would take on the duty.

Hothgarth, too, sat at the base of the helm to listen. It had been ages since Annaquinn's voice carried a sweet melody and not since the death of Annaquinn's mother had Hothgarth heard this tune.

Annaquinn's song soothed their souls. Though her audience could not comprehend the full meaning of her lyrics, she could tell by their expressions that there was love and sadness in her expression.

In that breathless moment, each person on *The Rising Stargazer* shared a bond. They had all experienced the loss of a dear friend. Faces of intimate memories flooded their minds. The knights of the Sangrahl thought about Sephus.

Annaquinn knew neither the joy nor the despair of these battle-hardened men. In her song, she felt for a moment she was a part of them, no longer looking in as an outsider. To the young Irish maiden, she carried a magic that would heal their worries and calm their fears.

Tuck walked down the ladder and sat next to Balladin. Neither of them said a word, but their eyes focused on the Irish lass. Her voice, her face, and the gentle sway of her body to the rhythm of the melody captivated them both.

When the song ended, the sailors hooted and cheered. They were not a typical rough bunch like so many who took on the life and death struggles at sea. Still, they were sailors and sailors celebrate when it was time to celebrate, each of them having sworn from day one that they were in love with the shipbuilder's daughter.

They demanded in unison a second song.

Annaquinn looked to her musicians for ideas. The man with the pennywhistle put forth a livelier tune of joy and celebration in order to offset the prior song of love lost and tragedy. Some sailors hopped in subtle fashion and clapped to the tune.

Marielle became lost in her thoughts, neither noticing nor caring about Annaquinn's unspoken love for Jacob Lake. She leaned her head against Jacob's shoulder.

"Jake?"

Jacob took his attention away from the entertainment and placed an arm around Marielle. "What is it?"

"Jake, we both know that I am not in the Seventh Age sending the Sangrahl's light into the world, but something about that is bothering me."

"What's that?"

"The world doesn't seem to be getting any better."

Jacob looked at her with concern. "What do you mean?"

"Look around you, Jake. There is harmony in this little circle, friendship with Tuck and Balladin, this ship, Angelou, and our love."

"I can see that. Why does that bother you?"

"Outside this circle, evil, selfish people still fill the world. I thought that when we delivered the Sangrahl in your Fourth Age, it would turn things around. In the Seventh Age, nothing had changed. I hoped that history might have changed, yet everywhere I look, nothing is different. Are we missing something?"

Jacob pondered a moment. "You may be right, Marielle. Maybe we're not doing something. If only we had Sephus."

"Yeah, or at least his book. Sephus would have told us we weren't doing something correctly. So, if we are mishandling this whole thing, then Sephus was also in the dark."

"It is a setback I failed to find Shoebottom and recover the two petras. It's also a shame I could not recover Sephus's book. I believe there is still information within that we might have missed."

Marielle leaned into Jacob a second time. She regarded Annaquinn with a little envy.

"Such talent… She's a lovely girl, isn't she? She has the most beautiful voice and I love the color of her hair."

Jacob cast his eyes from Marielle to Annaquinn and back again. "Would you like to dance?"

Marielle looked up at him, her eyes wide open. "You? You can dance?"

"Recall, I come from La Bellaroche! I can hold step with this beat if you can."

Marielle's face exploded with delight as the two of them got up, held both of their hands, and began a jig that was neither impressive nor inadequate. Marielle laughed with each turn around. The sways and twirls were much like the first night she danced in Jacob's hometown celebration, but this time, she got to be with a man she loved.

Marielle's silken tunic that stretched just past her knees, swayed with a gracefulness that shadowed each of her steps as if the tunic lived for such activity.

Annaquinn's voice flowed across the ship, penetrating both heart and mind. Her expression fell contrary to the merry tune when she saw the young couple dance. Her expression descended further when she saw how the dancing maiden was usurping the sailor's adoration away from the singer and onto the dancers.

When Annaquinn's gaze made the full inventory of faces across the main deck of the ship, they came to rest a second time on the two companions of foreign descent unfamiliar to the girl of the Celtic west.

Tuck and Balladin reflected neither the exaggerated attraction she found in most of the sailors nor were they disconnected. Their eyes drank her in as if tasting a fine wine for the first time. Tuck and Balladin were the only ones still focused on the Irish girl's singing.

A smile returned to Annaquinn's face. She kept her eyes locked on her two new admirers. *Perhaps,* she thought, *perhaps there are others to consider… if only my father felt that way.*

Far out into the Mediterranean Sea, they sailed. Annaquinn sang and sailors danced. Hothgarth put forth the customary ration of mead, enough to keep everyone feeling buoyant, but not enough to intoxicate.

At the end of the third song, Marielle sat back down to catch her breath. "Just a few and I'll be ready for another go!"

Jacob sat next to her. Someone had set two wooden tankards of mead where they had sat before, and Jacob handed one to Marielle. "Salut!" Jacob said, clanking his mug to hers.

"Na Zdravi!" said Marielle.

Jacob looked at her with amazement. "That's…"

"Czech."

"And you know this how?"

Marielle smiled and took a drink.

Far up in the crow's nest, the watchman called out. "Ship off the port side fore!"

The music stopped, followed by two beats more of a sailor's step. Everyone moved over to the port side of the ship. Their eyes scanned the seas ahead of them where the watchman pointed.

There on the horizon, the shadow of a ship listed and rocked against the moonlit sky. While ships on the North Sea were common, it was the watchman's duty to announce any sightings, as any ship sailing at night could be a threat.

The Rising Stargazer, boasted by Hothgarth to be the fastest ship in the Seven Seas, closed proximity with the vessel in little time. Neither Hothgarth nor the sailors feared pirates, even those who may be on the hunt in the wee hours of the night. Hothgarth had Jacob Lake and the Knights of the Sangrahl.

The dark ship on the horizon sailed towards them as though on a drunken course. With its bowsprit pointed away, it led everyone to believe the foreign vessel was unaware of *The Rising Stargazer*.

Marielle took the rails in both hands in between Tuck and Jacob. "I know that ship," she said.

Tuck looked at her. "You've only known two ships in your entire lifetime. How could you know this one?"

"I've known three, and that is one of them."

Jacob's immortal eyes focused on the encroaching ship. "Marielle is correct. Without a doubt, that is *Le Vin du Vie*."

"It would be a longshot," said Marielle, "but Shoebottom just might be on that ship."

Tuck said the words that Balladin was thinking. "Is it ethical to pirate a pirate ship?"

Annaquinn stood up, listening to all that was being said. Her song was over. There were more important events taking place than the music of an Irish lass. She turned and retired to her cabin.

Chapter 6
Pirating the Pirates

In the fifteenth century, cannons used to attack other ships were uncommon. Historically, while the more prominent military ships adopted siege weapons adopted from the Greeks and the Sicilians, gunpowder had yet to be a practical military product and so cannons were rare, especially aboard ships.

When *The Rising Stargazer* took on the midnight challenge of seizing another ship, the practical approach was for it to run alongside it, hooking an anchor onto a gunwale, and fight hand to hand.

What left the pirate ship like a duck on water were three gross advantages of *The Rising Stargazer*. The first major asset was *The Stargazer's* speed. If Bouffée le Ph'art and Flaque le Turd wanted to take flight and run, they were unmatched by Hothgarth's engineering genius.

The second asset was Tuck. His longbow and his keen ability to shoot an enemy down with accuracy from greater distances made him an awesome enemy to the Frenchmen's pirate sailors. Even in the dark, Tuck could perceive the shape of a figure from two hundred yards and make the kill with one pull of his bow.

The third asset was Jacob Lake. An immortal, Jacob not only feared no death from opposing bowmen, but the Fire Petra affixed into his celestial-crafted sword made his ability to stave off enemy arrows with ease and protect Tuck. Henceforth, Jacob would protect Tuck while Tuck minimized the inventory of enemy combatants.

By the time the two ships locked, the battle was over. The white flag raised and the few remaining pirate sailors laid down their arms.

Not knowing if Araqnis had made Shoebottom a cryptic, Jacob Lake boarded *Le Vin du Vie* first. Tuck and Balladin followed. With the surviving sailors ordered to sit at the port side, Jacob, Tuck, and Balladin found Bouffée le Ph'art and Flaque le Turd nestled between two barrels.

The two brothers sat with an arm on each other's shoulder, singing an old French military tune and swaying out of step with the song. A half-bottle of port wine rested in each of their free hands.

Bouffée turned his blurred vision up to his intruders. "Ah! We are drinking zee oh-kay-zee-on!"

Flaque lifted his bottle in agreement. "Oui, d'accord! To zee oh-kay-zee-on…" He buried what remained of the wine into his mouth.

Holding a sword to Flaque's throat, Jacob lifted the pirate's face and said, "Where is Shoebottom?"

While sliding down to a near unconscious state, Flaque le Turd cuddled his bottle in the crook of his arm and sang himself a sweet lullaby.

Bouffée grinned as he watched his brother metamorphose into a permanent part of the deck. He looked up at his captors. "Shoe-bot-temm not see for zeex months. He fire us for not keeping ze girl in ze cay-jeh."

While Bouffée took over the lyrics to Flaque's lullaby, Jacob ordered the sailors of *The Rising Stargazer* to stand guard over the prisoners. While Tuck searched the upper decks, Balladin searched the cabins. Jacob opened the center hatch and descended the ladder.

When he reached the bottom of the steps, he realized that someone had followed him down. He knew from the scent of her perfume who it was.

"Don't say a word," Marielle whispered, putting a finger up to his mouth. "I will be all right." She held one of the captured pirate's broadswords in her right hand.

The two of them wandered the hold, each with a lantern in hand. While Jacob took his search toward the forward end, Marielle approached the rear of the hold.

The cage that had been her prison for a week remained where Shoebottom had commissioned it. Marielle thought the jail would no longer be empty, rather filled with food stores and a smattering of useless treasures. As her eyes adjusted to the dim light, she could see it was as she left it. The wood and canvas cot that had been her bed stood as a memorial to her captivity.

Marielle opened the cell door and peered in. Memories of her capture flooded her memory. She saw no sign of the ragged dress Shoebottom had made her wear. Though the memories of her time there should have been gut-wrenching, Marielle's thoughts were of how she had outsmarted the genius villain Shoebottom. She had bested the master of the live chess match at his own game.

Marielle fingered the front crisscross ties of the blue-silken tunic she wore on her body. She had put that same tunic on for the first time when she made her escape. Then another thought came to her.

Closing the door to the jail, Marielle moved to the rear where her tunic had once hung. There on the floor was a bolt of dark, shimmering cloth. She lifted the material up and ran her fingers across it.

Jacob came up behind her, still holding his sword in one hand and a lantern in the other. "No sign of Shoebottom.

Balladin called down from the hatch that the captain's cabins hold only evidence of the two French pirates, but no one else."

Marielle turned to face him. "Madagascar silk."

"What?"

"It's the same material of the tunic Meeshayell gave you when he restored you to life and made you amaranthine. It is also the material of my tunic, the one I found hanging right there on that wooden hook. Jake! With this, we all can ride the wellsprings without being stripped of our clothes along the way. We could take this material and have tunics made for Tuck and Balladin as well."

Jacob marveled at the material. "Madagascar silk survives the time travel… who would have thought?"

"There must be living matter woven into the threads. If the matter isn't dead, it survives the journey, right? The real question is, is it ethical for us to take it?"

Jacob took the material from her. "You mean, is it morally wrong to be pirating pirates? My answer is this, what else might be useful down here?"

When they returned to the main deck carrying the bolt of cloth, the sky in the east lightened with the promise of dawn. A mist from the north enveloped both ships and hung close to the water's level.

Hothgarth ordered their captives into the foredeck cargo hold except for Bouffée and Flaque who slept lifeless and still between the same two barrels.

Balladin and Tuck secured the hatch. "What do we do with these criminals?"

Marielle stepped forward. "We will not burn the ship, right? I will not have them suffering."

Jacob said, "Let's release the drunken captains before sending it adrift. It will be a full day before they're able to recover their crew and ship. It is not our mission to punish criminals. Our quest, the Sangrahl, that is why we are here."

Balladin said, "I found no signs of Shoebottom in the captains' quarters. The ship's logs were in French as were the maps. Illustrations on the maps are extraordinary and appear to be accurate."

Jacob looked at the artisan illustrations and perfect penmanship. "Let's take the maps. They will be a gift to Hothgarth for diverting his spice trade in order to serve us."

As the first rays of the morning sun tickled the upper sails, Tuck and Balladin found Jacob and Marielle in the center of the main deck.

Tuck said, "The pirate ship is ready to send adrift whenever we're ready. In the meantime, what's the plan?"

Balladin said, "I think it is time we send Marielle back to the Seventh Age."

Jacob scratched the back of his head. "Normally, I would agree. Last night, Marielle mentioned to me that the Sangrahl's presence does not appear to be having positive effects on humanity. She believes we might have missed something critical and we have to put our heads together to find out what it is."

An unexpected voice addressed them from behind. "Perhaps it is within these pages."

The Knights of the Sangrahl turned around to see who had spoken.

Sitting on the upper steps of the foredeck, was Shoebottom. On his lap he held a satchel containing Sephus's book. He had no weapons.

He stood up and bowed, "My name is Hadrian Shoebottom and I am now your prisoner."

Shoebottom held out to them Sephus's book.

Chapter 7
Friendship Hanging by a Thread

Hothgarth had arranged the sleeping arrangements on *The Rising Stargazer*. The shipbuilder was not only ship captain, but moral captain as well. He kept wary eyes peeled for anything implicating physical contact with his daughter, Annaquinn, and now that a second female was guest on his ship, he kept her separate as well.

The three present females, Annaquinn, Marielle, and Angelou, shared the same bunk chamber despite his daughter's objections. While Annaquinn feigned being allergic to canine animals, it was Marielle whom she disliked.

Whenever Marielle spent time inside Annaquinn's chamber outside of sleeping hours, Annaquinn remained aloof and elsewhere on the ship. At times she would be near the helm reading a book. Other times she would be down in the galley, giving suggestions to the cook on how to make foie gras.

Marielle had chosen for herself an optimal place to sit alone when on the deck of the ship. It was the very same place she and Jacob had sat when listening to Annaquinn's song the previous night.

In the light of day, the starboard aft corner of the main deck kept Marielle apart from the distractions of the crew. She had arranged the crates for comfortable seating. With a few folded blankets, Marielle set up a place to put up her feet, feel the wind across her hair, and accompany a cup of jasmine tea, a fringe benefit of Hothgarth's spice trade.

Alongside Marielle was the bolt of Madagascar silk she and Jacob found in the underhold of *Le Vin du Vie*.

She held open Sephus's book across her lap for the first time since Shoebottom had relinquished the prize information. Thumbing through the pages, Marielle was hardened to decipher where they were to go next and answers to why the Sangrahl had little effect on the moral compass of human existence.

Marielle reclined, knowing that the Knights of the Sangrahl were interrogating Shoebottom in the basement cell of *Le Vin du Vie.* She chose not to join them in their quest for information, but knew, whether present or not, that Shoebottom would reveal nothing to them. Marielle would await her time with Shoebottom alone.

As she perused the pages, certain words flowed from her lips. *The Light shines like Fire in the darkness.*

She read further and found another stanza she had never noticed before. It beheld information about the immortal blades that existed in the world. The butterfly knives drew Marielle's attention, for she had been trained to use such weapons. "Where is this *Channel of Lost Souls*?"

Because women were a rare sight to sailors long at sea, anytime either Marielle or Annaquinn were in sight, the sailors watched them whether passing by or working the riggings from above.

When Marielle perceived that their attention focused towards the opposite side of the main deck, Marielle knew the reason. Annaquinn had just emerged from her cabin.

"Annaquinn!" Marielle waved as Annaquinn looked across the main deck with a perplexed expression.

Seeing Annaquinn's hesitation, Marielle called out a second time. "Please! Come join me!"

Annaquinn looked around her for an escape route, but decided it would be rude to refuse and would be an obvious sign of her disdain. Why did she loath Marielle so? Marielle had done nothing to offend her. She was simply in the way of Annaquinn's dreams.

Annaquinn sauntered to where Marielle sat. "Yeh wish to be served, Miss?" Annaquinn's voice was anything but ambient. "I could get yeh another spot of tea?"

"No," replied Marielle. "It is you that I want to see. Will you sit with me?"

Once again, Annaquinn looked around seeking an out. So many times her father, Hothgarth, would summon her without warning and it irked her when he did. Now she longed for the summoning that never came at the most opportune moment.

With an air of shyness, Annaquinn sat on a crate set far too close, but there were no other options other than the gunwale of the starboard side.

Marielle picked up the bolt of cloth and handed it to Annaquinn.

"What is it?" Annaquinn said feeling the fabric.

"Hothgarth mentioned you make your own clothes. Balladin and I would like to work with you to fashion tunics and perhaps a dress or two for our time travels."

"Jacob told me about the time traveling."

"This material survives the journey. Will you help me?"

Annaquinn felt the fabric with a new respect. "It is a fine material. Yeh are sure this will spare you?"

"This tunic I am wearing now is of the same material. I found them when I was a prisoner right over there in that underhold."

Annaquinn gave Marielle a wary look. "Yeh want to do the work… with me?"

"We will also need to make thread. Balladin has offered to help as well. He has a great many skills and will be most useful in putting together a warrior's costume for both him and Tuck."

"How did you make the tunic yeh are wearing?"

"This one I found already tailored."

"Not what we women typically wear, but it is very attractive on yeh."

"For me, I was thinking about a long, stylish dress so that I may fit in better when traveling about. I'm a knight of the Sangrahl, now, and this will be my mainstay. Still, a dress would help me fit in when in certain settings. Look here, I even have leggings and shoes made from the same fabric."

Annaquinn ran her fingers across the fabric a third time. Her lips projected a hint of a smile. "Could we be makin' one for me?"

"Will you be time traveling?"

Annaquinn shrugged her shoulders. "My father and I have been a part of this. Yeh never know what may come our way."

Marielle returned her smile. "Of course, and even if you never experience a wellspring, the color of this fabric will highlight your beautiful red hair."

Annaquinn tilted her head with inquisitiveness. "Yeh are bein' so kind to me? Why?"

"Do I have reason not to? You have been very important in our quest. You have the most beautiful singing voice and I hope to hear it again this evening."

"But I've been so rude towards yeh."

"You have? I just figured you preferred your alone time."

Annaquinn took hold of the bolt of silk. "My father, good man that he is, he never gives me the freedom to have friends outside of family. Ever since I was a young lass surrounded by three brothers, I have always had to find me own pleasures. Papa would have tanned meh hide if he knew the half of it! What few friends I had, were always hangin' by a thread."

Marielle sat up. "Well, I'll be a part of your family then. You could teach me to sing harmonies to some of your songs. We could be a duet."

Annaquinn's expression lit up like a firefly. "Truly? I would enjoy that. My mother used to join me in song. Can you sing?"

Marielle shrugged. "I guess we won't know until I try. Friends then?"

Annaquinn mimicked her shrug. "Perhaps… Just know then, we too may be hangin' by a thread. It is the way it is with me."

Chapter 8
A Role Reversal

For the first time in his life, Shoebottom kept his mouth closed. He had no words for Jacob Lake, Tuck, or Balladin. He refused even to regard them. His eyes and attention were only towards Marielle.

Two of Shoebottom's actions perplexed them. Why did he give himself up and why did he hand over Sephus's book? When Shoebottom gave no answer, they knew there was no hope of finding out where Shoebottom hid the Petras.

The only course of action was to place him inside the only cell available, the one Marielle had been a prisoner in.

Shoebottom sat on the same cot Marielle had slept on a year earlier. He sat with his eyes his eyes closed and his back against the flat corner bars.

Throughout the rest of the day, *The Rising Stargazer* remained anchored to *Le Vin du Vie*. Balladin leaned against the poop deck railing. Tuck approached him, wondering why his monk friend had been quiet for several hours.

"We cannot linger here into the night," said Balladin. "Somewhere out there, a cryptic creature is on the hunt. Our ship outruns its sea-faring velocity, but we do not know at what time it will catch up to us."

Tuck lifted a hand to the left side of his chest. It had been over a year since he had smoked a cigarette and still his hand moved mindlessly to the pocket where he had kept a pack.

"We have no cell to hold our enemy on Hothgarth's ship," Tuck replied. "Jake and I were just pacing back and forth with these same concerns. I say, let's kill him and have him done for. It's what he did to me."

Balladin regarded his friend with compassion. "Never stoop to his level, my good friend. Come, the sailors will keep full watch. Let's discuss the matter with Jacobi."

Though invited, Marielle had no interest in discussing with the knights Shoebottom's fate and whether he should live or die.

In the evening light, while Hothgarth's sailors kept an eye out for the possibility that the Gévaudan could appear out of the sea, Marielle remained alone in the cabin she shared with Annaquinn.

She remained on the far bunk with her ankles crossed and Sephus's book open across her lap. Thumbing through the pages, she sought answers to the questions that had been haunting her mind.

Why had nothing changed in the world of humanity? Why were people still blind to the will to do good over evil?

She closed the book, set it down next to the Sangrahl, and got up from her bunk. Peering outside the door, no one was in proximity. She opened the door and stepped out of her chamber.

Angelou, assigned to be her overnight guardian, stood up. The dog gave a wag of her tail and panted with a look of inquisitiveness.

"Angelou, you stay here. I won't be long, ol' girl!" Marielle closed the door behind her like a thief closing a safe. Through the walls of the main chamber next door, she could hear Jake, Balladin and Tuck discussing their dilemma.

The rest of the sailors tended to their normal duties. They had to manage two ships together, so Marielle stepped out into the evening sunlight. No one recognized she was there, so she walked to where gunwales held both ships together and climbed over them.

It was at this very rail that she had leapt into the sea and swam to the Irish shore. Valor was indeed a trait gifted to Keepers for Marielle could still not believe she had attempted such an escape.

No one noticed when Marielle opened the hatch to belowdecks and descended the wooden ladder to the bottom. She lit a second lantern for with only one, she could not see well into the cell.

"I expect you would show up right about this time." Shoebottom lifted his head from the cot in the far corner of the cell.

Marielle hung the lantern in a gap in the bars and pulled up a chair. "Jacob Lake believes I am the only one who might get through to you."

"Oh, did he?"

"I told him all about the last time we were in this setting. Hadrian, I find it interesting that here we are on opposite sides of the bars."

"A role reversal! Jacob knows you are down here?"

"Well, not exactly. I think he wanted to be here, but I came alone. Are you hungry?"

"You are ever the empathetic one. No, my hunger is more than satisfied by the look and smell of the foie gras your galley cook attempted to make. You should hire Bouffee's chef. Foolish as they may be, the Frenchmen have explicit culinary taste."

Marielle scooted forward and peeked between the bars. "Pull the cot closer. Unlike Bouffee and Flaque, I promise I won't bite."

Shoebottom did not hesitate, but jumped from his cot and dragged the wood and canvas cot across the floor until he was just a few feet from Marielle. "You realize, innocent girl, that I am close enough and quick enough to snag you through these bars and make a hostage out of you?"

Marielle did not flinch. "Do you detect fear in my eyes? I am prepared for that. My advice is you make no attempt, you just might lose your arm."

He suppressed a smirk. *Will this young woman ever cease to amaze me?* "Agreed, mademoiselle, I would not want to lose my arm to the likes of you. Now what can I do for you?"

"You gave yourself up. Why?"

"Oh, so you believe I am actually a prisoner to you and the Knights of the Sangrahl? You think these bars can hold me?"

"It does not matter to me whether you are a prisoner. I want to know why you came here and why you returned Sephus's book? As the others searched this ship for you and found no sign of your having been here, you could have remained a stow away awaiting the opportunity to kill any of us in the dark, and yet you appeared. You knew they would jail you. It's the only reason we haven't sent this ship adrift."

"I agree that jail cells are quite handy. I am happy you recognize my goodwill gesture of handing over Sephus's book."

"Yes, it is all so perplexing to me. Again, why are you helping us—or is there something else up your sleeve?"

Shoebottom revealed a confident grin. "Girl, do you know why I win most battles? I know my adversaries, while my adversaries do not know me. I predict their every move just I now predict you and your friends' movements. I even knew that as soon as evening came, you would choose this time to pay me a visit."

Marielle leaned forward and clasped her hands beneath her chin. "You believe I am that predictable, do you? Did you predict my escape from this very cell one year ago?"

Shoebottom locked his eyes on her. "I admit, my lady, you are the least predictable of them all. I would never have guessed you would be so resourceful as to carve a skeleton key from a wooden chess piece, befitting to unlock this very cell using only materials within your reach. Here at your disposal was all that you needed to escape, including a wire lantern handle, sharp and strong enough to carve into ebony. Very resourceful indeed!"

"And a stylish nobleman's tunic to boot."

"What I still have not surmised is how you got past Bouffée le Ph'art. He may have been drunk when he came down here, but the most resistant of his multitude of wenches have never worked their way past that hulk of a human primate, especially when accompanied by that gypsy girl."

"Candesol." Marielle smiled. "I'll leave that secret for you to ponder a while longer."

Shoebottom nodded. "You are the only one in my life's recollection who has ever impressed me. You slipped out of Dargo's grasp four times. Yes, Dargo kept count."

"I slipped out of your grasp twice. Care to even the score?"

"Difficult as it is to believe, I did not come here for you, neither to take nor to kill."

"Then why did you come?"

"When one desires to best the genius criminal mind, one has to think like one. Look at me and tell me my options."

Marielle stared, but made no answer.

"Woman child, if you're going to win the game, you have to learn how to perceive the whole chess board, anticipate the moves ahead. Ask yourself what my motivation is for handing over Sephus's book."

Marielle straightened up, attempting to keep her composure. "Very well, you win. I've never been good at the chess game."

"I will help you. Consider—If I truly wanted to win, I could have become a cryptic and serve Araqnis and this whole affair would with all of you dead. Araqnis attempted to convince me to drop our two Petras into the well and recreate himself into the dragon he once was. Araqnis would not hear of it. He wanted three petras and he wanted you. Consuming a Keeper girl gives him even more power than even all three petras. I will bet you did not know that?"

Without blinking, Marielle replied, "The picture is becoming clearer to me. What is not clear is why you are attempting to offer assistance while at the same time releasing the Gévaudan to hunt and kill me."

"That was Araqnis. Oh, don't doubt yourself. In my anger of having lost you from aboard this ship, I did take that rag you wore and allowed the hideous mut to mark your scent. It was not my best moment. Even a villain should never act with emotion."

"Araqnis then released the Gévaudan?"

"He did, but again, I gave the creature your scent. Not my best moment."

"Hadrian, I still cannot see the big picture. Why did you come here?"

Shoebottom leaned forward clasping both of his hands up to his chin. "Araqnis is most hungry for power, for with it he could destroy even the angelic being who put him in that well. To face this unsurmountable enemy, you must understand this. His hunger for power is his only weakness."

"Go on."

"Dear girl, you cannot win. Araqnis needs no Petras to find you. He sees with a lidless eye. He smells like a thousand bloodhounds. With just the Earth Petra, he will be quick as lightning. With just the Sky Petra, he can become invisible. He will find you even in that cliff-laden hidey-hole you once thought to be safe in."

"Go on."

"Even with all that luck and fortune that follows you, you cannot succeed against Araqnis should anyone free him. Neither you nor that petty group you consider knights can withstand his cunning and his prowess. If that dragon emerges from that well, it would be like a chess game in which your two knights, your rook, and you, who remain a pawn, are up against a king, two rooks, and four queens. The death of all of you is a mathematical certainty."

"You liken me to a pawn? You recall I bested Dargo, and I bested you. Can a pawn do all that?"

Shoebottom looked at Marielle with a hand concealing most of his face. "Are you listening to me?"

"Why would you care about whether we live or die? You may recall that you took me for ransom, and I bested you in that contest. So, am I still a pawn?"

"You are the conceited one! A bishop then…"

"A bishop's moves are predictable. Knights are much more invasive."

Shoebottom blinked at her. "Oh, have it your way! Four queens against three knights and one rook is still a suicidal endeavor. You cannot win. Even though I handed you Sephus's book to help even the score, it will never be enough."

Marielle folded her arms and cast her vision down to her unclad feet. The toes from her left foot played with the toes of her right foot.

"Hadrian, knowing you as much as I do, you are not here to help us. You don't care about whether we live or die. So, I have to ask, what would *you* gain from all of this?"

Shoebottom smiled. "At long last, you are playing the actual game! Never assume your adversary is on your side! You called it. I am still at the center of my universe. Ask yourself, what would Hadrian Shoebottom have to gain should he become a cryptic? Play out the scenario! Imagine, Araqnis is free to ravage the world as an unstoppable dragon. He destroys the Keepers and their knights, he consumes the Sangrahl, and all the light and goodness in the world goes out for all eternity. The world becomes exponentially evil with each passing week, and every living soul becomes the dragon's slaves. Soon there are no good people left. Where then would I be?"

"You are already evil, everything would complement you."

"Oh, you believe I do things because I am evil? Do you believe that all criminal minds are evil? Most criminals are survivors and nothing more. My drunken father murdered my mother when I was six. He beat me at will until I was twelve when I killed him. Why did I kill him? To survive! I have been surviving ever since, but that does not make me evil."

"Then explain to me how Araqnis's triumph would not complement you."

"The world has been my playground. I love the thrill of the hunt more than I love being paid. Money is only a way to buy food or find a better weapon. When the playground contains too many bullies, the playground is no longer a fun place to be. If you Keepers should win, I remain that solitary bully. The fun part is, the other children who play there don't even know that I exist. I continue to outwit and outsmart all of those God-fearing souls who believe that a miniscule jail cell like this one can hold me for long."

Marielle clasped both hands between her knees and straightened up. "All right then. We'll grant you that playground. Return the Petras to our possession. You read Sephus's book. What power do the Petras have in destroying the dragon?"

"Even with all three petras imbedded in Jacob Lake's sword, Jacob Lake cannot destroy Araqnis."

"So, we lose no matter what?"

"Read the book. The chapter on the Winged Warrior holds that answer."

"If we win, is that something you cannot stomach?"

"Neither side claiming a full victory benefits me. Either I am a criminal among criminals or I am forced to live the boring existence of peace and harmony. Your Sangrahl is not working, because you did not follow the real clues in Sephus's book. Like the schoolgirl you still are, you possess this adolescent belief that you cannot lose. That will be your downfall. Did you consider that a mortal cannot live forever with the amaranthine immortal?"

Marielle opened her mouth to respond, but no words came out. It was the first time in their conversation that caused Marielle to shudder.

"What would benefit me most," continued Shoebottom, "is if Araqnis dies, and the Sangrahl does not reach its fulfillment. Then and only then will I become the most notorious villain in human history."

"You would have to become a cryptic to do that."

Shoebottom pointed out his forefinger. "You know, that was also my initial thought. I thought that by becoming a cryptic, I would have the power to live in freedom for eternity. Then came along a most aggravating stanza that revealed to me that a cryptic finds himself a slave to the dragon's will. Though I could think on my own, I have no will but to Araqnis. Book of Sephus, page 327. Does that sound like freedom to you? That, dear girl, is why I will enter that crypt *after* you destroy him."

Marielle leaned back. "For the first time, I am finally coming to understanding your motivations. Still, there is something you are forgetting. A life of good can be far more rewarding than a life of crime."

"We're not going through that again, are we?"

Marielle fingered the ties to the front of her tunic. "Do you know that a woman has a super power within her that no man possesses?"

"If you are referring to trading her body for favor, that has never worked with me."

"No, nothing physical. I'm talking about something far more potent."

Shoebottom folded his arms. "I find that hard to believe."

Marielle said nothing more. For several seconds, she gazed without emotion into Shoebottom's eyes. Keeping her eyes locked on him, she scooted her chair closer to the bars.

Shoebottom angled himself back. Though he met her gaze, he fought the temptation to look away. *What is she up to?*

Marielle drew her long dark hair onto the back of her shoulders, keeping an affectionate gaze focused on her opponent. With her other hand slid from her shoulder down to her hips, before reaching through the cell and taking hold of Shoebottom's hand.

Shoebottom flinched at the touch, but Marielle held his hand firm.

"Imagine, Hadrian, that right now I am in love with you. You are my hero, my confidant. I entrust you with my life and my heart is yours. Because you are special to me, I find ways to make you happy. I anticipate your longings and bring a smile into your heart. You are the sunshine of my morning and the stars of my night. You and me, Hadrian, and no one else…"

Marielle pulled his hand through the bars, leaned forward, and cradled it beneath her chin. Her two hands caressed his fingers before she brought the back of his hand alongside the smooth skin of her cheek.

Shoebottom stared at Marielle, wondering for a moment if she was attempting to hypnotize him. A sweat broke out on his forehead.

Marielle kept hold of his hand across her lap and said, "Supposing a kiss from me was not for mere pleasure, but expressed a love I could no longer withhold—a love that I reserved for you and you alone. Imagine there was no man in the world more special to me than you. You were my light and my gladness, and no thought passed through my sweet memory without you being at the center of my heart."

Marielle let go of Shoebottom's hand and stood up. She took up her lantern and walked to the ladder. Turning, she gazed at him again.

"That, Hadrian, is what goodness feels like."

Shoebottom's hand remained where Marielle had dropped it. From the top of her head to the bottom of her bare feet, his eyes followed her as she ascended back up the steps.

Chapter 9
Fire in the Darkness

Inside the girl's quarters, Marielle returned to being alone with Angelou. She leaned down and kissed the dog on the top of the head and invited her up on the bed.

With the sun having now set beneath the horizon line, Marielle turned up the oil lantern, sat next to her dog, and leaned her back against the wall. While Angelou snuggled in, Marielle opened Sephus's book for the fourth time that day.

"There is very little in Sephus's writing I do not already know," Marielle said as if talking to Angelou. "I understand every part of the script except for one particular phrase."

A knock sounded outside the door. Angelou lifted her head.

Marielle called out, "Yes? Come in!" She looked up to see Jacob peering through the open door.

Jacob smiled, walked in. "How goes it? Did you find anything?" With his sheathed sword in one hand, he closed the door and sat across from her on Annaquinn's bed.

Angelou wagged her tail, but did not relinquish her comfortable nook between Marielle's legs and the back wall.

Marielle rotated Sephus's book on her lap with the open pages toward Jacob. "Jake, look at this peculiar phrase." She pointed out the phrase with a finger.

"The Light shines like Fire in the darkness."

"It is a peculiar phrase. What does it mean?"

"Jake, it is not the words that stand out, but how Sephus penned them. Why had Sephus written the words *light* and *fire* with capital letters? He did not do that anywhere else in this entire book. Even more so, why had Sephus worded this phrase at the end of the chapter about how he sought the answers. Here, look…"

"Scholaris gave me nothing further from his writings in the book shown to me in the Great Library of Alexandria. I had been there many times, yet the answers no longer enlightened me. The secrets remain hidden. The Light shines like Fire in the darkness."

Jacob leaned back, his eyes peering at nothing as he pondered the words. "It sounds like a hidden message, a riddle perhaps."

"You knew Fra Sephus better than I. Would he create some hidden message so that others, like Bo and Shoebottom, would have a difficult time deciphering it?"

"Or even knowing it was a clue at all. Yes, Sephus was just that clever. Poor Balladin, he feels himself as nothing more than a shadow compared to Sephus. I remind him that Sephus was just a novice at this when he was Balladin's age."

"So how do we decipher the clue?"

Jacob peered at the written words a second time. "I suppose we have to get into Sephus's mind. What would he mean by *light* and what would he mean by *fire?* I know, Marielle, light is light and fire is fire. There are a few metaphors that correlate to these two words, but the meaning is basically the same."

"I feel it has something to do with the reading of this book… or perhaps *how* we read it. Do you realize that during the first months when we were traveling around the Fourth Age, Sephus would leave this book inside his cave chamber hoping no one disturbed it when we traveled to the Fifth Age. I think that was all a ploy. Since that time, Jake, we have taken this book through time travel. Shoebottom had it on his ghost ship and yet it did not disappear like other non-living matter."

"Which means?"

"Which means this book, like your sword, has magical properties. I think the Fire and the Light are magical qualities and so long as we think along those lines, we can solve this riddle."

Marielle closed the book, keeping her forefinger as a bookmark. "Jake, will you kiss me?"

Jacob stood up and sat on the same bed, facing Marielle. He leaned over and kissed her gently on her lips. When he released his embrace and looked at her, she still had her eyes closed, a light smile still painted on her face.

Opening her eyes, Marielle said, "You know, it seems so odd that when we were strangers, we spent so many nights side-by-side. Now that we are together, I never have a chance to snuggle next to you."

"I feel that too. Worse still for me, both Tuck and Balladin snore. You know we would all share the same chamber if Hothgarth was not so strict about family values."

"As were the monks! Guess things are a lot more relaxed in the Seventh Age. I couldn't be with you either in La Bellaroche."

"Poor you, having to share a bunk with my sister Isabelle."

Marielle smiled at the memory. "I miss her. She was a better friend to me in those few days than all my friends at home combined. Jake? Have you thought about…"

Jake waited for her to answer, but Marielle stopped short. "Have I thought about what?"

Marielle took his hand into her own. "Have you ever thought about our future? Oh, I don't mean marriage and all. I'm still too young for that. We have another year before my Sangrahl period is up. I have just been thinking about you and me and how we might spend the rest of our lives."

Jacob's eyes looked down at their interlocking hands resting on the calf of her left leg. "Marielle, what has gotten you thinking about this?"

"I spoke with Shoebottom."

Jacob looked up at her. "Without an escort?"

"Come on, Jake, you know I'm trained now. I can take care of myself and don't need a constant bodyguard. I prepared myself for anything. Look, he still lives within that cell, and I am sitting right here with no mishap. Besides, I think I know this man better than any other."

"How long were you with him?"

"An hour, maybe more."

"He wouldn't talk to any of us, but he will talk to you?"

"You knew he would. One can make an impression on Shoebottom when one outwits him. He's a grandiose narcissist if you want my opinion. Play his own game at your own risk, but do something unexpected and you leave a permanent mark."

"What permanent mark did you leave on him?"

Marielle shrugged. "I escaped. Shoebottom can predict his enemy's movements and, like the chess master he is, he can see eight moves ahead of everyone else. With me, he thought he had it easy. I did not panic after my abduction, I kept my head, and in the end, I outsmarted him."

"This is the reason he spoke to you? What did he say?"

"Much of the first part was small talk. He mentioned something about an amaranthine not being able to spend forever with a mortal like me. It was peculiar that he even brought it up. I had to wonder if he wasn't jealous of our love."

"Shoebottom has loved no one in his life, nor has another loved him."

"I think he loved his mother. When he mentioned her, there was a faraway softness to his voice. I asked him why he had brought us Sephus's book and why he was attempting to help us by doing so."

"And?"

"Jake, he saw a world in which Araqnis, the dragon, wins. He said that if Araqnis receives even the two Petras and comes to life, we have no way of defeating him. None. He described it as playing a chess match against an opponent with four queens on the board. Then he confessed he could never enjoy his life of crime in such an evil world. Whatever Hadrian Shoebottom is, he is not stupid."

"What sort of world does Shoebottom want?"

"That's the funny part. He doesn't want the Sangrahl to succeed either. He prefers things like they are now, victories on both sides and a level playing field for which to pillage. Of course, he wants to become a cryptic, but according to this book, he would be under full control of Araqnis. He knows this now, which I think is why he remains mortal."

"You found all this out by talking to him?"

"I did."

"I can see why Shoebottom finds you impressive."

"You couldn't see that before?"

Jacob smiled. "My Marielle! You still surprise me around every turn. Balladin told me he has never seen a more talented student when you trained with the master. This evening you gleaned information from our enemy without batting an eye."

"Training is easy, Jake. The question will be, how will I do in actual battle? In training, when a person knows her opponent will not hurt or kill her, it is easy to concentrate. Someday I may have to face the reality of death in front of me."

"I hope that day never comes." Jacob leaned forward and kissed her again. "Know this, you faced Dargo in the cave. You had your focus when you escaped Shoebottom. I think you will hold your own when faced with death."

"No, Jake, I did not escape. I would have died were it not for Angelou and Balladin. That is the lie everyone has been telling. I failed in my attempt and survived due to sheer fortune."

Jacob gazed at her. "Marielle, we will talk about our future when the time comes. I have worried about that too. Right now, I don't have the answers. We are walking a path neither of us has encountered before. I love you so much, that is all that I know."

Marielle returned his gaze with a look of doubt. She believed him when he expressed his love for her, but she felt he had to know something more.

The attention bell sounded on the deck above.

"Something is happening." Jacob picked up his sword and raced from the chamber. Marielle and Angelou were close behind.

A mist had blocked out the light of the rising moon. Shoebottom was no longer inside his cell. Looking out into the moonlit sky, Marielle recognized the ghost ship's silhouette amidst the clouds.

From *La Constance,* just a hundred feet in the air, Shoebottom held a torch, revealing neither triumph nor solemnity in his expression. He simply stared down at them with uncertainty until the ghost ship disappeared into the clouds, the flame of his torch remaining the only thing still visible.

Shoebottom disappeared like a fire in the darkness.

Chapter 10
Balladin Lights the Fire

Jacob and Marielle stood outside the cell that held Shoebottom. The cell door stood open. On the cot was the only thing Shoebottom left behind—a parchment of paper.

Jacob picked up the paper and read it.

"I told you these bars could never hold me. Marielle, because you continue to impress me with your audacity and cleverness, I will share with you one of my many secrets. I keep certain tools in the souls of my shoes. That and my father's select admonitions in my childhood are how I came to be known as Shoebottom. I wish you the best of luck in your battle against the dragon. I will place flowers on each of your graves. Rest in peace. -Hadrian."

Jacob and Marielle regarded each other. "You certainly continue to make an impression on people!" Jacob said. "If only I had your talent."

"It has nothing to do with me," replied Marielle. "A shame we have no way to go after him."

"He has the time traveler that was meant for us Keepers. It's the reason Meeshayell gave us the wellsprings."

Tuck came up from behind them. "I think we need to let *Le Vin du Vie* go. I don't know how fast that cryptic creature swims, but we have delayed here long enough."

The three of them walked up to *Le Vin du Vie's* captain's quarters, where two of Hothgarth's sailors guarded the doorway. Each of the sailors suppressed a cagey grin.

Tuck glared at both of them. "What's so funny?"

The taller of the two sailors said, "Just listen."

While the sailors stepped aside, Tuck, Jacob, and Marielle leaned in toward the doorway. They could recognize right away the voices of Bouffée le Ph'art and Flaque le Turd singing. Although none of them had offered the pirate captains a ration of wine, there must have been a bottle, or possibly two, stowed away within.

"Hee-hee, ho-ho!" said Bouffée, "We write a new song!" His voice slurred as he spoke.

"Yes, oui-oui," replied the deeper voice of Flaque. "Eet will make us fay-mous, no? Let us zing it again."

"Not until af-terr we take another tip of ze bo-tell."

A momentary pause followed with everyone outside assuming two wine bottles were bottom side up. Flaque was the first to stop. "You won-derr, mon frère, if ze song be pop-yew-lair?"

"Bien sûr, mon ami, bien sûr! Zing it again!"

Quand je bois du vin clairet
Quand je bois du vin clairet,
Ami, tout tourne, tourne, tourne,...

"Zut alors! How many tournes, Bouffée?"

"I zhink you say, tree?"

"Tree, not four?"

"Tree... four! I forget."

"So... *when I drink some clairet wine, ever-ree-shing turns, turns, turns, turns...*"

"How did zhe fatty ham verse go again?"

"You mean, from zhat ham fat-tee, we eat, forget our sorrows?"

"Oui-oui, zhe sorrows. Zo, a pig makes us forget our sorrows?"

"Not a pig, zhe fatty ham… No! Zhe wine clairet… Or whatever!"

"Et Flaque, ever-ee-shing turns, turns, turns…"

"You mean for you right now?"

"Oui-oui!"

"Ah, bon! To long life to love and zhe bo-tell!"

"Zhat ees ze nexta verse."

"It ees?"

Tuck shook his head. "They sure don't appear concerned about losing their ship and everything on it."

"Not so long as they have wine," said Jacob.

Marielle said, "Let's open this door before they pass out again."

"And hope they never publish that song," said Tuck.

When the light of day through the doorway hit their faces, both of the pirate kings shielded their eyes. Bouffée was first to recognize them.

"Ah, ma jeune fille, ma belle! You miss me so much you come to rescue me, no?"

"You are free to go, messieres," said Jacob.

While the sailors prepared to release *Le Vin du Vie* from *The Rising Stargazer*, Tuck, Jacob, and Marielle remained hard pressed to get the drinking song out of their memories.

Hothgarth sailed his ship away from the idle *Le Vin du Vie,* knowing it would take the pirate kings time to sober up, release the crew kept in the foredeck cargo hold, and muster them to reset the sails.

He stood at the helm and said, "Where to from here?"

Jacob cast his eyes toward the sea. "Hothgarth, for now, continue your course. Marielle and I will use the map room to find out if Balladin has found something."

Marielle and Jacob walked into the captain's chamber where a map table rested. Two lanterns hung and swayed from the ceiling. Along with the lantern light, *The Rising Stargazer* was among the first ships in human history to have windows of fashion adorning the rear ship wall and this too provided sufficient light.

Balladin was pouring over the Book of Sephus on the table. He had opened the book to the same page Marielle had last read. "You were correct, Marielle, in that the Sangrahl has not been reflecting its light properly. The early Keepers all knew what to do, it seems, but lost something in translation since the first two ages. Look here at this curious phrasing. Many secrets remain hidden. The Light shines like Fire in the darkness."

Marielle placed her fingertips on the edge of the table. "Yes, Balladin, I noticed that too. Jake and I talked about it. What does it mean?"

"Fire letters."

"Fire letters?"

"It's just a hunch, but in the legends of yore, there were such things as moon letters, water letters, and fire letters. They require those elements to make invisible messages appear."

"Balladin, that's genius! Did you come up with that?"

"It is based on legend, so it might not have relevance at all, Marielle. We're pulling a rope in a jungle without knowing what's on the other end."

"But it is safe to pull that rope?"

Balladin took hold of the Sangrahl and examined its surface. "It has been transforming into gold this past year, a sign it is working its light. Maybe it's not that the world has gotten no better, but perhaps the Sangrahl has worked toward not allowing more evil in."

Balladin held the object with reverence, as if there was nothing more sacred than the carven stone material woven with gold. He set the Sangrahl on the table next to the book.

"Jacobi, I have a thought that occurred to me earlier. Do you remember how you knew to light this Lamp to blind Bo Eskatoll and his men?"

"Yes, Balladin, but…"

"How did you come to know this?"

Jacob stood for a moment pondering Balladin's question. "I have no direct answer to that. My conclusion was that when Meeshayell restored me to life and made me immortal, he disclosed to me certain answers to questions even Sephus could not provide. My mind told me, but I have no memory of receiving it. Same as with my silk garments. I knew they would survive the time travel, though no one told me this."

Balladin took up a candle and held it near the book. "My first instinct was that firelight would reveal a hidden print on the pages themselves. As you can see, this is not the case."

Balladin took hold of the Sangrahl and set it next to the book. He held the flame of the candle near the vessel. He hesitated when he noticed the others shielding their eyes. "Maybe the Lamp only shines bright when it is needed to do so."

He set the flame to the top of the Sangrahl. As if the Sangrahl contained lamp oil, a bright flame ensued with the intensity of ten candles. The bowl-shaped vessel held the flame suspended just inside the rim. It emitted a yellow aura illuminating everyone's face.

Marielle looked down at Sephus's book. "There is something more. Look!"

The lettering penned by Sephus himself gave way to a unique calligraphy that burned bright and orange across the pages.

"What is happening?" said Tuck.

"Fire letters," replied Balladin. "*The secrets remain hidden*, are words Sephus placed with intention next to *The Light shines like Fire in the darkness*. He placed capital letters on Light and Fire as he knew well an inquisitive and observant mind like Marielle's would pick up on the clues."

Marielle, ignoring everyone's gazes, stepped around the table to see the fire lettering that burned into the pages, but did no harm to them. "Balladin, I picked up on the clues, but you solved this! Sephus had written a whole other text. Here are the deeper secrets." She thumbed through the pages. "Balladin! Here is the location of the Sangrahl's delivery. We could go there right now."

> The final reception of the Sangrahl cannot happen until after the Fifth and Sixth Ages deliverances. Go to the village containing the Light to the Firmament. There you will find the wellspring that takes you there. Be wary! Final reception of the Sangrahl will come from the Seven at the Masa Mabedi, in that village ruin.

Marielle folded her hands against her lips. "This makes no sense! Why would we go to a village where we find a wellspring to take us there? If we're there, we're there!"

Jacob shook his head. "I noticed that too. Village that contains a Light to the Firmament? Balladin, do you know anything about this?"

Balladin shook his head. "This makes no sense. Masa Mabedi? Jacobi, you are the linguist, what does that mean?"

"It sounds like Turkish. I think Masa is a table."

Balladin said, "Here, Sephus speaks of the definition. Mabedi is a shrine. Masa Mabedi is a table shrine."

Marielle said, "Final reception? Did Sephus make a mistake here? Does he not mean, the *final deliverance?*"

Balladin sighed. "Sephus never makes a mistake. In the interim, I will study the rest of the book for other answers. In the meantime, what do these words tell us regarding our next steps?"

At that moment, Annaquinn knocked on the cabin door and opened it. She held a tray with four mugs of ale and half-slices of baguettes layered with butter and Swiss cheese.

"I beg pardon. The galley cook prepared these for yeh by my father's orders." She set the tray down on a side table as her eyes flashed with wonder and amazement at seeing the bright light of the Sangrahl flame and the orange Fire Letters on the pages of the hefty book on the table.

"What is all of this?"

Marielle moved to stand beside her. "Welcome to the world of our quest!"

"Such magic! This is what yeh've been ponderin' on all those sleepless nights? Marielle, did yeh find the answers yeh are lookin' for?"

"Some, but there are still riddles here we cannot decipher. You wouldn't happen to know where there might be a village ruin containing Light to the Firmament?"

Annaquinn looked at the four faces watching her. "Yeh are serious, then? I know of no village ruin with that name."

Tuck shook his head. "Well, that's it then. We reached another dead end."

Annaquinn wiped her hands on her apron. "I do know a village with a similar name, but it's not a ruin."

Everyone looked at her.

Annaquinn blushed. "It's called Lys mot Himmelen. It is Norwegian for light to the sky. It's a wondrous place, so named for the northern lights. Meh father and my brothers built a ship at a port near there when I was eleven."

Tuck walked over to her. "Annaquinn, where is this place?"

"In Norway, of course. It is inland at the end of a fiord."

Jacob addressed the entire company. "We have little else to go on. Annaquinn, tell your father to set sail for the town of Lys mot Himmelen in Norway."

Chapter 11
The Girl or the Spider?

"The girl or the big, black, hairy spider?" Shoebottom sat outside the abandoned woodland cottage he and Orface had made into a hideout. "Which one would you choose, Orface?"

Orface's stronger brow projected wrinkles on his forehead.

"Seriously, you dimwit! If you had to choose between a pretty girl and big, black, hairy spider, which one would you choose?"

Orface cast his eyes into the sky with one hand scratching his chin.

"Oh, for Pete's sake, Orface, you would choose the girl! Who in their right mind would want a spider?"

Shoebottom got up to organize his few possessions for the fifth time that morning. The quaint little cottage had belonged to a woodsman, as the wares of the forester were all that remained within the beam and plaster structure.

It sat in a wooded grove well apart from the main road Shoebottom had followed to the small primitive village in Brittany, which guarded and concealed the dark and gloomy graveyard. The cottage was void of a door and empty square slots were all that remained of its windows. The roof thatching was intact and kept out the rain that fell throughout that day.

Inside the one-room house, a fiery hearth rendered the two men warm. A kettle over the fire heated the mutton stew Shoebottom had prepared and was now setting on a makeshift table.

Such a rude lifestyle did not bother Shoebottom, as he never felt at home in a villa or a palace. To Shoebottom, villas and palaces were temporary strongholds Shoebottom could penetrate for some form of monetary or perhaps personal gain.

"Flying dragons," Orface said at last.

Shoebottom turned his attention and glowered at his minion. "What?"

"Orface like flying dragons better than spiders and pretty girls. Flying dragons don't bite like spiders and girls do."

Shoebottom pressed thumb and fingers into his eye sockets and shook his head. He dropped his bag next to the wooden bench and stirred the stewpot. "There is no hope for you, Orface!"

He scooped two helpings of the stew into wooden bowls and set them on the table. From Orface's race from his tree stump stool outside to the dinner bench gave Shoebottom the impression that to Orface, food was much better than dragons, girls, or spiders.

"I cannot get her out of my mind," Shoebottom said. He walked over to the stool by the window, where the weather continued to drizzle. He sat down, peering out, but looking at nothing. "So many women have I known in my time. I have killed a few of them for gain. Orface, why does this Keeper girl leave craters across the top of my head?"

Orface paid no attention. He had already reached the bottom of his stew bowl and was now eager for seconds.

Shoebottom did not look at Orface's outstretched arm. He tried to ignore the empty bowl held out like Oliver Twist, asking for more. Shoebottom knew better than to allow the half-wit to help himself, so he took the bowl without so much as a glance, filled it to the brim, and slapped it back down in front of his minion.

"In all of my days, not a single person has taken me down that pathway. My mother did, I suppose, but with Dad's incessant abuse, her sweetness and kindness were the reasons for her dying at such an early age."

While Orface dove headlong into his second helping, Shoebottom placed a hand to the back of his head, unconsciously scratching. He circled around the table without realizing that his own bowl of food would soon become Orface's third helping.

"Why, why, why?... Why does this girl impress me so? She outwitted Dargo. She broke through her prison and bypassed the love addict Bouffée. She looks at me without fear painted across her face."

You are my hero, my confidant.

In Shoebottom's mind, Marielle's face transformed into another's. Her dark hair and indigo blue eyes resembled the brown hair and brown eyes of his mother. Impoverished, she was thin of body, narrow of waist, and at age twenty-four, held the same youthful gaze Marielle had expressed in the days prior.

I entrust you with my life and my heart is yours.

Shoebottom's mother uttered those same words in a distinct accent. She crouched down to her little boy, wiped the homemade jelly from his mouth with the edge of her apron, and pressed gentle lips to the top of his forehead, tousling his hair with her fingers.

Because you are special to me, I find ways to make you happy. I anticipate your longings and bring a smile into your heart.

It was that same day that his father, drunk in despair at the loss of his family farm, had strangled the life from that beautiful face. Little Hadrian hid away lest he too become a victim. For days he cried at the loss until his hulking weasel of a father found him, forcing him to suck it in and carry on.

Was the memory of Shoebottom's mother the reason for Marielle's impacting hypnotism? No. Shoebottom knew there was something beyond what love a six-year-old boy has for his mother.

Marielle's words continued to echo inside his head. He could still see the contours of her body beneath the blue silk tunic and the smooth skin of the calves of her legs as she walked up the wooden steps. Most of all, he could see the magic of her eyes when she gazed at him.

Marielle was correct. It was not her physical beauty that perpetrated the forefront of his thoughts. It was something far deeper, something he could not wrap his mind around.

Shoebottom…

Araqnis's words entering Shoebottom's subconscience interrupted his revelry. He realized he was being summoned. It was a summoning he would not refuse. Perhaps the old dragon was ready to bargain.

Shoebottom's eyes returned to reality as the empty cottage came back into his focus. Two bowls sat empty on the still wooden table. The fire in the hearth had reduced to glowing coals. Rain no longer pattered the ground outside.

Shoebottom returned to the corner of the cottage where he had left his bag. The bag containing the Petras was no longer there.

Shoebottom looked beneath the benches and the table. His bag had walked away into the oblivion of space and time—that was how Shoebottom saw it. In a heatwave of panic, he searched the ground for what must have occurred to the treasures he had killed for.

Large, sodden footsteps over the wood-plank floor from the corner of the house to the outer door revealed the culprit.

The large, sodden feet belonged to no one but Orface.

Chapter 12
Lys mot Himmelen

The Rising Stargazer brought the Keepers and the knights to the banks of Norway. It was a world only a few of them had ever been, encapsulating the magic of Norway and of all of Scandinavia with the northern lights.

In the cold, misty night, beams of light shot into the sky, swaying to the dance of an inaudible beat. The aurora borealis colored the sky with shards of greens and golds garnished with hints of orange and red.

Balladin put an arm around his childhood friend and said, "Jacobi, with you and Marielle seeing colors in the stars above, this must be so much more spectacular than what I see."

"Indeed!" Jacob and Marielle could not pull their eyes from the wonder of it.

The Knights of the Sangrahl, along with Angelou, disembarked the ship into a world much different from anywhere they had traveled. Norway was nothing like the green, rolling hills of Ireland. Dark evergreen forests accompanied the night sounds of distant wildlife, small and large, in all directions. While the dark soil contrasted with white granite rocks, the red leaves of foliage complemented multi-colored autumn leaves set into the coniferous trees.

The September night air was chill, and there was a fogginess in the air. As each of them walked the forest pathways, the steam from their mouths puffed like smoke as they wrapped their cloaks about them.

The roadways, designed for horse travel, provided white painted signs showing at each crossroads where certain villages would lie. While the Knights of the Sangrahl followed one map they had requisitioned from the pirate ship to find their way, it took little time to reach a sign at a crossroads that read, "Lys mot Himmelen."

The light of the moon, accompanied by the northern lights, illuminated the tiny village. Lys mot Himmelen was little more than a cluster of cottages. Thatched roofs topped each of them. Their four walls contained a mix of rock over-layered with white-wash stucco. Green shutters with red painted tulips gave the homes a festive feel.

The company moved along the empty dirt street that wound in the nook of a hill. Already wary of a village watch, each of them was ready for any challenge that required either sword or diplomacy.

"No table or shrine here," said Tuck, scratching the back of his head. "Interesting that we have come full circle. In Ireland, we wandered through Viking ruins. Now we walk in their land of origin."

Jacob, inviting Marielle into the nook of his arm, said, "It is a peaceful and quaint little village. I don't understand why Sephus referred to this as a ruin."

"Annaquinn was not mistaken," replied Marielle. "This town is very much alive. There are lantern lights in many of the windows."

Tuck and Balladin looked around. Balladin took steps toward the northern village boundary. Spinning around to address them, he said, "Marielle, what else did Sephus say in the Fire Letters about this place?"

Marielle pondered the question. "There you will find the wellspring that takes you there. Balladin, this is still confusing. How can we go somewhere then take a wellspring to go there?"

"Unless there are two distinct villages, one inhabited and one a ruin. Possibly this one takes us to another."

At that moment, Tuck looked up. "Something's happening. Look!"

The company turned to look at where Tuck had pointed. The northern lights, in their magical sway, had gathered to a more prominent point in the distant forest. Though the aurora borealis continued across the arctic north, one particular golden strand appeared much closer and brighter than the others. It hovered over a particular niche between two hills.

Angelou was already ahead of them, as if she already knew what lie ahead.

Following the dog, they found a pathway meant only for foot travelers, for it was not wide enough for horses to pass in each direction. There were also low hanging limbs.

Angelou guided the group towards an opening, the niche between two hills, where a small body of water cast steam into the air. The dog stopped at the edge, wagging her tail.

Marielle bent to feel the water with her hand. "It's a thermal spring!"

"That's right," said Jacob. "Scandinavia is full of them. It's a good thing we're here so late in the night, the village likely comes here during the day to bathe."

Tuck shook his head. "Light to the Firmament. It is just as Annaquinn described it. A shame Hothgarth would not allow her to accompany us. She would have loved to see his. I have to ask though, is this really a wellspring?"

Balladin pointed to the far end. "It has to be, look!"

What appeared to be nothing more than a reflection from the northern lights merged into a faint green glow from deep down. The closer Marielle approached, the brighter the glow became.

"Are you all ready for a swim?" said Jacob.

Angelou spun around towards the east. Her ears were fully erect and her nose quivered. She let out a low growl.

A wave of fear encapsulated each of them, for they did not know if the dog sensed a human intruder, a wild bear, or something much worse.

He is coming... Jacob heard the words Marielle had felt the night she fled her home in the desert village when she sensed the approach of Dargo de Montebank. Jacob did not sense the cryptic man, rather the cryptic creature.

The Gévaudan must have sensed their presence as well, for it sent forth a high, guttural howl far off in the distant wilderness that only Jacob and Angelou could hear.

Angelou responded in like fashion. She let out a long howl to counter the cryptic creature. Her attention, all eyes and ears, gazed off in the direction where the evening was darkest.

"Angelou, hush! You'll give us away!" Jacob was now feeling the favorable opinion Marielle had given that the Sangrahl should enter an earlier delivery. Addressing the others, he said, "Whatever we decide, we need to move fast."

The howl resounded again from an offset direction. This time Marielle, Tuck, and Balladin heard it. The pricks that occurred along the backs of their necks reflected the penetrating angst inflicted within each of them.

Marielle cupped her hands over each side of her face. "I sense that creature is headed towards our ship!"

Tuck drew an arrow and fitted it to his longbow. He replaced the normal steel tip with one of the Tears of the Wanderer. Tuck was taking no chances.

Balladin, too, drew out his double swords, though he was certain the blades would give him no benefit against the immortal beast.

Marielle, still denied a weapon of her own, stood in the middle. "I think we should go into the spring."

Balladin replied, "Remember what happened the last time. That creature could follow us through time and space."

Angelou placed herself between the distant howling calls and the human companions she insisted on protecting.

Jacob, not wanting to lose his dog to the creature who would stand five times her own height, called Angelou to his side. The dog, for the first time in his memory, refused his command. He drew out his father's sword and positioned himself between his dog and the rest of the company.

"Angelou, heel!"

Angelou stood firm as if she heard no command. She growled again.

The Gévaudan closed the distance between itself and its prey well before a hint of dawn appeared in the southeastern sky. Then it appeared a half mile away at the top of a ragged ridge. Though it appeared as a black shape, the sight of it manifested in the imagination, glaring, glistening yellow fangs dripping with hatred.

Without a further thought, Tuck let fly an arrow. Whether guided by the magical power of the Tear or by his own talent with the bow, it penetrated the Gévaudan deep into its chest.

The Gévaudan fell. Its cries shattered the stillness of the air. It struggled on the ground, sending sticks and debris in all directions. To everyone's dismay, it got back up, more furious and determined than ever.

Tuck's arrow no longer stuck outside its chest.

Tuck fixed another arrow and another Tear tip.

Balladin took hold of his sleeve. "Your shot did little to daunt him. Careful you don't run low of your ability to distract it."

Though the cryptic creature made two attempts to charge at them, it hesitated each time because of Jacob's sword and Tuck's bow. It appeared even more wary of Angelou.

Balladin pointed one of his swords. "Dargo was leery of Angelou, thinking she was a wolf. This creature appears to do the same even though Angelou is not a wolf."

"What do they fear of wolves?" replied Tuck.

"I don't recall all that Sephus wrote. The bite of a wolf has some effect on the cryptic, how extreme, I do not know. Even Sephus was vague about it, as if he did not know for certain."

Each time the Gévaudan charged, its eyes bore into Marielle. Its target was obvious. The dog, the swords, and the arrow were mere distractions to what the Gévaudan coveted most of all, the Keeper girl. Circling, but keeping behind boulders and thick trees, the cryptic creature sought a way to reach her.

Angelou snarled and barked, keeping herself in guarding stance. She danced in response to the Gévaudan's stalking maneuvers, daring the creature to come closer.

"Angelou, come!" Jacob commanded in desperation of saving his dog. He wondered what had become of the dog's training.

Angelou ran down the hillside, barking a challenge to the cryptic creature.

When the Gévaudan got close to the dog, it leapt, attempting to crush her beneath its claw-fitted paws. As Angelou evaded the charge, it snapped its crocodile teeth, but was never quick enough to make a quick meal of the dodging canine.

Tuck took the Gévaudan to the ground with another arrow.

Angelou charged in. She did not reach the beast before it got to its feet again and lumbered back behind the hill. Angelou took chase.

"Angelou, no!" Jacob implored. What had gotten into her? She had never defied his commands in the three years they had been together.

Both the Gévaudan and Angelou disappeared into the woods.

"Jacobi, you and Marielle keep going," Balladin said. "Go deliver the Sangrahl if you can. Let's have this evil time put to rest."

Everything became quiet. There was no further sign of either the Gévaudan or of Angelou. The cryptic creature had disappeared over the same ridge it appeared on, with Angelou at its heels.

"Oh, Angelou!" Marielle covered her mouth with her hand. "Jake, what are we going to do? She doesn't stand a chance against that thing!"

"I have never seen her act this way."

Tuck held up a hand. "Jake. Marielle. As Balladin suggested, you all go on ahead. One thing for certain, that cryptic did not like the taste of my arrows. I'm going to track your dog and see if I can't save her. I will try to bring her back and meet you back at the ship."

Jacob said, "No, Tuck, let's stay together as a group."

"That dog of yours is special, Jake. I don't think we can afford to lose her."

Without a further word, Tuck took off and disappeared along the same path as Angelou and the Gévaudan. Even in the darkness, their paths in the moonlight would come easily for Tuck.

The first thing he noticed when he stopped where the Gévaudan had fallen, a broken shaft of his arrow remained on the ground. There was no sign of the Tear of the Wanderer.

Tuck continued forward, hoping for a chance to save Angelou. He followed their tracks over the same ridge and disappeared.

Marielle regarded Jacob with fear. "We have to go, especially with that creature not knowing we did so."

Jacob looked at his childhood friend. "Balladin?"

"There is no telling what you will find at the far side of that wellspring," said Balladin. "I will go back and make sure Annaquinn and the ship are safe and keep them anchored until you return."

Jacob and Marielle embraced Balladin together. They wished him Godspeed, turned, and entered the warmth of the thermal spring. Swimming out to the opposite end, they submerged into the green glow beneath the surface.

Balladin sheathed his double swords and set off through the village. When he reached the dock, what he saw horrified him. *The Rising Stargazer*, though still afloat, looked as if a tornado had torn through her. Sailors were already lingering about and attending to the repairs.

When Balladin reached the ship, he saw Annaquinn bent over the lifeless figure of her father. She looked up at Balladin with blood on her hands and tears in her eyes.

Following the scent path of Marielle, the Gévaudan had attacked the ship. Hothgarth died standing in its path.

Chapter 13
The Battle of the Crypts

Shoebottom followed Orface's tracks as fast as he could follow them. The previous rain that transformed the earth from dirt to mud made the endeavor easy. Orface's trail through the mud ran straight for the Gaul village.

When Shoebottom entered the grouping of primitive, thatched roof houses still left over from the Dark Ages, he followed Orface's muddy prints into the old tavern.

Opening the door, Shoebottom recognized the inn was empty, not only of customers, but the barkeep as well. The benches and chairs that accompanied the tables sat toppled or out of place. Cobwebs stretched across them as well as the tables, as if the place hadn't served a pint in ten years.

The side window that faced south sent sunbeams onto an ornate wooden table with two chairs in the far righthand corner of the inn. Brushing the cobwebs from his face, Shoebottom recognized Orface had stopped at the chess table, now vacant of any sign of Arthur Schachmeister.

Shoebottom leaned over the table. His eyes could recognize the ultimate moves of the same game he had played with the chess master. Apart from the dust and cobwebs, nothing had changed since that momentous match, as the game pieces were exactly as he and Arthur had left them.

He picked up the black knight piece, the one that had once been white, and placed it into his pocket. "A momentary delay for a souvenir of my victory here," he muttered.

Exiting the inn, he saw that the farm fields that had surrounded the village had again turned into an old-growth forest of wintery oak trees. He reached out and touched the bark of the first tree with his gloved hand. Orface had gone where Orface had never gone before—into the Forbidden Forest.

A rage welled up inside of Shoebottom as he realized just then that Araqnis must have called the half-wit to himself. A certified moron, like Orface, was bound to do anything he was told, so long as he received certain reward. Shoebottom knew that Orface wanted to see the dragon fly.

With a feeling of desperation, Shoebottom followed the muddy footprints into the same obscure pathway into the forest. A chill ran down his back the moment he heard the moaning sound from breezes that moved no branches. The farther into the Forbidden Forest he ventured, the more barren and dead the trees became.

Around the bend, he halted. There he saw the first hung skeleton corpse dangling and swaying from an unfelt wind. Its bones clacked with its movements.

When the cadaver lifted its skinless face and focused its eye sockets at Shoebottom, Shoebottom knew he was no longer welcome to the Specter of the Well and his dark and gloomy graveyard.

The rope that stretched the skeleton's neck snapped loose, and the skeleton landed in a heap on the ground. It slowly lifted its body from a crouched position and into a full stance. Picking up a wooden club, it took a step toward its intruder.

Shoebottom drew out his two swords from across his back.

When the bone-armored adversary swung the oak bludgeon, Shoebottom blocked the advance with his lefthanded sword and severed the skeleton's head with a counter swing from his righthanded sword.

The skeleton bones crashed to the ground as the skull rolled into the brush.

"I would imagine croquet was invented this way," he said. Stepping over the bones, he pressed forward in full defensive stance, further into the forest.

Around the next bend, two skeletons stood freed of the noose and awaited in hateful defense. One held another hardened club while the other held a sling.

Shoebottom's agility dodged the onslaught of rock and debris the second skeleton launched with his sling. With each dodge, he stepped closer until the first skeleton stepped towards him, brandishing the club.

Shoebottom's sword sliced through the shin bones of the first skeleton's right leg and the second skeleton's left. Both figures collapsed while Shoebottom severed off their heads with both of his swords.

At the fourth bend, the fourth skeleton stood still as a statue. Its jaws, rather than clenched tight, remained agape in the presence of Shoebottom.

Shoebottom pointed both of his swords and charged in, but to his chagrin, the skeleton turned and ran away.

The tips of Shoebottom's two swords dropped by his side. "The vanguard fought with honor, but the king's guard was a coward."

At the back of the graveyard, the same three mausoleums stood, but with a difference. The right side one held gates wide open, a reminder the Gévaudan was free to take on the epic hunt.

Gray, sorrowful cement sculptures, rough with a century of rainy weather, stood sentry over the mausoleums as if they grieved their permanent lot. None of them appeared welcoming to Shoebottom's presence.

In the center was the well. Surrounded by tombstones of persons long forgotten, the well had a singular visitor. Orface.

The half-wit stood looking down into the projected lava light from deep down. In his hands were two stones, blue and green, both of them dark, for there were no Keepers present.

"Orface, wait!" Shoebottom called out, taking a step towards the well. "Look, Orface, I have mutton on the grill, rare and tasty, just the way you like it!"

Orface looked at Shoebottom with an elated grin. Clapping his hands together, he nearly dropped the Petras into the well.

"That's right, Orface. It's your birthday and I have something very special planned for you!"

Orface's attention turned a moment back into the well. It was apparent Araqnis too was stating his case. Orface then turned back to Shoebottom. "Master make dragon fly?"

"Yes! Yes, Orface. For birthday, Chewbottom make dragon fly. We eat mutton, we drink ale, and we make the pretty dragon fly! Chewbottom promises!"

Orface let out a guttural laugh. He then turned his attention back to the well. "Not Chewbottom, but Wacknis! Wacknis make dragon fly!"

"No, Orface, Wacknis not make dragon fly, he is lying to you. Chewbottom always tell the truth. Birthday, Orface! Over here, mutton leg, and almond cookies!"

"Almond cookies?" Orface's stronger brow lifted, making his eye look larger than the other.

"Yes, Almond cookies!" Shoebottom took more steps, closing the distance. A few more and he could wrestle

Orface to the ground. He could see the half-wit listening into Araqnis's words and he knew he had to act fast.

"Wacknis say for Orface birthday, he get to ride on flying dragon. Wacknis wins! Heh-heh-heh!"

"Orface, NO!"

Shoebottom rushed in, but before he could take hold of Orface, the petras dropped deep into the Specter of the Well. A massive shock wave shook the ground, sending Shoebottom backwards a distance of three times his height.

With his swords cast away and his mind spinning into blackness, he held his head until he could regain his equilibrium. He crawled to his senses and leaned his shaken body up against a tombstone. There, set before him, was a different scene.

The first thing Shoebottom noticed as his vision returned into focus was Orface making his way into the middle crypt.

Orface turned and grinned at Shoebottom. He held a golden skeleton key in his left hand.

The next thing Shoebottom saw was a dragon. It was not the oversized type of dragon one imagines or reads about in the knight's tales. This one had a body only twice the size of a grizzly bear.

The dragon lay just outside the well as if sleeping. The Petras, now shining bright blue and green, rested inside a golden amulet fixed around the dragon's neck.

Chapter 14
The Return of the Dragon

At first, Shoebottom did not know how to proceed with what he saw. Araqnis had come to life. This time without Shoebottom being granted cryptic status. The world was now poised to fall off of its trajectory. The people of Planet Earth would never be the same.

Shoebottom possessed the photographic memory, which very few people possessed. He had examined and read every page of Sephus's book. He knew the dragon would be weak and would require sleep during the first hours of his recovery.

Shoebottom also knew the Petras would give the beast unspeakable power, enough to conquer the world in all three of the remaining ages. Whether Shoebottom cared for the fate of the remaining Keepers, he knew they did not stand a chance.

How could he imagine being the most notorious villain in human history if all people were criminal? Even if he worked for the good, how could he be the heroic type Marielle had spoken about if there was no one worth defending?

Shoebottom drew out his dagger. It was the same one that Araqnis had given him when Shoebottom was first commissioned to pursue the Petras. Because the dragon had surmised that a poor, underpaid assassin had no chance of winning over a rich and well-supported nobleman like Bo Eskatoll. Shoebottom received his dagger from Araqnis as a way of giving Shoebottom a small advantage.

Shoebottom knew from Sephus's writing that such a dagger would never harm Araqnis if used against him, not unless the one wielding the weapon was himself a celestial. A mere human like Shoebottom could never deem to harm Araqnis. Not even Jacob Lake or Dargo de Montebank could do the celestial creature harm. Hurt or kill a cryptic, perhaps, but never a celestial.

Holding the dagger in his right hand, Shoebottom came up with a different plan.

He worked his way in stealthy steps toward the sleeping Araqnis. It was the same careful maneuver he had used a hundred times when sneaking past guards inside a well-fortified castle. In this manner, Shoebottom never made a straight line towards his quarry, but took a circular path no different from a stalking puma.

Cut the amulet chain from around the dragon's neck. That was Shoebottom's plan. Once he recovered the Petras, there was no telling what he could do with them. Sell them perhaps? Use them perhaps? Maybe he could pass them onto the Keepers just to even the score a bit. *Araqnis won't miss them...*

Neither his footsteps nor his breathing made a sound. Shoebottom often boasted to the idea that not even his thoughts made a sound when he was on the hunt. Step by step, he edged closer to the dragon's neck, the glowing blue and green Petras revealing nothing of his presence.

A short distance to Shoebottom's left, Orface emerged from the middle crypt.

Shoebottom stopped just short of reaching Araqnis. He noticed something about Orface had changed.

Orface grinned like the Cheshire Cat, all teeth and not much else. There was a sinister gaze behind that grin.

Don't forget I am putting a birthday party together for you. Shoebottom willed Orface to hear his thoughts for he dared not speak the words. Shoebottom held up a hand hoping Orface would say nothing.

"Ha-HA Chewbottom! Orface now cwiptic! Wacknis promised it be so!" Orface's exclamation could have awakened earthworms six feet under the ground.

Orface brandished a wooden club he had taken earlier from a fallen skeleton warrior. He clapped the club with brute force against his own skull, laughing out loud each time he heard the clammer of the impact, but felt no pain. The club made no impression on the idiot cryptic.

No brain, no pain, Shoebottom thought while wincing at the noise his onetime minion was making in alarming repetition.

Araqnis stirred.

Shoebottom closed in. It was now or never. He linked his dagger into the golden chain of the dragon's amulet and began sawing the metal. An immortal blade will not dull with use and can break certain objects of the celestial realm, but it did not do so fast enough.

Orface closed in with his club. "Look, Chewbottom! Orface very powerful!"

Shoebottom continued to saw the chain with his dagger, but still, the chain would not break loose. He quickened the speed of his sawing.

Araqnis, realizing what was happening, lifted his head. Grunting, he swung his head and collided into Shoebottom, tumbling him to the ground.

"Orface!" commanded Araqnis, still too weak to fly. "Kill Shoebottom!"

Shoebottom got up to his knees, attempting to brush away the pain. He looked up in time to see Orface closing in.

A swing of Orface's club swooped with an intended deadly impact, but Shoebottom was still agile. He lifted his body in a rear retreat like a panther evading a swipe of a tiger's claws.

Orface noticed Shoebottom's dagger, leaned down, and picked it up. The one asset Shoebottom had left in defending himself against this first time cryptic was now in Orface's hand.

Orface examined the dagger with a look of glee, threw away the club, and walked towards Shoebottom with a blood thirst.

Shoebottom made a dash through the Forbidden Forest. Even a half-wit cryptic with an immortal blade would be no match for Shoebottom's speed.

At the far end near the inn, Shoebottom stopped to catch his breath. A heavy heart accompanied him for the first time since his mother's death. What remained ahead of him? Shoebottom could no longer think that far in advance.

He continued to run until his feet and legs could no longer carry him. Along the meadows of Brittany, Shoebottom collapsed onto the ground. His lungs had never required so much air and he came close to passing out.

As the evening sun disappeared into the night, Shoebottom sat up. His head still pained him, but he cast his eyes towards the heavens. In the sky towards the west, a silhouette emerged of a flying dragon, soaring and swaying with a new confidence.

Araqnis was alive and in search of the Keepers.

Chapter 15
Myra and the Masa Mabedi

Jacob and Marielle rose from the light of the wellspring into another dark place. Like the wellspring in Le Mont St. Michel, it echoed their voices against stone.

Marielle reached out with her free hand and touched the sides of narrow walls. Her other hand held the Sangrahl contained inside the wooden box. Her feet found no foothold, and she continued to kick in order to keep her body afloat. "Jake! I can't feel the bottom!"

"I have a handhold, hang onto me."

Marielle grasped the darkness toward his voice until her hand met with his shoulder. Feeling the strength of his hold, she glided her body into his, wrapping an arm around his shoulders.

"Are we back in Le Mont St. Michel?" Marielle's teeth chattered in response to her shivering from the icy cold water.

"No, this is too tight a spot. This one is manmade." Jacob threw one of his arms up higher until his hand met with a depression in the hand-hewn stones surrounding them.

"You can see that?" Marielle said. "My eyes cannot see a thing."

"It's one advantage to being immortal. I can still make out things in the dark. Hold on tight!"

He lifted both of them with his superhuman strength. While Marielle clung to him, his other hand pushed up the great stone lid that encased them in complete blackness. Bright light poured in from the morning sun.

Marielle took hold of the edges of the rectangular cavity they had emerged from. She let go of Jacob's shoulders and pushed herself over the edge. She pulled her soaked body wrapped tight by the saturated blue, silken tunic, to the ground.

Jacob leapt over the same white stone wall and sat next to her. He placed his strong arms around her to stave off her shivering.

Looking about them, nothing was familiar. Here, the coming sunrise was farther along than at the Scandinavian coastline they had just left. White columns of alabaster marble, painted salmon pink with the color of dawn, surrounded them. Hewn blocks made up partial walls of the surrounding structures and paved thed ground beneath them. An abundance of weeds permeated the cracks between each of the avenue stones.

"We're in some sort of ruin," Jacob said.

"Now we know why Sephus mentioned a village ruin. This one is much different from the Celtic and Viking ruins we encountered in Ireland. I wonder what this place is."

Marielle's shivering subsided. She felt the sun rising in a temperate climate wrap its warming gaze about her. She turned away from Jacob and stood up.

Keeping her eyes up and down the barren streets, Marielle wrung the excess water from the hem of her tunic and from the ends of her hair. She slipped the silken shoes from her feet, allowing the water to dump out. She set them in the sun to dry.

Jacob got to his feet and wrung the water from his own sodden tunic. He peered back into the rectangular cavity they had climbed out of. "Marielle, this is the first wellspring we've encountered that lies in a manmade structure."

"What is it?"

"It looks like a cistern, a place containing well water for a cluster of houses."

"Or maybe it is a well. The water could flow there naturally and they built the rectangular cavity around it."

Keeping his sword sheathed, but strapped across his back, Jacob took Marielle's hand as the two of them explored their surroundings. Their bare feet made water footprints on the marble streets as they moved into the heart of the village ruin.

Each of the dwellings were of the same marble, all of them broken after hundreds of years without repair, almost none of them containing a roof. Some of the marble blocks sat at angles or had separated themselves altogether.

Fragmented and scattered Greek columns were all that remained of an old temple. A few of them stood in their original position, but no longer reached their colossal height. The large, half a head of a goddess sculpture glared up at them with one eye still intact. She did not appear happy about her permanent predicament.

Marielle gazed at it as if expecting it one eye to blink. "Athena?" she said to Jacob.

"Perhaps Artemis."

While Ionic columns remained in fragments around the village's pagan origins, stone prisms adorned what had once been homes, workshops, and marketplaces. On the north side, a Greek amphitheater stood with most of its shape and structure still intact.

Marielle stopped, her eyes still taking in the ruins with wonder. "Where do you suppose we are?"

"Not just where, but *when*... There is something familiar about this place, like I have seen it in a history book or something."

"Yeah," said Marielle, "I feel like we've been here before, even though I know we have not. Jake, I'm worried about Angelou. Against that cryptic creature, Angelou would not stand a chance."

Jacob nodded. "I fear for her as well. She's a special girl, though. Maybe she's too quick for that enormous beast. I also fear for Tuck. So long as the Tears of his bow hold out, he may be okay."

"That enormous beast seemed awfully quick to me." Marielle's eyes met with Jacob's. "I know. We need to focus on the present moment. It's times like this that I wish that our mission was over and life could return to normal. I miss watching sports and eating pizza. I miss going to a movie theater to see a long-anticipated new film."

Jacob squeezed Marielle's hand. "For us, there will never be a normalcy to return to. One cannot engage in such a meaningful purpose and expect to fade into society as if none of this ever happened."

Marielle stopped them and pointed. "Look at those cliffs there. The inhabitants of this village carved temple fronts right into the marble cliff and the windows appear to be caves."

"Tombs, I would imagine."

"Doesn't sound like our Table Shrine. Where do you suppose it is located? We were counting on our Simple-Minded One to guide us."

Jacob turned his gaze in every direction. "Let's keep going. I think the signs will come to us. We just need to trust in this destiny."

They followed along the main street toward the amphitheater to see if there was any sign of the place called Masa Mabedi, the Table Shrine. The stone-laden buildings were of a larger size than the ones Jacob and Marielle passed earlier. It was a sign the more affluent and elite of the town had lived there.

"Jake, what would 'going back to normal' look like to you?"

"You mean, what would I do once all of this is over?"

"Yes."

Jacob considered her question. "You know, what I would want to do and what I can do cannot be. My mother Katherine lost her husband and her son just a few years apart. Both of these women, the only family I have, suffered so much loss these past few years. In the Medieval age, a union between a man and woman is much more a prerequisite for survival."

Marielle nodded. "I could see that. It's not at all like in my age where so many conveniences come at the push of a button."

"Being both seamstresses, they fare all right having a trade. It just makes me sad to think about them living out their years without me and without Papá. I would have very much liked to live out my years in La Bellaroche."

"If you could, is that where you would want to go?"

"I'm a knight. I will always be one to take up the quest in defense of the weak."

"There is no way back to the Fourth Age?"

"You know there is not. Sephus made it clear there are no wellsprings open to that period anymore. All that we have access to are these last three ages."

"Would you remain with me in the Seventh Age then?"

Jacob's silence made Marielle uneasy, and she let go of his grasp. She looked down across the cobbles. She walked forward, finding something that had not seen before.

At the edge of the lane was a large stone with chiseled lettering.

MYRA

"Jake, this is where…"

Jacob caressed the carven lettering with his hand. "Yes, of course! I should have guessed it long ago. Myra is the original town of St. Nicholas."

"Truly?"

"We're in the place where St. Nicholas lived his earthly life."

Marielle pointed. "Right over there, a structure that looks like it was once an old church."

"What better place for a Table Shrine, huh?"

They walked over to where three walls remained standing of a stone-laden church, neither majestic nor modest. An octagonal apse surrounded a large hand-hewn stone table at the center.

The top of the table contained an engraved circle at the center. From that circle, seven engraved rays pointed in every direction making seven congruent trapezoids.

Marielle placed a delicate hand across the church's broken doorway. "Masa Mabedi," she said. "This has to be the place. Why was this written in Turkish?"

"I believe Myra was in Asia Minor, not too far from Greece. It may well be somewhere in Turkey where we are standing now."

Marielle's feet padded across the stone church floor until she reached the hand-hewn stone table. Keeping her body facing away from Jacob Lake, she concealed the tear that flowed down her cheek.

Chapter 16
Two Keepers Too Few

When the midday sun reached its zenith in the blue sky, a beam of its light stretched through a hole in the old church ceiling and illuminated the Table Shrine.

"Marielle, look over there." Jacob touched a light hand over Marielle's upper arm.

As a last droplet of water fell from a lock of her hair onto his hand, she turned her eyes to where Jacob was staring.

Across the square towards the tomb cliffs, a ghostly figure appeared. Though his appearance was human in every sense, his skin and white woolen attire glowed with the light of the sun. Behind him, two more figures appeared, each dressed in identical fashion, as if the three of them belonged to the same order.

The lead figure had a familiar appearance that both Jacob and Marielle recognized, but could not place. He was short of stature, with a full head of thick, dark hair and an equally dark beard. His eyes locked onto them, recognizing their awe and confusion. In response, he smiled as if he was an old friend.

Within his hands, he held an identical Sangrahl, the Lamp of Light, and with it, he approached the old church. Walking through the rear wall and into the apse, he stood behind the table at its head and awaited the others to follow.

The second figure was of African descent. He carried himself like a tribal warrior in a time before his people became slaves of western cultures. His face held the painted features of a prominent one in his village, a chief perhaps.

Within his hands was a Sangrahl identical to the first. He stopped and stood at the first figure's right hand.

The third figure was of Asian descent, Indian or perhaps Burmese. He approached the second figure's right side.

When the three of them stood side-by-side facing Jacob and Marielle across the Table Shrine, they looked up at their two visitors. An apparition of the Sangrahl appeared in Jacob's own hands. Though it remained in a ghostly aura, he could touch and feel it as if it had solidified.

"Jake, I think they are imploring you to join them," Marielle said, taking out her own Sangrahl from the wooden box. "This appears to be the delivery point for the final Sangrahl!"

"Yes, I believe it is, Marielle! If this should work, this will destroy the evil forces of darkness."

"Will Araqnis perish then?"

"I do not know. One thing for sure, though, the cryptics will be no more."

The first figure smiled as Jacob said these words.

"Go and join them, Jake! Count them. These are all the Keepers that came before you!"

Jacob walked over and stood next to the Asian figure, who bowed with a charismatic smile. As Marielle looked on, the first figure, in reverence, placed his Sangrahl in the middle circle of the table. The second Keeper placed his Sangrahl in the same place, superimposing the two Sangrahls into one. The third followed.

Jacob Lake felt the power of the vessel within his grasp. When he stretched his hands across the table to merge his Sangrahl with the others, he felt the energy of the three together surge through him like an electric charge.

Marielle approached the table with her Sangrahl. She swelled with gladness as she realized that the watch must indeed be over and that her placing the Sangrahl could both end the quest of the Keeper of the Seventh Age and save Angelou from the Gévaudan.

When she stretched her hands holding the Lamp above the table, the first Keeper held up a hand. The smile drained away from his face as he looked across at the two empty spaces between Jacob and Marielle.

Two Keepers are missing!.

The three figures faded away one by one, starting with the Keeper of the Third Age and followed by the Keeper of the Second Age. The Keeper of the First Age sent Jacob and Marielle a nod, as if everything that was happening was just as it should be. He then disappeared with the others.

The superimposed Sangrahl at the center of the table disappeared last, its aura lingering like the scent of a girl's perfume long after she had walked away.

Alone, Jacob and Marielle stood desolate and lost in their places at the Table Shrine. Jacob's eyes met Marielle's imploring gaze.

"What just happened?" Marielle's voice squeaked from her breathlessness.

Jacob furrowed his brow in response. "I... I don't really know."

They stepped back, but kept their bodies facing the shrine. "The first Keeper, I felt like he knew us. He revealed that two of the seven Keepers are missing."

Jacob stepped back and sat down on a stone slab, fingering the hilt of his sword. "Hothgarth's son was the Keeper of the Fifth Age. It remains a mystery how Dargo figured out who he was. He killed Korynn long before he became the Fifth Keeper."

"No…" Marielle held a hand across her lips. "How could this be?"

"It was one of the few things Meeshayell gave to my memory when he breathed life into my body. Meeshayell told me of my nature and that I am now amaranthine. He told me of the silken tunic and silken shoes that I was to wear to protect me from the nature of time travel. I even knew where to find you in the alcove hideaway and that you were faring well there. In my mind, I saw Korynn's death."

"You knew of my existence in the alcove?"

"Yes, I saw images of you. It made my heart swell to see you so happy in your solitude."

"But you saw me as I was?"

"As always, you are so beautiful to me."

Marielle set down the Sangrahl back inside its box and pressed both hands across her cheeks. "What was I doing?"

"You were sitting crisscross next to your hammock on a flat sandstone rock. It was early morning, and you were talking to Angelou and petting her. You said to her, 'you will always be my Angelwolf.'"

"Oh!"

"What is it?"

"It's just that I always think that I'm alone and there you were, looking in on me."

"It was just a glimpse, Marielle, one that Meeshayell must have chosen. It was a beautiful scene that I was privy to for only enough time to hear your words about our dog. The question we should ask ourselves is, what do we do without a Keeper of the Fifth Age? Korynn is dead. The second question is, did Dargo also kill the Keeper of the Sixth Age? If not, where would we find him?"

Marielle looked up at Jacob. "Too many questions have inadequate answers. As for the Keeper of the Fifth Age, Sephus mentioned in his book that a surrogate Keeper exists should a Keeper lose his life. The next younger sibling of a Keeper becomes that surrogate. For me that would be my sister Shelly. For you it would have been your sister Isabelle."

Jacob thought about what Marielle had said. "Then Korynn's surrogate Keeper would be…"
Marielle nodded. "Annaquinn."

Chapter 17
Tears of the Bowman

Tuck took pause in his hunt for Angelou. He cast his eyes into the twilit sky. Something had changed in the world, like an omen of misfortune or a dark cloud approaching.

Whatever the Southern Ute felt, his intuition told him that the darkness had just taken its upper hand. Whether Tuck felt the presence of the dragon, he could not tell. Dragons were beyond his perception, as dragons were mythical. Tuck asked himself why he saw a dragon at the forefront of his thoughts?

He shook his head at the irony of once again being alone in his corner of the quest. It was by his own choice this time round. No one but him could go after the highly valued Angelou, hoping to spare the dog from an impending death from a creature that required no rest.

Tuck took on his journey alone, because the other Knights of the Sangrahl had other priorities. Annaquinn had lost her father and required a protector. She also was susceptible to a world dominated by men to have *The Rising Stargazer* taken from her. Balladin would remain by her side.

The first mate and sailors of *The Rising Stargazer* had seen Balladin fight. They would keep their distance when the monk was present.

Jake and Marielle had to take the Sangrahl to the delivery point indicated in Sephus's book. It was everyone's hope that if the Keepers could fulfill the Sangrahl's destination, they could hope to defeat the evil that worked to penetrate every facet of life in the final thousand years of the Sangrahl's existence.

He followed Angelou's track along the ridge of the coastline of Norway. There was a chill in the air and Tuck wrapped the newly fashioned Madagascar silk cloak around his silken overshirt and slacks. Though he held no reason to find a wellspring for which to travel, he was glad of the new attire.

Angelou's tracks soon merged with the track of a much larger creature. The Gévaudan and the angel wolf danced and dodged each other without either claiming the victory. Deeper impressions of the Gévaudan's paw prints showed the cryptic creature used the stamping of his paws as much as a snapping of its teeth.

"That poor dog," was all Tuck could say. He saw their trails moved further west, but still kept close to the fiords. "She will soon wear herself out and the cryptic creature will have her."

Tuck had little hope that Angelou could have enough sense to locate a cave in which to retreat to when she got weary. He could not understand what had gotten into the ol' girl. She had never bolted away from her Keepers in such a way and never failed to come when Jacob Lake gave her the command.

"Jacob Lake saved my life," Tuck said out loud. "I feel the need to restore such a favor by sparing his beloved canine."

Sensing something other than a dragon's presence, Tuck hunkered low and strung an arrow to his bow. Looking about for the danger that lurked, he fixed one Tear of the Wanderer on his arrow tip.

"Show yourself, if you dare!" he called forth.

As if obeying Tuck's command, the Gévaudan appeared a quarter mile ahead. It zigzagged right and left, its body following courses not directly related to its prey target. Its head, however, never failed to focus its attention towards Tuck.

"So, you have a special bloodlust for young women, have you? First Marielle and then Annaquinn. You failed to have either, so you go after her father as her scent must have been a part of him."

Though Tuck addressed the Gévaudan, his words were for his own ears..

Tuck steadied his bow. *One piercing of a Tear of the Wanderer collapses him, but fails to kill. It recovers rather quickly from the wound I impose. What about two Tears shot in succession? If I can get it to be out in the open where it cannot evade a second shot...*

The Gévaudan did just as Tuck had hoped. Though he felt uncertain such a ploy could cost him his life, it was worth the chance.

A few more zags and you'll be in perfect range, Tuck thought.

The Gévaudan had his own plan. Though he was working his way to the place Tuck had in his sights, he knew that once an arrow flew, if the creature could dodge it, it would only take a few seconds for it to close the gap for the kill. No man can reset a bow with an arrow that fast.

Tuck took aim and set off the Tear-tipped arrow.

The Gévaudan saw it coming and dodged to the right.

The magical force of Tuck's arrow caused it to turn in mid-flight, follow the Gévaudan's lightning-quick course, and penetrate into the creature, causing it to fall.

What an incredible magic these Tears hold!

Tuck put together a second arrow, this one too affixed with a Tear and set it forth.

While the Gévaudan got up, the second arrow met its mark, causing the Gévaudan to stumble a second time.

Tuck took several steps forward. For a moment, he believed he had killed the cryptic creature. Just in case he was wrong, he affixed a third arrow.

The Gévaudan got up, snarled in anger towards Tuck, and dashed into the woodlands before Tuck could reach it with a third shot. It pushed its way through trees and underbrush while Tuck kept aim just in case it made a second attack.

The sound of snapping trees and crumbling rocks continued until Tuck heard them no more.

A sobering thought entered his brain. *Where was Angelou?* Because the dog appeared nowhere near the cryptic creature, Tuck believed Angelou was dead. Regardless, he would follow the dog's course until the signs showed a confirmation or a denial of Tuck's suspicions.

Besides being a master of the bow, Tuck's unique talent lied within his instincts. From deep inside his core, he knew when good things were on the horizon. He also knew when terrible things were to be in play.

Tuck sent his vision across the horizon line about him. He sensed something was near, something safe. Following his sixth sense, he turned to set himself on a different path.

In a tight grove of trees, he found it. An obscure pool of an artesian well sent clear water into a stream that would flow into the fiord a half mile away. At Tuck's presence, the pool glowed blue from far into its depths.

Tuck smiled. "I'm not even a Keeper, yet a wellspring welcomes me as if I were one!"

Tuck formulated an idea. "What if I could get *Ugly* out there to follow me into this wellspring?"

Tuck thought that perhaps it could work. If he led the Gévaudan into thinking he was no longer armed, the cryptic creature would take on the offensive. Tuck set down his longbow and quiver on the rim of the artesian well.

He returned to the open area and stood out in the middle. "Hey Ugly!" he called out. "Hey you, with the malicious attitude! I'm right here and I'm not armed anymore! I am a Ute and it is a good day to die!"

Minutes passed. Tuck remained where he stood, but his ears were more attuned to what was around him than his eyes. Even his own nose could pick up the Gévaudan's scent, for the Gévaudan smelled of roadkill along an Arizona highway in the middle of summer.

The roadkill smell reached his nostrils first. Then came the sound. He heard the crackling of Gévaudan paws in the deep, dense forest.

Tuck took a few steps back. He knew that if he appeared scared, it would stimulate the cryptic creature's resolve to make an attack. What Tuck did not expect was where a surprise attack would come.

Tuck instinctively cowed down low when the creature jumped onto the rocks thirty yards behind him. Turning, he saw the monster at full speed towards him, giving him only a second to react.

Tuck twisted and jumped between two large spruce trees, the claw of the Gévaudan grazing his left leg, splitting it wide open. Tuck fell to the earth and, despite the wound, jumped to his feet and scrambled forward.

The Gévaudan tore down what trees stood in its way. Anything growing that was less than a foot in diameter, the creature pummeled with brief delay in its progression towards Tuck.

Tuck's foot pained him to delirium, and he found he could no longer place any weight on it. He hopped forward just short of the wellspring pool.

To Tuck's surprise, the Gévaudan too, had stumbled. Overly confident of the kill, it had pushed its massive legs forward too fast, its front left paw slipping beneath it, causing it to fall onto its mammoth jaws.

Tuck picked himself up first, crawling to the edge of the wellspring. He turned to gather himself, knowing he should not enter the springs too soon, lest the trap not work. If he entered too late, he would find himself in the jaws of the cryptic creature.

The Gévaudan collected itself and returned to a four-legged stance. The beast glared at Tuck with a hatred Tuck had never seen, even from Dargo. Taking careful steps like a tiger on the verge of a catfight. It growled a deep guttural growl, showing teeth that were all crocodile fangs.

The moment the Gévaudan hinted a crouch, Tuck knew it would pounce. Tuck grabbed his bow and quiver and slipped into the wellspring. Just as the starry sky disappeared with the shadow of the Gévaudan, Tuck allowed the wellspring take him down under.

Tuck had no way of knowing where the wellspring would take him.

Chapter 18
Scraping the Bottom of a Shoe

Jacob and Marielle sat on a flat marble stone bench halfway up the seating heights in the grand amphitheater ruin. Their silken tunics, now mostly dry, they felt the need for a respite and wanted to gather their wits.

"Not exactly the North Pole, sleighs and reindeer," Jacob said, feeling the warm, humid air. "I wonder where all the stories came from."

"I read a book about St. Nicholas once. Everything wrapped around Santa Claus as a Christmas figure all started here. Look over there, many houses where he dropped coins into children's shoes left out overnight on the doorsteps. And over there may well be the home of the three maidens without a dowry. The stockings over the fireplaces began with that story and how Nicholas used a portion of his inheritance to help them marry rather than see the girls sold into slavery."

"You know all of this?"

"Just a little, enough to invigorate my imagination as a girl growing up. It is interesting, Jake, that you, a Keeper of the Middle Ages, should know all about the modern view of Christmas."

"I have gotten to live in both worlds."

"As have I, though I did not spend but a few days in your time."

Both of them sat in silence.

Jacob shifted to face her. "Marielle?"

"Yes?"

"You've been thinking about your life after being a Keeper. What do you dream about?"

Marielle shook her head, casting her body forward so that her elbows rested on the top of her knees and her chin rested into the palms of her hands. "You know I would have to just carry on, Jake. I have a life too. I would return to my family, who have only known from a few obscure letters that I'm doing all right. There are relationships there that would require some healing. After that, who knows? There's finishing high school. There's college."

Marielle gave a despondent shrug. "There are boys and marriage. I would go on my Marielle way."

Jacob's heart sank as he knew what Marielle was thinking, but he had no way to console her. It pleased him that by nature, she was not the confrontational type and would remain gentle within her independence, even when she found independence to be laced with melancholy.

"Going your Marielle way does not sound like a happy course."

"Jake, how many happy people do you know?"

A stranger's voice rang out from the backstage of the amphitheater. "Love looks not with the eyes, but with the mind; and therefore, is winged Cupid painted blind!"

Both Jacob and Marielle sat up in unison. They spied the stranger, all dressed in black, as he emerged out onto the block, marble stage. Jacob clasped the hilt of his sword. Marielle placed a quick hand over his to keep him from drawing it.

Shoebottom bowed in their direction. "*A Midsummer Night's Dream*, act one, scene one. That's some fellow named Shakespeare, is it not?"

He stood at stage center as if the amphitheater was full of spectators. Rather than regard Jacob and Marielle, he turned his gaze across the arena as if speaking to hundreds of people.

Jacob stood up. "How did you find us?"

Shoebottom looked at Jacob and Marielle for the first time. He shuffled across the stage towards them, as if the interruption was part of the act. He gestured a hand towards his two solitary spectators. "Lord, what fools these mortals be!"

Marielle whispered, *"Act I, Scene I of the same play."*

Jacob regarded her with an astonished expression.

Shoebottom pointed a dramatic finger towards his two spectators. "Shakespeare, as you may know, is well beyond my future. Shakespeare didn't exist in the Fourth Age." Shoebottom laughed in spite of himself. "Some would say that William Shakespeare was a man ahead of his time. In actuality, he's a man ahead of mine!"

Marielle remained where she sat, making no expression towards him. If Shoebottom had become a cryptic, Jacob still held the advantage. Jacob possessed the Fire Petra and the sword of Meeshayell.

"I asked you a question." Jacob kept his right hand on the hilt of his sword. "How did you find us?"

"Oh, keep your pants on! I am not a cryptic, dear boy, look…" Shoebottom drew his dagger and made a small slit on the palm of his hand. Drops of blood splashed on the stage at Shoebottom's feet. He took out a handkerchief and wrapped his wound.

Marielle felt herself cringe, hoping this narcissistic psychopath would not start saying, "Out, damned spot, out!"

Shoebottom tied his bandage tight. He looked at his two adversaries from top to bottom. "I see you two found the Madagascar silk. Brilliant—even for you! I made a suit myself, only mine is in black. It definitely helps with the time travel."

Shoebottom took three more steps to the edge of the stage and stepped one of his boots onto the bottom stone seat in the front row.

"Do you know how I know about Shakespeare? I travel a lot. I gather all the information my little brain can carry. Unlike your Sephus, I do not need to write it all down. It's all right inside here."

Shoebottom pointed to his head.

Marielle tugged at Jacob's sleeve. "Jake, sit down. Let's hear him out."

"What if this is a trap?"

"It's not a trap. If Hadrian had wanted to harm us, he would have done it with stealth."

"The blue tunic looks especially attractive on you, Marielle," Shoebottom continued while Jacob sat down. "My birds tell me you'll be sewing together enough material for a fashionable dress. I am guessing you will spend your life wearing it."

Marielle gripped the white alabaster marble beneath her. "What brings you here, Hadrian?"

Jacob turned and whispered. "You call him Hadrian? Since when are you two on a first name basis?"

"Shhh! Just listen. His purpose for being here will become clear soon enough. Keep your eyes open for a metaphorical chess move."

Shoebottom took steps up the stone stairway between the theater rows, stopping himself at a midpoint. "Did you read Sephus's book? Did you discover the meaning of the riddle about the Fire in the darkness? Did you ask yourself the question, why would Sephus capitalize on these particular words?"

Marielle said, "I did. Yes, we found the Fire Letters. What do you know of this?"

"And what about this clever little phrase about reception at the place of deliverance? Did you figure that one out?"

Marielle squinted at him. "No. And how on Earth would you know about that? You did not have a Sangrahl to light in order to…"

"Oh, I'm so disappointed in you, dear girl. I thought you were smarter than that. Around every turn you impress me, but not this time." Shoebottom continued towards them, but stopped short of where Jacob sat positioned between Marielle and Shoebottom.

Marielle clasped her hands across her lap. "You're the smart one, Hadrian, you tell us."

Shoebottom smiled. "How little the two of you know about me, after all these years of bickering and fighting. I mentioned to Bo Eskatoll after he killed Sephus that riddles are not my thing. I gave him the book because of Sephus's last page prophesy. Too bad for Bo the prophesy came true and did not apply to me. I am superstitious that way."

Marielle shifted closer to Jacob. "Petras!"

Shoebottom stared after her, awaiting the rest.

Marielle said, "Petras allow you to read the Fire Letters! You can read the fire of the Sangrahl through the Petras!"

Shoebottom pointed a triumphant finger towards her.

Marielle said, "You said you were never good at riddles and yet you solved this one."

"Solving these riddles is up to you, Keeper girl, and I am certain you, if not the two of you, will figure it out. I watched you as you walked the streets of this once prosperous community. No holding hands amidst gently falling cherry blossoms. I see no lover's arms wrapped around each other. There are no sighs of starry night affection as you gaze into each other's eyes. You two have a great deal to work out."

Jacob drew his sword and with the hilt end, pushed Shoebottom back onto the stone seating across the aisle and steps. He held the base of the blade to Shoebottom's throat. "Speak your piece and be gone with you!"

Marielle stood up. "Jake, please..."

Shoebottom smiled up at Jacob Lake. "You are much quicker than I remember. I have never found one so agile since... well, since I came into being. If it is answers you seek, it is answers I will give."

Marielle took hold of Jacob's arms and pulled him back. "Jake, he's not here to do us harm. I know enough about this man from the long conversations we've had."

Jacob took his sword blade from Shoebottom's throat. "I should kill you for kidnapping Marielle and putting her life at risk. I should kill you twice for mortally wounding my friend Tuck."

"As well you should, dear boy," agreed Shoebottom. "You may find it hard to believe, but I, too, make mistakes. Yes, I know, you find that hard to believe! I abducted your sister out of her bed in La Bellaroche, thinking it was Marielle. The assassins I sent forth to kill you and Balladin at the chapel ruin failed despite the favorable odds. I failed to bring Araqnis all that he required of me. Yes, I am nothing more than a complete failure."

Jacob took steps back and lowered his sword. "All right, Shoebottom, you've established yourself as a failure. Why are you here?"

Shoebottom sat up, brushing the dust off of his lap. The cynical expression washed from his face and he stared at both of them with expression of a doctor about to hand out the terminal prognosis.

"Araqnis is now free. The dragon is on the hunt and the dragon will have you two as his prime target. He will kill anyone who stands between you and himself. Dear girl, you implored me to do good for the cause, well here I am! I gave you back Sephus's book and now I am telling you, your death is imminent unless you can find a way to outmaneuver a dragon. Separate yourselves from your allies, they will only become mint sauce in Araqnis's roasted lamb."

Jacob sat back down, but kept his sword across his lap. "Why are you telling us this? Why would you want to help us?"

"Here we are, scraping the bottom of my shoe. Your girl here knows the answer."

Marielle shuffled her body. "So that you can be the most notorious villain in human history."

Shoebottom pointed his finger at her like a wide receiver just after a seventy-yard touchdown. "You are the smart one in the group. Your lover here is looking perplexed. Later, after I have gone, explain to him the deductive reasoning behind your conclusion. In the meantime, we all have our fires to light. I suggest you figure out a way to outrun a celestial creature who can skip the ages like a rock across the water! He can zip from one place to another in the blink of an eye. He can render himself invisible. How, pray tell, willst thou counter such a foe as he?"

"The question I ask of you, Hadrian Shoebottom," Jacob said, "is what role in all of this will you play?"

Shoebottom looked away, but shook a pointed finger at Jacob Lake. "That, dear boy, is for me to know and me alone. I warn you, that although I have played a part on your side, never trust me."

"I can assure you of that."

"One more thing. Araqnis is already sealing off every wellspring he can find. He plans on cutting you off from time travel. You cannot waste any time—no pun intended!"

Shoebottom turned from them and skipped his way down the marble steps to the stage. At the center of the stage, he stopped, turned around, and like the principal actor addressing a full house, said, "If you smell sulfur, Araqnis is near. In the meantime, receive where you deliver and deliver where you receive! There is so much more to Sephus than we all give him credit for."

He scampered back to the Greek columns downstage, wrapped his arm around one of them like a Romeo, and addressed them one more time. "All the world's a stage, and all the men and women merely players. They have their exits and their entrances. And one man in his time plays many parts. *As You Like It*, act two, scene seven."

For a moment, Jake and Marielle kept their eyes on the stage long after Shoebottom disappeared from sight.

"I still do not trust him," Jacob said standing up. He held a hand to welcome Marielle to her feet.

Marielle stood up without taking his hand. "Neither do I, Jake, but I believe he has a thing for me. That may be what could save us. We should get back, maybe see what we can do for Angelou and Tuck."

As they walked side-by-side down the long stone steps, Jacob said, "Tuck will be fine. So will Angelou. Marielle, why did Shoebottom want to help us? He said you would know the answer."

Marielle felt the pleasant, sun-warmed steps beneath her unclad feet. The early autumn sun nestled into the western horizon, washing all the stone ruins in a repeat color performance from earlier that morning.

"Hadrian knows that if Araqnis wins this contest, kills all of us, and destroys the Sangrahl, his criminal playground will no longer be fun."

"Fun? He thinks all of this is fun?"

"He's a peculiar one, Jake, but I think something I said to him got through. The way he was being playful on the stage, I've never seen him like that before. He bases his logic on the Keepers becoming the victors so that he can still enjoy taking advantage of the wealthy for his own gain. He's becoming more like a Robin Hood."

"You are indeed the smart one in our midst. What did you say that got through to him?"

Marielle stopped to face him. "I offered him friendship."

Chapter 19
The Sangrahl Quarry

Tuck felt the healing effects of the wellspring on his seven-minute journey. He emerged to the other side, fully restored from his leg injury. He wondered if the trap worked and the Gévaudan attempted to follow or perhaps even fell into the pool.

Tuck knew the wellspring would have killed the Gévaudan. He would not know if the cryptic creature entered the wellspring until he returned. He would remain at his destination at least until his enemy had time to give up the hunt.

The pool at the end of the wellspring was square and narrow, much narrower than the artesian spring he had left behind in Norway. The stone about him was smooth to the touch, pure white to the eyes, and hewn from human hands. An arched ceiling blocked out the view to the sky.

From the open end, Tuck peered around, wary of the possibility he was not alone. It would take a full day for the wellspring to accept him back inside to return to Norway, so Tuck was careful not to intrude where an enemy would take exception from Tuck's presence.

Though it was the middle of the night when Tuck was in Norway, he could tell it was the approach of dawn where he arrived. Looking around, he found himself in a place very much unfamiliar to him.

"Early morning hour," he pondered. "That could only mean I had moved east in the wellspring transfer. The Middle East?"

Geometric patterns edging the archways confirmed Tuck's estimation. The walls that surrounded him gave the impression he was inside a place of worship. The chamber's mosaic floor, intact walls, columns, and ceiling, and covered windows were clear indications he stood in some form of an ancient church or synagogue.

He had indeed landed somewhere in the Middle East, but where? Even at that hour, the air was warm and dry. A fresh desert air met his senses.

He stepped out of the pool, which he guessed was for spiritual cleansing—a ritual common in nearly all Middle Eastern cultures.

In the twilit darkness, he thought he had landed in another ruin site. Looking about him, he could see that was not the case. The floors, walls, and ceiling appeared clean and recently constructed.

Though he could see that he was in an antechamber near the entrance to the structure, Tuck could not see well enough in the dark to tell what the rest of the furnishings and architecture revealed.

Walking to the front wooden doors, he unlatched the bar across them, set down the beam, and creaked open the main door. Peering out, he knew he was alone in the early morning hours.

Dripping water from his body to the ground, he stepped out into the gray light. The sky to the east turned pink from the pending sunrise.

He expected to find a town surrounding him, but everywhere was a desert. A dirt road laden with camel and horse prints paralleled the solitary building leading both east and west into the arid wilderness.

Tuck circumnavigated the sanctuary building made of block stones and containing many archways. They were not the barrel-vaulting archways found in the Middle Ages, but the block-arches found in ancient Rome or Greece.

On every side was a flat desert landscape, barren and sandy, with only sparse patches of greenery. Small hills stood sentry along the horizon. The ground surrounding the religious structure where Tuck stood must have been an oasis, for palm trees adorned it on all sides.

To the rear of the building lay the only other sign of human existence, a stone quarry.

Why a stone quarry? Who would build a place of worship next to a stone quarry?

The quarry, dug into the same white rock that built the stone sanctuary, was an elongated impression, six feet or more into the ground. Its floor was mostly flat, but filled with the white dust of the rock material. Its walls stood at a perfect vertical angle, but wound around to the right. Several fluttering canvas canopies sheltered the quarry from sun, wind, and rain.

Stepping down into the open entrance to the quarry, Tuck recognized what appeared to be pottery—bowls, mugs, plates, and large, lidded jars, each set on various wooden planks against both walls. The pottery was not from clay and hardened in a fire kiln, but chiseled and carved out of the pure white stone.

He knew he should not be there. Tuck was not a swordsman like Balladin. Should anyone come by and find him there, they would mistake him for a thief and attack him on the spot. His longbow could take on any enemy from a distance, but not from such tight quarters.

Tuck walked along the recessed corridor, admiring the flawlessness of the potted plates, mugs, bowls, and jars. The workmanship was perfect in Tuck's eyes and he wondered about the artisan who had such a gift.

When he rounded the corner to perceive the quarry's terminus, Tuck froze when he found he was not alone.

A small man stood facing away from him at the far end, chipping away in delicate precision at a small jar. He wore a white, cotton *thoab,* or long dress-like cloth, adhered in the middle of the man's waist by a black braided belt made from horsehair.

By his dark hair and smooth, olive complexion, Tuck guessed the man to be no older than forty. There was something familiar about his mannerism, but Tuck could not place it.

Tuck froze when the man turned and noticed him. Tuck held tight his longbow, but did not string an arrow to it, for the man in front of him carried no weapon.

The stranger held a steel chisel in one hand and the cup he was working on in the other. He looked at Tuck. At first, he winced with surprise. He expected no one that day. Then he smiled as if he had known Tuck for years. He set down the cup and chisel and spoke in a Middle Eastern tongue Tuck did not recognize.

Tuck shook his head, "I am sorry, I do not understand."

"No, of course you don't," said the stone mason. "You are a stranger to this place."

"You... you speak...?"

The stone mason nodded. "I speak many languages from around the world. Dialects too!"

"How so, since you are a simple stone mason?"

"Stone masonry was my trade from youth. My father was a stone mason and so, here I am!" He jumped from his stool. "What brings you to such a desolate place at this hour of the morning, pilgrim?"

Tuck shuffled his feet. "I happened here by accident."

The man nodded as if with approval. Slapping the dust from his hands, he walked to where Tuck stood. His eyes surveyed the details of Tuck's silk attire, his bow and quiver, and his face. "Yes, a man like you would not intend to come to a place like this! I always say there are no coincidences. I believe I know why you are here."

Tuck shook his head. "If you know, then you know more than I."

The mason nodded with a broad smile. "Come! There are olives, bread, and oil for breakfast. There is something over there as well that I would like you to have before you depart."

"I was not intending to depart. I am here for a day."

The stone mason looked up at him. "Then you must stay for a day. I have something for you and you have something for me."

"Sir, I have nothing to give."

"I believe, sir, that you do. Come!"

The stone mason was a head shorter than Tuck, who in his age was an average height. He pushed past him with the energy of a child towards a plate filled with cookies. He turned down a dig row between the shelf planks that Tuck did not recognize earlier.

At the end, the man stopped to where a tent covering protected a small wooden table and chairs framed with wood. On the table was a plate of olives, a shallow bowl filled olive oil, and two loaves of hard-crusted bread.

The stone mason washed his face and hands in a basin of water and dried them with a white linen cloth.

"Please, sit and enjoy yourself," the proprietor said. "We have much to talk about."

Tuck realized he was famished and had not eaten in two days. He sat on the chair that rested in the righthand corner. Taking hold of one loaf of bread, he broke off a piece and dipped it into the oil. Tuck paused when he realized the mason was murmuring a prayer over the meal.

The stone mason sat down in the remaining chair and poured water into two drinking cups that were of the same stoneware of his craft. He handed one to Tuck.

With bread dipped in oil already in his mouth, Tuck took the drinking bowl in his other hand to wash it down. The first thing he noticed was the sweet flavor of the water.

The olives were unlike anything Tuck had ever tasted and he staved off desire to consume the entire plate.

Before the stone mason spoke another word, Tuck recognized another piece of stoneware that sat empty in a niche behind where the table rested. The bowl was identical in shape and size to the Sangrahl.

"What is this?" Tuck said. "You made this?"

"I did. I made its twin as well, but its twin has gone on to a much higher purpose."

"The Sangrahl?"

The stone mason said nothing, but dipped his own bread into the oil and ate along with three or four of the Greek olives, spitting out the pits into a small stone plate. "When you finish with your visit, I want you to have it. Do not think that it is sacred, but I know you might need it."

Tuck looked at the Sangrahl-shaped water glass. He then looked at the quarry proprietor. "Who are you? What is it you want from me?"

The stone mason popped two more olives in his mouth and dropped the pits from his lips before answering. "Like you, sir knight, I am a time-traveler, only I travel to gather as much information as I can. As for what you can give me, I require your bow and quiver. It is the only way you can have use of it when I make it available to you later on."

"My bow and... Why would I give this up when I have need of it on the journey ahead?"

The stone mason gave him a broad smile as if the question was more pleasing than seeing a newborn baby.

"Time travel is a funny thing. If you ponder it long enough it will make your head spin. How does one find such fine weaponry deep inside a cavern in the Fourth Age when it had yet to be invented? How again shall you find it with you at the edge of the wellspring you entered just now?"

Tuck's brow began to perspire. "How do you know about... Who are you?"

I have yet to learn your name. As for me, I am Jospehus Àrmitéa. You know me in a later time as Fra Sephus."

Chapter 20
The Wellspring Seal

When Araqnis awoke, metamorphosed back to his original dragon shape, he had not experienced freedom since his epic battle with Meeshayell. After the passing of a few hours, he lifted his head and for the first time in two thousand years, he could see through his dragon eyes.

The world is a much different place when seen through clear vision rather than imagined deep inside a well.

On that first day of dragon consciousness, he recovered his strength and lifted his bat-like wings and began flapping them.

His first flight showed he was still weak as he sauntered through the air like a buzzard sniffing the air for roadkill. Little could Araqnis accomplish on his first day's hunt for the Keepers.

Soaring into the night, Araqnis soon picked up speed. At first he was lax to control his direction and he slowed his velocity lest he careen in reckless fashion into the side of a mountain.

By the third day of his release, he had full control of his flying ability. He could reach the far horizon fast as a lightning bolt, the speed of which allowed him instantaneous time travel.

The hunt for the Keepers would take less than a fortnight.

What inspired the dragon more than speed and time travel, was the power of the Petra gemstones embedded in a golden amulet around his neck. Earth Petra green gave Araqnis a strength he had never felt before. Sky Petra Blue allowed Araqnis to enter and exit the vibrations of visual perception... Araqnis could be invisible.

He had been a caged bird for a thousand years and was now free to wallow in his newfound strengths. At the initial outset, he reflected on all that he had been, finally influencing someone to restore his true identity. He never imagined it would come from a half-wit.

In the time that he and the Winged Warrior fell wounded to the earth, they found themselves in different predicaments. While the Winged Warrior became vulnerable, blind, and human, Araqnis found himself as a spirit deep inside a well.

Feeling the power of the Petras for the first time, Araqnis could imagine where his archenemy, Meeshayell, possessed the upper hand in their battle. Meeshayell, being a *celestial* or highest order of creation, would still possess a hidden power, one that he disclosed to no one. For if his enemy knew both his vulnerability and his assets, he would never survive.

"Meeshayell's only superpower left is his ability to hide like a coward!" Araqnis smirked in response to his own words.

Araqnis too had his own superpower. Even while locked deep inside a well, Araqnis could call forth any mere human or animal and transform both of them into cryptic immortality. Doing so, however, came at a price. Araqnis had to impart a portion of his own power to the cryptic. Sacrificing oneself for the good of another was not the way of evil beings.

Although Shoebottom failed to bring him the girl and the Petras, Araqnis had other ways of regaining the powers he imparted. He saw in the half-wit a trouble-free cryptic. Anything Araqnis asked of him, Orface would do without question. Unlike Dargo, Bo, or Shoebottom, Orface had no ability to think through his own destiny, so Araqnis left him with simple instructions.

"Come Orface, come to the well… Drop in the Petras, Orface. KILL Shoebottom."

Orface, however, was not the intelligent ally Araqnis desired. The half-wit did nothing more than linger about the cemetery, focused only on his latest instruction, to kill his former master. Until Orface succeeded in the simple task, Orface was useless to Araqnis.

Ignoring this temporary setback, Araqnis focused on the path ahead. Darkness was now on the world stage to overcome the light.

Taking a different course in his flight, he sniffed the air. No Keepers present in this age. Araqnis would have to go in search of them in the consequent ages. They would not be easy to find, not yet.

Araqnis thought about Hadrian Shoebottom. The cryptic candidate had brought Araqnis far more than Araqnis was willing to admit. Along with the Petras embedded around the dragon's neck, Shoebottom offered a genius plan of action.

"A dragon's fire can seal a wellspring which turns its waters into stone. Isolate them into one age with nowhere to run."

The first of the three continental Earthsprings was a half a day's flight and rested in France. Araqnis glided down to it and sat at the edge of the shore. "First, we will close off the Fifth Age to them at every port."

Near to the pool, a creek ran by. A man and his lady sat on the shoreline preparing breads and cheeses for their family outing. With their horses hobbled close by, the man stood up at the sight of the dragon. His hand clenched the hilt of his sword, but he was too shocked to draw it out.

Dragons exist only in fairy tales and legends and not in real life!

His two preadolescent sons, halting their sparring match with wooden training swords, noticed their father standing and heard the muffled cry of their mother. They, too, saw the dragon.

"Dragon!" they cried out in delight. "Tuons le dragon!" The pointed their practice swords at the celestial creature. "Nous serons des héros!"

Araqnis ignored them and their wooden swords, but their father did not. He intercepted his two sons and, taking the rest of the family, scampered deep into the woods for cover.

Araqnis watched as the inhabitants crunched the forest floor with intrepid footprints. *Such fools, these humans!* He grinned his dragon grin.

Without the Fire Petra, his fiery breath was at its minimum. Good for roasting sheep and horses, but not for killing immortals. It was certainly good enough for what Araqnis had in mind at that moment.

He heaved in the air, the furnace at the back of his throat roaring into life, and he blew his fire into the Earthspring.

Steam poured forth and the small pool solidified into a rock cavity.

Araqnis blew a second course of flaming air and the rock at the bottom of the pool cavity turned into rock glass, black and shiny. Obsidian was Araqnis's personal favorite.

He cast his attention to the blue Petra embedded in the amulet and disappeared. A moment later on a far hilltop, he reappeared. With just a fleeting thought, he disappeared a second time and reappeared in full flight, high in the sky. Invisibility would be his greatest asset. If only he had the Fire Petra, his power would be paramount!

    Araqnis set his sights toward Romania and the second Earthspring. There were two that remained on the continent and several continents. What would be most daunting would be the blue water wellsprings of which were in abundance. One by one, he would sense their locations. One by one, he would seal them.

He would seal them all.

Chapter 21
The Kulning Call

Annaquinn sat alone on the forecastle deck of *The Rising Stargazer*. With a Norwegian breeze blowing the frosty night air about her, she sat gazing up at the aurora borealis, the northern lights.

"I remember seeing them when I was a girl," she said, recognizing that the footsteps that approached her with little sound could only belong to Balladin.

The monk, now dressed in his warrior monk's tunic, shoes, and leggings of Madagascar silk, sat on the wooden deck next to the girl. "Here, I brought you something to eat."

Annaquinn turned and her eyes regarded him in amazement.

Balladin smiled and handed her a metal plate of bread, butter, and cheese. Alongside the main fare were slices of autumn harvest apples, sprinkled with cinnamon.

Handing her a mug of jasmine tea, Balladin looked at the maiden to see if she had been crying. "How is it with you?"

"Yeh're not just the first man to offer me service, you're the first person. Yeh don't believe food prep is for women only?"

Balladin sat down beside her. "I never grew up with women. The monks were a brotherhood, and we did everything for the good of the community. Outside of our training in meditation and the martial arts, we cleaned, sewed, and prepared our own food."

Annaquinn set the plate and cup on an adjacent crate. She studied his expression of disbelief. "Yeh know yeh are serving a woman?"

"I am serving a friend. Woman or man, child, or elder, it makes no difference. People should live to serve. My only exception, I do not serve the rich or the privileged who look at a foreign man expecting such a humble role."

Annaquinn took part in the food offering, happy that Balladin had brought some for himself as well. She had never tasted jasmine tea before and, with a touch of honey, thought it to be the best hot beverage she had ever tasted.

"The lights in the sky, Balladin, have yeh ever seen them before?"

"Sephus told me about them once, but I found his description difficult to imagine. Now I am seeing it for real. Truly amazing!"

"I have seen them many times in my father's travels. He brought me here for the first time when buildin' a ship for the prince of Sweden. I was nine, I think. I thought the glowing lights to be a magic conjured up by a great wizard somewhere up there in the icy wilderness."

Balladin smiled. "Perhaps it is so."

Annaquinn turned in mid-bite to regard him. "Do yeh believe in magic?"

Balladin shrugged. "It depends on what you define as magic. The monks mastered an internal energy called chi that gave them amazing ability with strength and incomprehensible speed. To me, that was a type of magic. The Sangrahl heals. A wellspring will span space and time. There are cryptics and Petra gemstones. Whether a spiritual grace or a type of magic, it exists."

Annaquinn took a sip of her tea to wash down the bread and cheese. "The northern lights are especially beautiful decorated with all those stars."

Balladin gave her an inquisitive look. "Annaquinn, what color are the stars?"

"What do yeh mean? Stars are white... well, most of them. Some of them sparkle with color and I recall a star to the south shimmerin' in red. Mostly, they are white."

Balladin nodded. "I am sorry about what happened to your father."

Annaquinn looked down at her plate. She set her teacup on the deck. "I cried my tears. There is not much else to do."

"You loved your father?"

"Meh father had but two ambitions in life, shipbuildin'... and shipbuildin'."

"That's one ambition."

"No, that's two. Concerning his family, he loved us so long as we were part of his shipbuildin'. There will never again be another vessel like the *Stargazer*. She is a work of beauty and many would pay a fortune for her if they knew how incredible she is."

"What is your ambition in life?"

Annaquinn set her empty plate down. "Yeh know, yeh are the first person to ask me that. My father kept me from the things in life I wanted to do most. He kept them from me, but he could not keep me from dreamin' dreams."

"Which are?"

Annaquinn sighed. "I was fifteen the first time I fell in love with a boy. He was handsome and kind and worked for a time with meh father. I fall in love, and father sends him away. So, at sixteen, I fall in love a second time. Father sends him away. Every year I think I love a man and every year meh father keeps him from me. Then I turn twenty, getting too old for marriage. Jacob Lake comes into our lives and father gives me the go ahead. 'Fall in love with him', he tells me. I come to find out that the one man I am allowed to love, is in love with somebody else. She's a beautiful girl, this Marielle. She has eyes that see right into yeh're heart, but with a gaze of acceptance. I wanted to hate her, but I cannot."

"Marielle, Jake, and Tuck. These are my only family."

"Yeah?"

"Your father is gone now. You are free to love whomever you wish."

Annaquinn cast her eyes back into the heavens. "I never thought of that. Balladin? Could you ever be one to love a girl like me?"

Balladin allowed his own eyes to view the sky. Neither of them looked at each other. "Yes," he said. "I loved a few girls in my time, but like you, could never love them. It is not a family and children that I seek. I think as I get older, I will become one of those sages who sits on mountaintops pondering the meaning of life."

Annaquinn smiled, showing most of her white teeth. Her smile broke into a laugh as Balladin laughed with her. "I know there is some truth in your statement."

"We love to hear you sing," said Balladin, wanting to divert the conversation away from love.

"Do yeh?"

"Your voice is sweet as an angel's."

"Oh! Yeh know how to make a girl blush! Do yeh know about the girls of the north?"

"This is my first time to Norway."

"Swedish and Norwegian girls sing too, but often with a different purpose."

"Oh?"

"It's called kulning."

"Kulning?"

"It's a high-toned melodic call. It began with the tribes of long ago. I want to say it began with the Vikings. The wolf clan believed the northern wolves gave them protection and power. So, they would *kuln*... It's a single voice song, always by a woman, to call the wolves. The wolves have all gone far to the north. So, now kulning is for calling cattle. It works too, you should see it."

Balladin lifted his knees to his chin. "Can you do it? Can you kuln?"

Annaquinn pondered his question. "Yeh know, I knew a girl here when father built a ship in Sweden. Her name was Marta. She was older than me, but we were friends. At thirteen she kulned to call the cattle, and she taught me how it worked. My mouth dropped open the first time I heard it. It has no words, just meaningless expression, or at least that was my impression. But the mere sound of it, melodic and haunting, just took me aback."

"She taught you?"

"Yeah. It's been many years, but the two of us would kuln the cattle. It never failed to draw them to us."

"Can you show me?"

"Yeh... yeh want me to kuln?"

"Yes. I want to hear what it sounds like."

Annaquinn took the last sip of tea, got up and walked to the gunwale, her dress swaying in time with her flowing red hair in the northern breeze. She cast her gaze into the night, then looked over her shoulder at Balladin. "All right,

I will try it, but know this! This might wake up a few of our sailors or it just might lull them back to sleep."

Annaquinn placed delicate hands on the rail. She faced the shore of the dark Norwegian wilderness beyond. Holding a hand up to her face, she sang out.

Oh-Wah-HOO-week-deh!

Her voice boomed into the darkness, echoing across the wooded hills.

Ah-HOOO-hey-koo-weh! EEEh-HEY-wah-hoo!

As Annaquinn's voice penetrated the forests, cattle brayed far into unseen distant meadows. It was a fitting voice to the northern lights and all that represented the north countries.

Balladin got up, his ears mesmerized by the clarity of her voice traveling long distance across the fiords and mountains of Norway.

Far off into the distance, they heard another answer. The pack of wolves mimicked Annaquinn's song.

Annaquinn turned and concealed an excited chuckle from beneath her cupped hand. "Did yeh hear that?"

Balladin placed his hands on the railing and gazed off toward the distant howls. He nodded with an enchanted expression.

"The world sure is an awesome place."

Chapter 22
The Surrogate Keeper

Balladin took a firm hand to his double swords when he detected someone approaching out of the wilderness. "Tuck? Is that you?"

Jacob and Marielle appeared along the shore. Balladin called to the crew to send out a dingy to pick them up and bring them to the ship.

Once the dingy reached *The Rising Stargazer* and the two Keepers climbed the rope ladder, they met Balladin on the main deck. Jacob said, "Tuck? Angelou?"

Balladin shook his head.

Marielle stepped up on the deck and gazed out into the forest. "My Angelwolf, where are you and what are you doing?"

Jacob looked around the ship. Hothgarth's sailors had gathered in response to hearing Annaquinn's kulning and the arrival of the Keepers.

Annaquinn stood on the forecastle deck and leaned against the rail at the top of the steps. She covered her mouth, concealing her elation that Jacob and Marielle were alive despite the horrifying danger they had all faced. Where was Tuck and the incredible dog Marielle kept company with in her cabin?

"Galley cook!" Annaquinn called to the main deck. "A meal and ale for our guests!" She descended the stairs to meet with the newcomers. "Or would yeh prefer a cup of port wine?"

The galley cook approached Annaquinn with disdain. "I don't take orders from a woman."

"This is now meh ship, you will take my orders or find yourself another berth!"

Hothgarth's first mate, Mr. Fletcher, glared at the galley cook. "She's your captain now."

The galley cook cast his squinting eyes around for anyone to back up his resolve. None of the sailors dared to say anything, so the cook disappeared in the galley in order to follow the orders given to him.

Mr. Fletcher addressed Annaquinn. "What will your orders be then, Miss?"

Balladin stood next to the first mate. "I think we should address her as Captain Quinn."

The sailors cheered the girl's new title.

Mr. Fletcher barked orders at the rest of the sailors to return to their posts.

"Yeh are a fine officer, Mr. Fletcher," Annaquinn said.

Fletcher gave an uneasy bow. "At yeh're service, Miss… er, Captain Quinn." The first mate turned with a touch of apprehension and disappeared into the galley to make sure the cook put forth a proper effort.

Balladin, Jacob, and Marielle joined with Annaquinn on the upper forecastle deck in a circle of spice crates. Annaquinn, though surprised to be invited, assumed she was part of the circle only because *The Rising Stargazer* was now hers to command.

Balladin said to Jacob, "What should we do about Angelou and Tuck?"

"I see no way to help them, Balladin," Jake said. "The Gévaudan has his sights on Marielle. Tuck is doing everything he can to keep it distracted until we can kill it."

"Your sword, Jacobi, the Fire Petra. You could kill it."

"We will have to think on that. Yes, I could take my sword and go after it. If we find Tuck, maybe the two of us could destroy it. The problem is Marielle."

"Yes," said Annaquinn. "When yeh took yer leave to findin' Lys mot Himmelen, that creature came to this ship before any of us knew what was happenin'. My father was dead and none of us even saw the attack."

Jacob nodded in agreement. "If I go and Marielle stays, there is no way to protect her. Balladin, Marielle still carries no sword."

Balladin drew out one of us double swords to hand to Marielle. Marielle raised a hand against his intention.

"No, Balladin. You are best when you have two. I saw you battle the pirate sailors on the beach in Ireland. As well, the swords of Hothgarth's sailors do me little good as they are slow and weighty."

Balladin put back his sword. "Maybe I should go after Tuck now that you are back."

"Let's consider it," said Jacob. "In the meantime, we have much to tell."

Jacob and Marielle relayed their story of Myra and encountering the apparitions at the Masa Mabedi, the Table Shrine. They talked of Shoebottom and his warnings about the release of Araqnis into the world. Even Jacob did not doubt the truthfulness of his information, for Meeshayell had spoken of the inevitable rebirth of the dragon.

"This brings us to you, Annaquinn," Jacob said.

Annaquinn straightened up. "Me? If it's yeh're wantin' use of meh ship, she is at yeh're service. I am no more a spice merchant than anyone here."

"It is not just the use of your ship that we ask of you."

"Is it to be my singin' then?"

Marielle scooted closer to Annaquinn. "My good friend, you are more a part of us than any of us could imagine. Your brother was one of us, a Keeper, the protector of the treasure I now hold in my hands."

Annaquinn looked at the Sangrahl Marielle held. She had seen it a few times before and knew a little of its importance from the stories Jacob Lake had told her the first time they traveled together.

"Jacob told me my brother Korynn was a Keeper. What's that got to do with me?"

"In the order of the Keepers," continued Marielle, "when a Keeper loses his or her life, a next younger sibling becomes the surrogate Keeper for that age. Annaquinn, that's you."

"Me? What am I to do? I know nothin' about bein' a Keeper."

Jacob scratched the side of his beard and regarded Annaquinn with a serious look. "Have you had a dream of late, a place with still water, a glowing of blue or green beneath its surface?"

Annaquinn stared at Jacob. She clasped her hands together as if in prayer and leaned her body forward, the top of her forehead against her hands. "Two nights ago, I dreamed of a Roman ruin, an old bath house with hot water coming from the ground. It was a place meh family and I had been to when I was fifteen. Meh brothers and I took a swim there. In my dream, the water turned from clear to a moonlight blue."

"That's it," said Jacob. "That's the place. Captain Quinn, can you find it again?"

Annaquinn looked around at the others. "I... I think so. It is just across the sea on the east coast of Great Britain."

"It is imperative we get you there now. Could you set sail?"

"At first dawn, but..."

"Jake?" Marielle broke in. "We have another problem. I've been smelling it all night."

"Sulfur?"

"Yes, like rotting eggs. It's not very strong, but I can feel him hunting for me."

Jacob sat back. "Araqnis."

"If we follow Annaquinn to Great Britain, we may compromise not only ourselves, but Annaquinn's mission to deliver the Sangrahl of the Fifth Age."

Balladin nodded. "What would you suggest?"

Jacob said, "I suggest we leave you in charge of accompanying Annaquinn to Great Britain and the Roman Bath Wellspring and deliver the Sangrahl. Marielle and I will create a diversion and hopefully throw the dragon off your trail."

Marielle said, "But Jake, what if Araqnis senses the Sangrahl and takes them first."

Jacob shook his head. "We would be lost either way. The dragon has a greater lust for finding Keepers than destroying the Sangrahl. I believe he has an even greater desire in finding me as I have one of the two items he wants most."

"The Fire Petra."

"The Fire Petra is a dragon's most coveted possession. Balladin, we cannot protect you even if we all remained together. I know we agreed we should never split apart ever again, but this is the only way."

Annaquinn said, "Where will yeh two go? And what about yeh're friend Tuck and his dog?"

Jacob locked his eyes with Marielle's. "It will be a game of cat and mouse. We will have to remain on the move. So long as wellsprings remain open to us, we will have to continue to elude the dragon's pursuit until we can find a way to kill him."

Marielle said, "Meeshayell?"

Balladin nodded. "No telling where he is. The problem is, even if he comes out of hiding, he requires all three petras to recover from his injuries and regain full power."

Marielle said, "Then the Sangrahl is our only hope. If Annaquinn can deliver it to the Roman bath and we can find the Keeper of the Sixth Age, we just might have a chance."

"As for Tuck and Angelou, for all we know, they could be dead. Balladin, after you and Annaquinn fulfill the Sangrahl of the Fifth Age, return here. If either of them is still alive, they will look for us where we left them."

"The Table Shrine, Jacobi," said Balladin. "Once the Sangrahl fulfills its quest in the Fifth and Sixth Ages, you must make a run for the Masa Mabedi in Myra."

Marielle lowered her head. "I don't see how we can pull this off."

Jacob shook his head. "I know. To this company, I tell you this. We are now sailing a sinking ship with no buckets to bail out the water. We're running out of answers. Balladin, prepare Annaquinn for the journey. Marielle and I have one more fire to light."

Chapter 23
Fire Letters

Balladin remained with Annaquinn at the meeting circle on the forecastle deck while Jacob and Marielle disappeared into the captain's chamber.

Annaquinn wrung her hands across her lap. "Brother monk, I know nothing about being a Keeper. Jacob told me just a little about the whole quest. What must I do?"

"Jacob and Marielle are attempting to uncover hidden messages in Sephus's book, and I will join them soon. After that, Marielle will pass onto you the Sangrahl treasure. As Keeper, you are to keep this close to you and visible so that its light shines against the evil ways of the world."

"That doesn't sound too difficult. Then what?"

"We take it to the place you dreamt about, the Roman thermal spring. It is also a wellspring, so if the dragon comes for us, we may use it to escape. No telling where we would end up as it is a wellspring and not one of Sephus's mapped out Earthsprings."

"There is a difference?"

"Only that one glows blue and sends you where it wills. That dress you were making from the silk. Did you complete it?"

"Not yet, but what's wrong with the one I have on?"

Balladin shook his head.

Annaquinn's eyes widened. "Oh!"

"Finish it, in case you need to travel through time."

"I am certain we will have time durin' the journey. Yeh will help me finish it?"

Balladin nodded. "I am at your service."

In the Captain's chamber, Jacob and Marielle opened up Sephus's book to the page where Sephus's elusive clue rested. While Jacob lit three candles, Marielle took out the Sangrahl and placed it next to the book.

Marielle sat at the table. "Let's hope this works a second time. I am ready."

Marielle cupped her hands over both of her eyes while Jacob picked up a candle. Seeing that Marielle had her eyes covered, he placed the flame of the candle into the top of the bowl.

"It's all right, Marielle, you can open them."

Marielle took her hands from her eyes. She looked first at Jacob, then gazed into the lamplight.

The Sangrahl, resting next to Sephus's book, carried a torch flame worthy of the Olympics, neither bright nor dull. Like before, the flame itself appeared as suspended in the air above the Lamp's opening.

"Marielle, give me your hand." Jacob took hold of her hand and placed it close to the flame.

Marielle resisted the pull, yet she felt only a minor amount of heat projecting from the flame. She allowed Jacob to level her hand within the flame. No pain or intense heat burned into her flesh. Rather, the magic fire felt as thermal water flowing across her palm.

"Unbelievable!" she said.

"Yes."

"How did you know it would be harmless?"

"Harmless only to Keepers. When it burned bright on the Irish plain, I picked it up in a way that should have burned me, but like you, I felt only a comforting warmth."

"But you're immortal."

"Let's take a look."

Marielle took her hand from the fire and gazed at the pages of Sephus's book.

Overlaying the lettering in Sephus's hand were letters etched in glowing embers across the page. Sephus's script faded away as the fiery lettering took over every page in the book.

Marielle turned the pages over and over, marveling at the delicate, illuminated print. She looked up at Jacob. "Is there ever a time when we don't discover something new about the Sangrahl and stand in awe of it?"

"I believe there is still so much mystery yet to be known about this small treasure. Marielle! Our time is short."

Balladin knocked on the outer door before entering. He also gazed upon the flame in wonder. "You found something?"

Jacob gestured an outstretched hand towards the open book.

Balladin stared into the pages. "It did this before. The words are in an ancient script. I believe the book reads us, finds out which language we speak."

The lettering began as an ancient script of an origin none of them could recognize. It then transformed into another script similar to the first. Then it transformed again.

Balladin said, "Oh, look! That's Greek."

"Yes," agreed Jacob. "It is as if it's looking for our language. Yes. There's the French dialect of my youth in La Bellaroche."

Marielle called out. "Now it's transforming into English. This is amazing! Let's get quill and paper. We do not know when we may see the Sangrahl again."

Page after page, Jacob and Marielle read the script of a delicate hand neither of them could recognize. The print was not by Sephus's hand, but from something of a higher realm. Marielle kept her thoughts to herself when the script touched on the Firespring and the dangers of going there. She did not want to admit she had once found herself close to being drawn into it.

"Wait!," said Marielle. "This is important."

> Regarding the Masa Mabedi. This is the Table Shrine where the Sangrahl first left this earth in the First Age. Thanks be to God. It is from this place in the Sixth Age that the cumulation of the Sacred Object of all ages, the Sangrahl, may be joined to become One. It is here in this sacred place and time that the unification of all seven Keepers enjoins as one.
>
> Once the Keepers in each of the six ages light the Lamp, set them upon a hill, and deliver the Lamp at the designated place and time, the Seventh Keeper will receive the Sangrahl for one final year.
>
> The final Sangrahl will come to her in Myra, where she shall receive and keep it lit throughout her period. Bring Light, Bring Light! Goodness shall shine in the hearts of men and women across the world.

The three of them all regarded each other. Balladin placed gentle hands on the table. "We've been missing the most important thing."

Marielle nodded. "We should have been lighting the Lamp and placing it high on a mountain or hill this whole time? That explains why the people of our time have not changed."

Jacob shook his head. "There was one problem."

Balladin and Marielle said, "Dargo."

"This writing came into this book long before the coming of Araqnis and the cryptics. If a Keeper lights the Sangrahl and places it in a place for all the world to see, the Keeper then gives him or herself away and becomes a target."

"Did you know this, Jacobi?" Balladin said.

"Sephus protected me. He knew we were doing it wrong, but first wanted to see if there was a way to do away with the cryptic Dargo. He mentioned the lighting of the Sangrahl, but I never understood until now what he meant."

Marielle held her hand over the flame of the Sangrahl, again feeling its flowing warmth. "Gentlemen. We cannot light it still. Even now we are being hunted by something much greater than cryptics. Balladin, have Annaquinn conceal this and mention nothing about its lighting. If you are safe, light it just before delivery. At least it is something. In the meantime, Jake and I have to stall that dragon and figure out a way to defeat it."

Balladin shook his head. "Without the Petras and without Meeshayell, there is no way to defeat it."

Jacob looked towards the door. "We must be off then. Annaquinn? Is she ready?"

"Annaquinn is preparing the ship now for departure."

Out on the deck, the smell of sulfur was stronger than before. *He is coming*. Jacob and Marielle could sense it.

Annaquinn approached them. "What is that smell?"

Marielle walked up to her. "My surrogate Keeper and friend."

Marielle leaned in and gave a long, warm hug to Annaquinn.

Annaquinn could not hold back a tear from streaming down her cheek. "Yeh know I hated you once."

Marielle released her embrace and held Annaquinn within her gaze. "And now?"

Annaquinn blushed a little. "We are sisters now… and friends always."

"Survive this quest so that I may hold you to that! I hand over this treasure into your capable hands. It is both a gift and a burden. Bear it well"

Marielle gave Annaquinn the box and walked over to Jacob's side.

Jacob placed Sephus's book inside a satchel made of the silk. He felt the sword at his side glowing with the presence of Marielle. "Fare thee all well and Godspeed. When your mission is complete, come to Myra in the Sixth Age. That will be our rendezvous point."

He turned to leave, but Marielle had one last word.

"Look out for our Angelou and Tuck. Bring them back to safety!"

Balladin held out his hands. They all placed their hands together into one clasp. Balladin assured them, "Annaquinn and I will first sail the coastline hoping to find Tuck before moving on to England."

Chapter 24
The Wolf and the Cryptic Creature

As rain fell across the whole of Scandinavia, Tuck returned to Norway through the same wellspring he had entered when he came to find Sephus in an earlier dimension. His mind spun in the contemplation of his unexpected encounter with a young Sephus.

He found himself holed up inside a cave and warming his saturated body by a fire. Though he had given up his bow to Sephus, he found them afloat in the wellspring upon his return, just as Sephus promised.

He made a fire near to the entrance hoping that it would also stave off the cryptic creature. He sat alone nibbling pine nuts he had gained along the way and reflected on the last time he had been alone in the rain.

"This is an ominous feeling," he said to no one. "The last time I was alone in a stone laden place in such weather, Shoebottom deceived me and stabbed me with a knife."

He looked at his quiver and then into his pouch. Though his quiver still held ten long arrows, his pouch was close to empty. *Only two Tears left.*

Though he had chosen not to expend the Tears of the Wanderer too readily, the Gévaudan had accepted the challenge, charging in every opportunity it found, forcing Tuck to defend himself by expending the magic gemstones he carried. Though his bow staved off each attempt at his life, it was only a matter of time before Tuck would run out of the Tears of the Wanderer.

Tuck found the cave and, although it was not deep, he hoped it was enough to grant him a reprieve from the constant threat from the elusive, cryptic creature. What was worse, the Gévaudan required no sleep, as Tuck had not slept in three days.

The wellspring through which he had gone was near to the cave. Tuck knew if he had to, he could use it a second time for his own protection.

Each time he drifted into sleep, a distant howl penetrating the trees and echoing off the hills would rattle his senses. He would awaken again and take out just the arrow and affix it with a Tear gemstone.

"If it comes into here, I'll stab it rather than shoot it." Tuck let his eyelids droop once again until the howling became alarmingly close—or worse, until the howling stopped altogether, leaving Tuck with no idea how close the creature stalked.

Putting another log on the fire and closing his eyes tight, he wondered once again about Angelou. He had not seen the dog since the second day of his hunt. Because the Gévaudan had charged him three times since, Tuck assumed Jake and Marielle's beloved dog had long since perished.

He slept through the night and awoke gladdened to find himself still alive when the sun appeared in the sky. With the Tear-tipped arrow still clasped in his hand, he peered out the opening of his shelter. The rain had moved on and so had his fire.

Tuck stepped out into the sunlight, feeling the wonder of the beauty of the northern countries for the first time. He had focused too much on the danger ahead of him to have even noticed the natural beauty before him, but now his senses inhaled the enchantment of his surroundings.

He looped his bow across his back and held the two remaining longbow arrows in each hand. He would not waste another Tear, but use them as daggers should the time come.

Angelou! Poor girl. You must have met a foolish end.

It saddened Tuck, knowing that if he made it back to the Keepers, he would have somber news indeed. The dog appeared to have teased the cryptic creature into going farther north and Tuck had tracked her as far as he was able, without a certainty of his own death. The Gévaudan took the bait. Now Tuck walked along the shoreline of an unknown fiord.

"Perhaps I should head south. With luck I may come in contact with *The Rising Stargazer.*"

As his reflection met him along the gentle water, he could see how the stress and lack of sleep had worked into his image. The peacefulness of the light breeze and small waves across the rocky beach gave Tuck a false sense he was out of danger.

Turning around, he saw the place where the wellspring had welcomed him. His last point of escape remained a warm beacon. Then he noticed something different.

There was a strange dark aura projected above the wellspring. The aura contained a shadow that concealed all that rested in the forest beyond.

Tuck shivered at the reality of it. "So that's it! That's how that cryptic creature time traveled in unison with the rest of us. He entered that aura into that dark place!"

Tuck strung one of the two arrows to his longbow. He took aim at the aura and sent the arrow flying towards it.

Upon impact, a flash of light sent beams of light in every direction. The aura no longer stood above the wellspring. Tuck had only one remaining Tear with which to defend himself.

"There you go, you rat bastard. You no longer have a way to follow us!"

Tuck sat on a large rock facing the water. To his left was the path from which he had come. He imagined *The Rising Stargazer* awaiting him somewhere along the shoreline.

"I failed you, Angelou. I have no way to protect you even if you survived this. I should return to the ship."

Tuck stood up. To his right was the remaining track he had yet to cover.

"No, I cannot go on without some proof, some answer to the puzzling questions. Angelou's tracks still run before me. I have to go on, even though I know it will cost me my life."

He bent into the lapping water and washed his face and neck. "Yes… even if it costs me my life."

He got up to return to the north and the last place he had seen Angelou's track, when the hair on the back of his neck stood up. He turned and froze.

There between himself and the woodlands, the Gévaudan stood, staring.

In the daylight, the features of the creature came more into focus. Its dull, charcoal-colored fur appeared matted as if never washed of the blood of its many victims. Its long, clawed paws were the size of two of Tuck's feet. The black, elongated fur across the top of its head and back stood up like knife points.

The worst part was its eyes. Mimicking the sharpened edges of its yellow fangs, the pupils were diamond shaped and filled with malice. The edges of the corneas were blood red half-concealed by the heavy upper lids.

It licked its lips, assured of victory. It recognized that Tuck had his back against the water with no place to run.

Tuck remained still. He gripped his remaining arrow in his right hand, but at that moment, knew it would do him little good. A swipe of one paw would be crippling and painful. A thrust of its jaws and he would know what it felt like to be consumed by a shark.

The Gévaudan's lips quivered and it let out a low, guttural growl. It took a step to one side that still closed a portion of the distance between them. Then it took a step opposite, each time weaving its way closer to its target.

Tuck knew that although Marielle was the scent marked on the beast forever, his bow and Tears had marked him as the cryptic creature's mortal enemy. The Gévaudan would never stop until both he and Marielle found themselves inside the creature's mouth.

From one side to another, the Gévaudan zigzagged ever closer, pushing Tuck farther against the shoreline. To swim was useless. They had witnessed the Gévaudan's ability at sea.

Tuck placed himself low amidst the rocks and sand. He knew the Gévaudan would charge, he would put up a fierce resistance, kill the bloody creature if he could.

The Gévaudan moved in ever closer. Saliva dripped from its teeth.

Just as he was about to pounce, a rustle of tiny steps sounded along the beach. Angelou appeared and closed in. She growled and barked at the cryptic creature with stone-laden resolve.

The Gévaudan back away and faced the oncoming dog. As they had done in the days prior, the two of them danced and lunged. The beast leapt to where Angelou challenged it, but missed the dog by an inch.

As Angelou circled it, the creature resumed the chase. The Gévaudan had two choices, man or wolf. It chose the mortal enemy and chased Angelou into the forest.

Tuck stood up and, in the silence, he marveled at what he had just seen.

"I know something," he said out loud. "With luck it will be your undoing!"

Far out on the horizon, he spied an approaching ship. Tuck ran out onto a jetty to get a better look. He was certain by the masts it was *The Rising Stargazer.*

Chapter 25
Kulning Cows and Wolves

Two sailors from *The Rising Stargazer* approached the shoreline where Tuck awaited them. They rowed the dingy into a deeper pocket of water along a large rock outcropping, allowing Tuck to meet them along the edge of the natural jetty.

In the boat, Tuck could see the elated looks of Balladin and Annaquinn leaning against the ship's starboard rail. As the two of them stood close together, Tuck thought for a moment of the possibility that a romance was brewing between them. Annaquinn was, after all, grieving. Grieving invites comfort and the need for comfort invites affection.

He climbed the rope ladder where Balladin offered him a sturdy arm, followed by a brotherly embrace. To Tuck's surprise, Annaquinn followed suit and wrapped her arms around him.

The sailors, from the rigging to the decks, stopped to watch. They knew it was uncustomary for a young woman to wrap arms around a man who was not family.

"We thought over these past days that you were dead," Annaquinn said, releasing her embrace. "What can I do for you?"

"Where are Jake and Marielle?"

"The Seventh Age," replied Balladin.

Tuck scowled. "We had all agreed we would not split apart. Why are we divided?"

"I will tell you everything, Tuck, but first, have you seen Angelou?"

"This morning. That dog saved my life. The cryptic creature is more deadly than a full- grown tiger. For some strange reason, it was more engaged with the dog than coming after me. That creature could have made a meal out of both of us, but I was a much easier target."

"The Tears did not work?"

"The harm was inconsequential. Why are Jake and Marielle not with you?"

"The dragon is out of its celestial prison and is hunting for them."

"What?"

"The smell of sulfur. We saw his silhouette against the night sky. Jacobi and Marielle made it to the Masa Mabedi, the place where the Sangrahl's final delivery is to take place. Ghost Keepers of the first three ages appeared to deliver the Sangrahl to Marielle, but the fifth and sixth Keepers were missing."

"Because they have yet to deliver the Sangrahl in those ages?"

Balladin nodded.

Tuck leaned against the rail. "So, what now?"

"Annaquinn, according to Sephus's way, is now the surrogate Keeper to her brother Korynn. As soon as the crew turns this ship around, we're headed to the Sangrahl delivery place in England."

"Annaquinn, you have the Sangrahl?"

"I do," said Annaquinn. "I did not expect this."

"They orientated you to the weight of your role?"

Balladin clapped his hand on Tuck's shoulder. "I took care of it. Jake and Marielle took flight to the Seventh Age in order to lead Araqnis away from Annaquinn and allow us a running start. They will meet up with us later on at the Table Shrine."

Tuck shook his head. "We will deliver the Sangrahl, but there is one thing you are all forgetting. There is a Keeper of the Sixth Age. If we get the Sangrahl to the delivery point, logic would follow that the Keeper of the Sixth Age has his treasure to hold. With a dragon on the hunt for Keepers, he will need our protection as well. Balladin, it's what we swore an oath to do."

Balladin nodded. "Your plan is already on our schedule. We will see this through to the end, even if it means dying for the cause. The Gévaudan came here before Angelou disappeared. Hothgarth is dead."

Tuck heaved a deep breath. "I almost lost my life already. Annaquinn, I am sorry to hear about your father. Are you now in charge of this ship?"

Annaquinn tilted her head inquisitively. "I am. The *Stargazer* is now mine in my father's stead."

Balladin smiled. "The crew and I are addressing her as Captain Quinn."

Tuck smiled. "Captain Quinn, will you take the *Stargazer* up the northern shore?"

Annaquinn smiled with a feeling of importance. "I will do whatever pleases the Knights of the Sangrahl. Mr. Fletcher! A word if yeh may!"

"The Sangrahl is our priority, Tuck," said Balladin.

"Give me an hour. Angelou is still out there. When last I saw her, she was still very much alive."

"If we find her, so will the Gévaudan. Legend has it the cryptic creature has an uncontrollable appetite for young women. If he sees Anna… if he sees Captain Quinn here…"

"I have just one Tear left. I used the last one to destroy the Gévaudan's time portal. At least he cannot time travel. Know this Bal, Jake and Marielle would never forgive us if we didn't do all that we could to rescue their dog."

"Jake and Marielle would never forgive us if we all lose our lives and the Sangrahl to boot."

"Then we will do all that we can to stay alive."

Balladin and Annaquinn regarded each other. They nodded in agreement.

"I'm never one to be a leader, Tuck," said Balladin. "I am here as an advisor as Sephus was."

"You are among the best, my friend!"

"How will we get Angelou to come to the ship? She would not even listen to Jacobi's commands?"

"I don't know, Bal, I guess we'll address the challenges as they come."

As Captain Quinn had commanded, *The Rising Stargazer* continued forward along the shore as the evening shadows approached. Off in the distant forest, they could hear snarling and the breaking of timbers. The watchman from the crow's nest sighted activity and called the coordinates.

Out onto the beach, two creatures, one large and one small, dashed and circled around each other. The Gévaudan, feeling livid by this bothersome canine, growled and gritted its fangs while it took chase.

Angelou, for reasons the Knights of the Sangrahl could not fathom, had guided the cryptic creature towards them along the Norwegian shoreline. She dodged this way and then that, keeping just enough distance between herself and the cryptic creature. Whenever she had room to stop, she would bark the challenge, infuriating the Gévaudan further and causing it to continue the chase.

Tuck shook his head. "She must have hidden herself for rest these past days when I could not find her. Now, she thinks she has the stamina to outrun him forever. We've got to do something."

"What if you take it down with an arrow? Angelou would then have room to move."

"And do what? Her bite couldn't do any more harm than my arrows."

Balladin took an abrupt hold of Tuck's arm. "Tuck, that's it!"

Tuck looked at him. "What?"

"The bite of a wolf! Dargo was always afraid of Angelou. Why?"

Tuck shook his head. He recalled the cryptic did not dare enter Jacob's cottage so long as he suspected his dog remained within. Was it to be the same case with the Gévaudan?

"Angelou is just a dog, Bal, what's this have to do with wolves?"

Tuck turned around, but Balladin was no longer there. He watched as Balladin caught up with Annaquinn, whispering into the girl's ear.

Annaquinn's face contorted with perplexity at Balladin's request.

Balladin took Annaquinn's hand (another anomaly to the sailors who watched them) and guided her towards the steps leading up to the forecastle deck. He looked over his shoulder towards Tuck, beckoning him to follow.

"Anchor the ship!" called out Annaquinn to her first officer. When the first mate hesitated with a look of bewilderment, Annaquinn addressed him again. "Yeh heard me, Mr. Fletcher, anchor this ship!"

One of the sailors released the capstan that held one of the anchors. It rolled with a clatter and splashed into the deep part of the inlet sea, just thirty feet from the shore.

When Tuck caught up with them on the upper deck, everything became quiet. On the shoreline battlefield,

Angelou and the cryptic creature had disappeared into the woods and, for a time, made no more sound. The birds ceased to chirp. The wind became placid. A heavy fog poured in across the water towards the shoreline.

Annaquinn took hold of the forecastle rail. In the stillness, her clear, melodic voice rang out in a range of notes.

"Oh-Wah-HOO-weeh-neh!"

Her voice echoed across the forests and hills like ocean waves at high tide.

Tuck looked at Balladin.

"Kulning," said Balladin. "It is a way Nordic girls call cattle."

"Cattle? What do cows have to do with all of this?"

"Kulning was once a way a wolf clan communicated with wolves in the days of yore."

"EEEh-HEY-wah-hoo!"

Whenever Annaquinn's echoes ceased, everything remained in stillness.

"Ah-HOOO-hey-koo-weh!"

Far into the distance, every listening ear on *The Rising Stargazer* heard it. A barely audible howl from yonder distant horizon echoed Annaquinn's kulning.

"Keep going," said Balladin to the maiden.

Annaquinn's voice rang out louder than before. *"Mey-wahh-hey-noh! Oh-Wah-HOO-weeh-neh!"*

One wolf howl became two and from two to a multitude. Each time Annaquinn's voice sang out, the wolve's howls became more audible than before.

"They are coming!" said Balladin.

Annaquinn continued to kuln as the wolves' howls got ever closer. To everyone's dismay, another sound rang out.

Mooo!
Three cows appeared out of the southern plain to join in the chorus.

Between Annaquinn's kulning, the cry of an approaching wolf pack, and three unsuspecting cattle, Angelou appeared once again along the beachhead. She was bleeding from a gash along her neck, but still holding onto energetic resolve.

The Gévaudan followed, but now with hesitant steps. It had its sights no longer on Angelou, but turned its head in several directions. A myriad of distractions engaged the cryptic creature all at once.

First were the cows, a quick and tasty meal and of many the Gévaudan had already engaged in. There was Angelou, the incessant menace it had been swatting at like a pesky fly. There was the smell of Annaquinn somewhere in the sea's direction. There was the faint smell of Marielle still lingering about the ship.

On top of it all, a new realization penetrated the Gévaudan's reality. The deadly bite of the timber wolf was a cryptic's worst nightmare.

The meandering cows decided the kulning calls were no longer about them and moved away down the beach in resolve to not get eaten that day.

Angelou dashed into the water and swam towards the ship. Behind her, two wolves appeared along the edge of the forest.

The first wolf, by his tall stance, and broad shoulders, was the alpha wolf. It was his voice that rang out first. It was his eyes that surveyed the battle scene. It was this white and silver wolf who called the shots.

By his side, was the alpha wolf's mate. She was equally regal in her appearance with a darker, silvery coat.

The Gévaudan's shackles raised, and it set its front legs apart and its front body low. It snarled in challenge at the two wolves.

Annaquinn ceased her kulning calls when she saw three more wolves appear alongside the alphas.

The wolves' eyes bored into the cryptic creature. They made not a sound, but surveyed their challenge with careful deliberation.

By the time Angelou reached the ship's hull, the entire pack, forty-three in all, had emerged out of the forest. They looked to the alpha male and female to control the moves. Between them was a clear and concise communication that required no sound or signal.

Altogether, the wolves moved in, surrounding the Gévaudan on all sides. Now they howled and barked, carefully positioning themselves as if hunting a wooly mammoth.

The Gévaudan jumped into the thick of them, swiping its claws and snapping its jaws. In the ensuing battle, the Gévaudan's snarls and growls were its battle cry.

It was still too quick for forty-three wolves. He leapt across great distances, outmaneuvering them around each turn. He stomped onto the top of an unwary wolf, snuffing the life out of it. The cryptic creature's strategy was simple, wound them one wolf at a time until they are too few to do him harm.

It was at that moment when the Gévaudan cast its gaze toward *The Rising Stargazer* that Tuck felt a cold reality. If the cryptic creature leapt over the surrounding wolf pack and made it into fiord, he would not only escape his adversaries, he would swim to where Tuck stood and kill everyone aboard the ship.

Tuck had one Tear gemstone left inside his pouch. Tuck knew all that the wolves required was the stumbling of the great, cryptic creature.

The Gévaudan bound down the beach toward the water.

Tuck set his longbow one last time. The twang rang out in harmony with the voices of the wolves. It flew across the water like a shooting star across the heavens, meeting its mark just where Tuck had intended.

At the edge of the shore, just feet from the water's edge, the Gévaudan fell to the earth. In a convulsing shock, its legs and paws flailed in desperation.

The pack of wolves halted at the unexpected spectacle as the Gévaudan struggled against the earth. The pack to the Gévaudan's rear closed in. The alpha male and female darted in. The others followed.

Three of the rear guard snapped the Gévaudan's rear legs. Two more sank teeth into its lower rib cage. Soon, others tore into the creature's soft underbelly.

The cryptic creature jerked like one who was drowning in a merciless sea. Forty-two wolves were soon on top of the creature giving it no way to recover it once upper hand.

Annaquinn could no longer watch the spectacle and turned away. Though she carried no love for such an evil creature, she still could not bear to absorb its audible suffering.

It did not take long before the wolf pack completed the kill. They stepped away when the Gévaudan made no further movement. Because its flesh was undesirable to the wolves for feeding, the wolf pack abandoned the carcass for the carrion and crows to feed on.

In the aftermath, the wolves walked down to the beach. In the passing moments, they focused their attention on Annaquinn, the woman who had called to them. The alpha wolf poised itself and let out a triumphant howl. His mate did likewise. The others followed in unison until the full song echoed across the entire region. In the silent echo that followed, they turned and disappeared into the deep forest.

Tuck took Angelou into his arms from the sailor who extracted the dog from the seawater. "Good girl!" he told her repeatedly as Angelou whimpered and cried.

Balladin beckoned Annaquinn to bring the Sangrahl and water. While *The Rising Stargazer* raised anchor and turned away from the terminus of the fiord and towards the mouth of the North Sea, Balladin poured water from the Sangrahl over the dog's many wounds, restoring her to full health.

"What a brave little girl!" each of them said as three pairs of hands caressed her fur.

Angelou sat up, licking their faces, and giving them a wag of her tail. She nestled her furry head into them, letting each of them know she still loved them.

"We could never doubt your love or your devotion, ol' girl," Tuck said, holding tears back from his eyes. He knew he had played his part to keep her alive as she did to him. Tuck would never look at Jacob Lake's dog again without intense admiration.

As *The Rising Stargazer* took to the sea and pointed her bow towards England, a dragon circled in the skies far overhead. Araqnis had followed Marielle's scent to that region, but could not discern why her scent had dissipated.

From that faraway place, Araqnis's eyes and ears perceived the war of the wolves, knowing full well the deadliness of their bite against his cryptics. He felt the fall of the Gévaudan and a part of Araqnis died along with it.

The dragon belched forth a cry of anger that spanned across the Nordic countries from Denmark and Norway to Finland to the east. Araqnis was more resolved than ever to destroy them all.

Chapter 26
A Silence in Ghost Hollow

Shoebottom sailed *La Constance* hoisting the whitest, newest sails. The moonlit night energized his time-traveling ship to the midlands of France, where farm and forest intermingled like brothers.

He directed *La Constance* down to a familiar place only a day's ride of where the long-abandoned village of La Bellaroche once stood. It was the Seventh Age, the twenty-first century, and much had changed in the world since Shoebottom's time.

Ghost Hollow, however, had changed little. The old-growth trees and limestone cliffs still held the creek-carven valley in its primitive impersonation. The restricted opening contained the same vein of rock and rubble that caved in the Cave of Bulls. It remained the same steadfast sentry to Dargo's three-hundred-year prison, except for one minor difference.

The intrusion gave way to a cavity large enough to bring a sliver of light into the cave after 900 years of weathered erosion. Ever since Balladin and Tuck had expelled the opening of the cave to trap Dargo within, no outside air had reached its inner bowels until now.

Shoebottom jumped off the time traveler and, with a myriad of tools accompanied by a bottle of Bordeaux wine, stopped at the opening to listen in. Knowing that the opening was still too small for the onetime cryptic to escape, he leaned down and called Dargo's name.

Only hollow air echoing Shoebottom's voice made a reply.

With pick and shovel, Shoebottom attacked the cavity like a prospector discovering the mother lode. Rock and debris poured out of the hole until it was large enough for a man the size of Shoebottom to slither his way in.

Lighting a light and carrying the green bottle, Shoebottom adjusted his eyes to the darkness within. On the ceiling, and revealed by the lantern light, the painted bulls, cave hunters, elk, and lions, appeared to dance with elation—free at last.

The cave paintings remained a marvel to behold, but they were not the purpose of Shoebottom's visit. Through a narrow corridor, he worked his way deep into the hollowed impression. At the cave's terminus where a wellspring threw forth no blue light, Shoebottom stopped.

"Ah! There you are ol' chap!"

There, at the edge of the pool, was a large skeleton once belonging to Dargo de Montebank. It rested face down with its skull turned to one side. Its arms and legs sprayed in four directions as evidence the dying figure must have been standing when it died and fell to the earth. Dargo's black attire clung brittle against its spine and rib cage.

Shoebottom sat down near the skull on a bench-level rock. He placed a corkscrew into the bottle cork and began twisting it in. "How long has it been, dear boy, since I last paid you a visit? What's that? A thousand years? Oh, you exaggerate! It couldn't be more than a few hundred."

Pop! The cork whizzed and collided against the far wall, echoing sound waves into every crevice. If the painted deer, the victim of the cork's target, had been alive, Shoebottom would have bagged it.

He bent over and took hold of Dargo's skull. He twisted it until it snapped loose from the neck vertebrae attached there since Dargo's beginnings. Shoebottom held up the skull and examined it.

"Why Dargo, you look a bit pale! Tell me, are they not feeding you in here? For such an enormous head, you did not carry a tremendous intellect."

Shoebottom turned the skull upside down and poured a generous serving of red wine into it. He lifted the skull to his mouth. "Here's to the good old days!" He drank down the wine.

He placed the skull right side up onto a level shelf across from him so that it faced him, its jaw and teeth in a permanent grin of irony.

"You know, dear boy, Araqnis assured me you would turn to dust the moment I became a cryptic. As you well know, it was not I who ceased your incessant suffering by replacing your life's immortality, but a village idiot not much smarter than yourself. The interesting thing is, that village idiot outsmarted me as well."

Shoebottom took up pebbles and pitched them towards the skull, attempting to score shots in Dargo's eye sockets. "The girl? What girl? Oh! Dear boy, you mean the girl Keeper! What has become of her? You'll be happy to know she is faring very well—very well, no thanks to you. A lovely girl, Marielle…"

Shoebottom stopped pitching the pebbles as his eyes gazed into the unknown. His shoulders drooped a bit as he thought of her. "I never thought a young woman could impact me in such a way."

Dargo's skull made no reply.

Shoebottom took a swig of wine from the bottle. "Having lived for centuries as a cryptic, I am sure you would understand. I know you've been in love many, many times.

What's that? You haven't? A handsome boy like you? Oh, come now!"

Dargo's skull made no response.

Shoebottom stood up. He took yet another swig of the Bordeaux and stepped over the oversized skeleton. He could tell that the remnants of Dargo's black leather attire were brittle and delicate after centuries of decay.

Dargo's belt remained tight about the hips.

"Really, ol' chap, you should put more food into your diet. You are way underweight for a man your size." He bent over and picked up the dagger, still sheathed, and tucked into the belt. Going back to his place near the lantern, he sat down and took out the blade.

"Funny how well preserved an airtight space is. This blade looks as if crafted yesterday." He fingered the edge, careful not to cut himself. "This is the blade that killed Jacob Lake. It may well be up for a repeat performance. Look here…"

Shoebottom held the blade up to the grinning skull. "There is still a stain of blood right here. Didn't your father teach you to wipe clean your weapons after battle?"

Shoebottom took a final swig of the bottle and placed the empty bottle into one of Dargo's skeleton hands. He returned the skull to the ground as it had rested previously.

"My dear boy, you appear to have drunk yourself to oblivion! This is sure to baffle the archeologists for years."

Shoebottom sheathed the dagger and held it up. "This is what I came for. There are only four noted immortal weapons in Sephus's book, and you had one of them. Yes, Jacob Lake's sword is the third one mentioned, but even I would be hard-pressed to wrestle it out from under him. The fourth? Something called a butterfly knife. Yes, I know, ol' chap. Sounds like a dinner plate utensil."

Shoebottom turned, picked up his lantern, and headed towards the exit. He turned again and bowed in gratitude to his old master. "Fare thee well, and good health to you! I apologize for permanently borrowing your prize possession, but I have a dim-witted cryptic to kill."

After Hadrian Shoebottom worked his way out of the hole and set the sails of *La Constance* back to the Fifth Age, Ghost Hollow would never be the same.

As the howls and groans of a ghostly voice no longer permeated the walls of the cave, the opening was soon to beckon a wanderer, a man gathering wood or children out playing hide and go seek. Whichever the case, someone would find the cavity opening, crawl in, and announce an epic Paleolithic discovery.

As with Lascaux, anthropologists will list this particular Cave of Intoxication into the archives of anthropology. Many would believe, until carbon dating proved otherwise, that the large skeleton found on the cave floor, had once been a caveman.

Chapter 27
A River of Lost Souls

Just before Jacob and Marielle entered an Earthspring that would carry them back to the Seventh Age, they spied the dragon Araqnis for the first time.

The dragon soared high above the earth like a treasure boat at sea, looking for the sunken Titanic. Flying in progressive circles, it followed its senses for a treasure no sunken ship could rival.

It appeared only as a shadow against the moonlit sky. From its pattern of flight, it was clear to the Keepers; the dragon had a proximity of where to find them.

With Sephus's book bound tight within a silken satchel, Jacob Lake and Marielle Eckenrode dove deep into the green-glowing springs and far out of the range of a fire-breathing dragon.

As had been the case with every trip, the springs enveloped them with a feeling of serenity, of healing, and of hope. For the first time in their relationship, they held hands beneath the water, acknowledging each other's twilit silhouette as the warm current coaxed them along the seven-minute swim.

They emerged in a place both of them recognized—Baker's Bridge of the Seventh Age.

The deep waters of the channel of the Animas River had never been more welcoming as the two of them reached the surface.

Sunlight poured in as they had entered the space 660 years into the future, but eight hours earlier in time. Though it appeared to be the middle of the day, Jacob and Marielle were happy to find no one witnessing their emergence from deep down.

"I spied something on the river bottom just as the Earthspring closed," Jacob said.

"What was it?" Marielle kept her body afloat with her hand skimming the water and her legs in constant motion.

"I can breathe for a long time under the water, I'm going down for a second look."

As Jacob swam down beneath her, Marielle picked out a satisfactory shore and swam towards it. She wondered what the inhabitants of Durango, Colorado would think if they saw a couple wearing silken, sopping wet, medieval tunics. No matter, she thought, we're not here to make an impression.

She sat against the steep shoreline as Jacob's image appeared out of the depths. When he reached the surface, he was carrying what appeared to be a small treasure chest.

"You found something indeed!" Marielle said, leaning forward for a better look.

Jacob swam to where she sat. "It seems every time we turn around, we're soaked from head to toe!"

Marielle smiled with the realization that even a dragon cannot follow them through a wellspring.

Jacob stepped out of the water. "You recall in Sephus's book that there are just four immortal weapons available to the amaranthine? I believe this is one of them."

"Why would you think that?"

Jacob sat next to her. "When Sephus wrote of their origins, he mentioned 'the Channel of Lost Souls.' Look, the workmanship of this chest is much like what had carried the Sangrahl."

"That's right! I saw that too," Marielle said, pondering. "Yes, that makes sense! This is the Rio de las Animas, the River of Souls."

"Not the River of *Lost* Souls?"

"I think *perdidas* is implied, but that's what I remember."

Jacob sat next to her. He unlatched the lid to the box and opened it.

Inside was a red velvet lining molded to hold two very shiny weapons. They were identical to each other in every way. Each had a black leather-bound handle. The hilt, hand guards, and short, flat, and rounded blades shimmered silver in the midday sun.

"Butterfly knives!" Marielle ran her fingers across the dull top and sharp edges. "They appear as if they are new."

"Immortal blades are just like that. I've carried my father's sword for years and there is never a mark or blemish anywhere."

Jacob handed the box to Marielle. "Now you have your weapons."

Marielle straightened up. "Me? But…"

"The master of the temple in India said you were especially good with butterfly knives."

Marielle took hold of the swords in each hand. "He said that, didn't he?" She slashed them into the air with the precision of her training. "Master was never one to compliment, just to make one feel good. In fact, he was often blunt and painfully honest in his assessments!"

"Now you can slay the dragon." Jacob smiled.

"Hardly!" Marielle returned the blades. "Where did Tuck leave his Humvee?"

Jacob stood up. "Come on, it's over this way."

Marielle followed him down a two-lane road a half-mile walk to where Tuck had stowed his vehicle in a friend's driveway. She looked about the familiar atmosphere not far removed from her own hometown.

"Jake?"

Jacob slowed down to allow Marielle to walk by his side.

"You propose we return to the alcove, my hideaway camp in the Grand Canyon?"

"Shoebottom knew of its location, but I doubt he would have shared that with Araqnis. Even a dragon might have a hard time locating us there."

"He uses his sense of smell or some other internal sense. He will know a way to find me."

Jacob stopped. "I know no other place. I favor this location, because there is a wellspring there and we can at least escape through if he comes. I know of no safer place. How many times can a dragon search the ages in search of us. At the very least, it's the only other wellspring we know and a way to flee if we need to."

Marielle pondered his words. "I think we should go to Havasu Falls. Tuck used the Earthspring there to reach me. Jake, I'm not too certain the alcove is the safest place."

Jake moved forward. "There is another reason for going there. I see a path from the wellspring to Le Mont St. Michel and from Le Mont St. Michel across the sea to Norway. It's the shortest range to return to Myra."

Marielle nodded. "I would imagine Sephus's chamber would be even more difficult for the dragon to locate. To the alcove then. At least we know it will take the dragon some time to figure out where we are. If stone eludes the Petras, perhaps it stifles the senses of a dragon. I will concur then. Let's head quick as we can to the alcove."

Marielle stopped and opened the box containing the butterfly knives. "One more thing."

Jacob turned. "What's that?"

"We're passing by Lake Powell on our way to the North Rim. I want to stop and see my family."

Chapter 28
The Key That Opens the Crypt

From Ghost Hollow, Shoebottom rode across the French countryside, heading back to Brittany in the northwestern corner of France. His journey took him through the mountains of the Loire River, the Gate of Poitou, and the city of Poitiers.

During Shoebottom's lifetime, Poitiers had passed from French to English rule and back again like a tennis ball during a Wimbledon tournament. Through the narrow cobblestone streets and past with its Romanesque cathedral, Shoebottom could care less about who ruled who, so long as Shoebottom was free to go his own way.

From Poitiers, he continued his journey through Angers and into the heart of Brittany in the northwestern region of France. He chose horseback rather than continuing on *La Constance,* because traveling the moonlit skies could place him too close to a happenchance flying dragon. Dragons were especially menacing when dragons targeted one for death.

Evading dragons was now among Shoebottom's special new talents while Shoebottom was in search of Orface. If Shoebottom was on Araqnis's hit list, Orface was now on Shoebottom's.

Whether Shoebottom fought for the noble cause solidified by the Keepers or for something more internal, even Shoebottom did not know. *The power of sweet friendship from such a gentle soul!* Marielle had complicated Shoebottom's personal bylaws. Life was no longer simple.

Her impacts on his past and present projected his resolve forward for reasons he could not fathom.

No hanging skeletons guarded his passing when he reached the Forbidden Forest. Their bones still decorated the ground along the winding pathway. Though Araqnis was no longer present, the cemetery of the Specter of the Well remained darker and gloomier than ever before.

"Orface?" Shoebottom called out like he was calling a cat. "Here, Orface! Where are you hiding, you elusive imbecile?"

Shoebottom entered the bone orchard. In his right hand, he held tight to Dargo's immortal dagger. "I know you are here, Orface. You're not smart enough to walk your own path. Araqnis may have commanded you to destroy me, but I know you much better than he."

Shoebottom's instincts commanded him to stand still. He sensed something intangible approached him, something not Orface, but far, far worse. Shoebottom backed himself against a barren oak tree.

Araqnis materialized a short distance in front of him. He did not move, but grinned like a snake anticipating the passing of a frog.

Shoebottom straightened up. "Why, dear boy, you pay me a visit. Impressive disappearing act, Your Dragonship! Normally, anyone in my shoes would tremble, but I figure if you wanted me dead, you would have killed me already."

"Shoebottom, you are ever the one with prowess," said Araqnis. "Apart from the Fire Petra, I am at my full strength, no thanks to you."

"You know, ol' chap, I have a keen sense of injustice. Because you did not keep your end of our agreement, I chose to not uphold mine. If you would like, we could express grievances against each other with a good family counselor. No? What if we visit a local justice of the peace to mitigate our dispute?"

Araqnis grinned more. His long, silvery fangs glistened in the twilight. "Yes, you are the clever one I have always wanted serving at my side. You know, Shoebottom, I could still make you my cryptic. Don't you want to live forever?"

"I noticed you said, *my* cryptic, not *a* cryptic. I'm not certain being a cryptic is much fun when serving one such as you. No offense intended, your Dragonbreath."

Araqnis retained his grin, but the hissing toilet sound emitted from inside his throat.

Shoebottom folded his arms, but pointed a finger up in the air whenever he made a particular point. He paced like a litigator in a courtroom. "Our bargain included me beating Arthur Schachmeister in a second chess match. With the Fire Petra inaccessible to either me or Bo Eskatoll and Marielle denying opportunity to die, the chess match remained the third option. You added this option to our agreement, because if I had failed in the first two options, you did not wish me alive. I not only succeeded in all that you offered me, but I had two Petras to boot."

Shoebottom addressed the tombstones surrounding the two of them. "Ladies and gentlemen of the jury, you can all clearly recognize that it was His Dragonship, not I, who broke the contractual agreement by not upholding his end of the deal."

Shoebottom turned, and whispered an aside to the dead oak tree, "I got the twelve of them in my pocket! The plaintiff doesn't stand a chance."

Araqnis's hissing stopped. "I still want you on my side, Shoebottom. I can do nothing with a cryptic village idiot. It was you who suggested I seal the wellsprings and trap the Keepers into a single age. Thanks to you, the Fifth Age is no longer accessible to them. I am corralling them all into the Seventh Age. I have you to thank for that."

Shoebottom turned to face him. "I have upped my price now that the Black Friday sale is over. What would you offer me? Cryptic status was not enough."

"I cannot offer you even one Petra. I know that's what you desire, but I am a dragon who covets power above all."

"Your power precedes you, Your Dragonship. I had little idea you were approaching without being seen. Very impressive! If no Petra, then what else could you possibly place on the bargaining table?"

"Being my cryptic is all I offer. You can live forever. You can be the most notorious villain in human history. No one can stop you. The challenges in the life game of chess are unlimited."

"Hmm, very tempting—very tempting… You see, ol' chap, there remains one major issue besides the fact that I now have the jury on my side. For a time, I had in my possession Fra Sephus's informational book. I take just one read through and the information imprints itself into my memory forever. What did I discover in those pages, you wonder? I thank you for asking! If I accept your offer and become a cryptic, I am forever under your tutelage and worse still, I am under you full control. You can control me like a string puppet marionette to do your will as you see fit—not much fun for a man of talent."

"You would still be the most notorious villain in human history. I would make sure of it."

"For a dragon who sees much of the world from a well, you miss the very thing I told Marielle just a week ago.

If you, in your evil ways, create a world filled with evil, I am just another criminal among criminals. What fun would that be?"

Araqnis lifted his head high. "You don't understand the brevity of your situation, Shoebottom. I am not asking, I am demanding. Since breaking our contract, I might as well break it further. Now here is my final offer. Be my cryptic or die."

Shoebottom peered at the tombstones. "The jury now has my unwavering sympathy. The judge is threatening you with contempt of court. You might want to hire an experienced attorney rather than argue your feeble case on..."

Before Shoebottom could look Araqnis in the eyes, a dragon's armed wing careened across Shoebottom's body, sending him flying across the ground, twice the distance as before. He collided with a broken stone sculpture of a saddened angel.

Araqnis took on the full limit to a sinister grin, exposing every pointed tooth. "Hadrian Shoebottom, I see you have chosen death. I could snuff out your life altogether, but I see you are on the slow path there! Your wounds are mortal. I bid you, enjoy the pain of dying. I did not wish to make that easy for you, you made your choice and I have made mine!"

Shoebottom's body trembled and flinched without his control. One leg and one arm were broken. Three of his ribs were cracked. He felt the internal bleeding beneath his shattered ribs.

For the first time in his adult memory, Shoebottom regretted having kept his sarcastic mouth open. Hard, disturbing memories of his father strangling the life out of his mother appeared in Shoebottom's throbbing memory.

Araqnis spit in Shoebottom's direction. Seeing there was no further hope for him, Araqnis turned and flew into the sky, leaving his number one cryptic candidate alone to die.

Lying convulsing at the base of the sculpture, he attempted in vain to will his body still. Even the abuse of his father never rendered such intense pain as this. To Shoebottom's dismay, his predicament went from bad to worse. He looked up and saw Orface standing over him.

The half-wit cryptic smirked at his former master while holding the same old club in one hand and Shoebottom's original dagger in his other.

"I knew... I would... find you here," Shoebottom said between heaving breaths.

"Wacknis make dragon fly. Wacknis say kill Chewbottom!"

Orface stepped on Shoebottom's broken leg, causing Shoebottom to cry out. Orface let out his half-wit chuckle and did it again. It was great fun to see his former master squirm so. Orface had undergone such behavior from his own peers growing up. Now it was someone else's turn to suffer.

Feeling the merciless attack by a person who at one time never intended pain on anything, Shoebottom knew he could not bear to allow his predicament to continue. When Orface turned his attention to stepping on Shoebottom's left broken arm, Shoebottom's still intact right arm took out Dargo's dagger and lodged it to the hilt in Orface's chest.

Orface stumbled backwards. With shock written across his asymmetrical face, he looked in horror first at Shoebottom and then at the knife in his chest. His body collapsed from beneath him.

As the cryptic lifeblood drained out of him, Orface's eyes perceived the better days when Shoebottom roasted him spicy mutton legs, gave him monthly birthday presents, and treated him like a friend. Orface concluded that being a cryptic and being bad was not the fun Orface thought it would be.

He sat with his upper body against the empty Gévaudan crypt, his eyes now gazing towards his old master with intense regret and affection. "I sorry, Chewbottom," Orface whispered. "I sorry Orface so bad…" He let out a final breath and was no more.

Shoebottom rolled onto his belly. In agony, he wriggled to where Orface's body lay. Reaching up with his right arm, he fingered the small chain around Orface's neck and took hold of the cryptic key.

Better to be under Araqnis's control than to be dead. Shoebottom could bear his pain no longer.

He crawled his way into the middle crypt with the key now around his own neck. The final thoughts of Hadrian Shoebottom's mortal existence were of Marielle.

Chapter 29
Vacancy of Home and Heart

Streetlights illuminated the dark, soggy street when Jacob pulled the Humvee across the street from Marielle's house. The cloudy skies and accompanying drizzle did little to lighten the weight the young couple felt that evening.

Marielle sat in the passenger seat, staring at the house. Her life appeared before her like a movie running backwards in slow motion. "In my life, I faced two villains, one a cryptic out to kill me and one a genius kidnapper. Yet here I sit, afraid to go in."

"Will you be going in?"

Marielle sat in silence with her eyes fixed on the house. "No, Jake. You make a good point. If they see me, my parents would never let me leave. It is better just to see how they are doing."

Marielle got out of the vehicle.

Jacob followed her with his eyes as she approached her home with caution. With their backpacks stored in the back seat of the Humvee, Marielle now wore the same hiking attire she had when living in the Grand Canyon alcove. Seeing her in the same old ripstop shorts and button-up shirt brought Jacob the memories of the first time they fled into the wilderness.

His heart sank to find her so sad, but he was at a loss for how to comfort her.

Jacob got out from the driver's side. He had also changed into his familiar back-country slacks and shirt. He followed Marielle's hesitant approach to the very home she grew up in.

Marielle looked around to ensure her activity did not appear to be suspicious to any neighbor or passerby. With the dark street empty, she kept her focus on the unveiled window of the living room. She did not go right up to the window, but sidled toward the front yard weeping willow, ducking beneath its ropey strands before placing a delicate hand against its smooth bark trunk.

Through the window, Marielle could see four people snuggled up on the couch. With an oversized plaid blanket on their laps and popcorn bowls on their laps, a blue light flickered across their faces from a TV screen movie they were watching.

Marielle flinched when she felt Jacob's hand on her back. She did not know he had followed her.

"This is your family?" he whispered.

"My mom is on the right, my dad is next to her, and the girl snuggling into my dad is my sister Shelly."

"And the boy?"

"Andy, the boy Shelly always had a crush on since middle school. They are holding hands, so they must be dating. Wait! Shelly has a boyfriend? When I was her age, I was not allowed to date!"

Several minutes passed as Marielle watched them. A tear appeared in her eye.

"Jake, I want to see the back yard."

"We really should go, we…" Jacob looked at her and recognized her expression of resolve.

Marielle walked the shadows of her front yard towards the side of the house and entered the wooden gate that separated the front yard from the back yard. With each step, her eyes surveyed the details of her childhood playground.

Jacob followed.

"See those the trees and bushes, Jake?" Marielle whispered. "That's where Shelly and I played hide-and-go-seek. We built a playhouse there that eventually collapsed. There's the old swing set my parents never got rid of after we outgrew it. Over there is a sandbox Shelly and I made sandcastles in."

Jacob envisioned the little girl, her straight dark hair glistening with sunlight, her small, rounded six-year-old face with deep blue indigo eyes. "So blessed were you to have a happy childhood."

Marielle walked to the middle of her back yard and gazed back at the house. She pointed to the second floor and said, "The larger window with the light still on, that was my bedroom."

"What do you mean, *was?*"

"The posters on the wall, they are not mine. They must have given the room to my sister. Look there. the open window of the bathroom has Shelly's pink robe hanging on the hook outside the shower. Jake, it's like I am no longer a part of their world. My family has moved on from me!"

Jacob put an arm around her. "Where would you be right now if you had stayed, and Dargo never chased you from your home?"

Marielle thought about it. "I guess I would be on my way to college. I had three colleges of interest and the promise of scholarship offers from each of them. My grades were straight A's, and I had my whole life planned in front of me."

"Shelly would move into your bedroom, regardless?"

Marielle pondered his words. "They know I'm still alive as I got a letter or two to them, explaining that I was never abducted, but that I was part of a secret government mission."

Jacob smiled. "That was really your bedroom?"

"Yes. I got it on my thirteenth birthday. It was a sort of rite of passage."

"And the bathroom where you showered and brushed your teeth?"

"Yes."

"I'm really glad I got to stop to see this part of you. You came to La Bellaroche and got to see my life growing up. Now it is my turn to see yours."

"I would have preferred it if I could have introduced you to my family. I know that if I hadn't resisted the temptation to knock on or open the front door, they would have kept us for hours. Dad would have insisted on calling the police. Mom would never let me go."

"They do still love you."

Marielle looked down. "Let's go."

They walked together through the porch light shadows until they both sat next to each other in the Humvee.

Marielle looked at Jacob. "Where to from here?"

Jacob looked at her. "When we get the Sangrahl and no longer bear the fear of dragons or of cryptics, we can light it so that all the broken families can find healing. We will go to the alcove and give the Keepers of the Fifth and Sixth Ages their chance to succeed."

"You think it will be that simple?"

"Marielle, it has to be. Without the light, what else is there? Evil can come to us in many forms."

"What about you?"

Jacob glanced at her. "What do you mean?"

"Have you not been lying to me all along?"

"If I have, it is not with intention."

"Jake, how old will you be in a hundred years?"

Jacob looked into her eyes. "Why are you…"

"How old?"

"Uh… a hundred twenty-three."

"And how old will I be then?"

Jacob sat in silence.

Marielle turned her face from him, gazing out the front window. "You saw Sephus's words about cryptics and amaranthines. We could never marry. I could never bear children. Yet you love me as if this were all still possible! You have known all along you and I cannot remain together. You're an immortal and I am not."

With sadness, Jacob nodded.

"Jake, how could you lie to me? You lead me on pretending you're still in love with me, yet you know all along that we have no future together."

Tears flowed down Marielle's cheeks. "I wish I had never come to be part of all of this. I want to go back to my normal life and never be around immortals again."

Jacob took his eyes from her and towards the road ahead.

At that moment, he had no answers.

Chapter 30
Broken Agreements

During the course of the following day, Shoebottom wandered alone. He did not recognize where he was nor did he care. Though he was unsure of all that had occurred to him in a fortnight, he wandered without sleeping. He noticed that his restored legs did not tire from the long jaunt. He noticed that his lungs no longer required more air when he exerted his energy.

When evening came, he entered a forest and followed the path that penetrated it. He stopped a moment when he recognized firelight in a forest opening. Knowing he no longer had need to fear for his life, he proceeded forward.

Araqnis sat in the opening, a fire from its own breath blazed in a fire ring before him. He reclined against a large burr oak picking his teeth with the bone splinter of something he had just eaten.

Shoebottom entered the fire light. "Why is it every time something evil wants to talk to me, they light a fire in a forest clearing?"

Araqnis did not look at Shoebottom, but kept his eyes toward his own future. "You responded to my call. You passed your first test as a cryptic."

Shoebottom placed his foot on a large rock and leaned into it. "So, you won. You got your cryptic albeit against my better judgement. You can now rule the earth. My question is, what do you need me for when you have it all?"

Araqnis spit out the bone splinter. "There is something you can still give me, Shoebottom, something no other cryptic could do."

"What is that?"

"Your experience of the human world. I am a dragon, I have only seen things from a distance. I know nothing about the ways of man."

"Well, it is quite simple, really. You're a dragon. You just go around blowing fire at everything until there is nothing left."

"I have known other dragons who think like that. It's not my way. Your genius mind, genius in the way you relate to a situation and think your way through it, that is what I covet from you."

"Well, I tell you what, Your Dragonbreath, let's slice open the top of my head and you can just borrow my brain for a while. How's that?"

"I see being a cryptic hasn't changed your sarcastic nature, Shoebottom. It was clever of you to think about sealing off the wellsprings. Cut off their escape and they don't stand a chance."

"Sounds like a lot of work, if you ask me."

"It is a lot of work, but I have most of them done now. A few more and the Keepers and their knights will have nowhere left to turn—all because of you, Shoebottom."

"Have the Queen give me a ceremonial metal."

"There are still some things I can learn from you, Shoebottom."

"A brilliant intellectual like you? Oh, come now!"

"You know you are beholden now to me."

"I do. It's the reason why I resisted this whole cryptic idea in the first place."

"You have no choice to answer my questions with honesty when asked."

"Another unfortunate fact."

"If you were in search of Marielle, where would you go?"

Shoebottom stood up taking his foot off the rock. "You're doing just fine in your plan. Just… keep doing what you're doing."

"Shoebottom…"

"No, you're doing great."

With a lightning-fast claw, Araqnis nabbed Shoebottom's body and held him up to its jowls. "Don't think that because you're immortal you cannot be killed," Araqnis glowered. "You may survive any incursions this earth plays against you, but all I have to do is squeeze!"

Shoebottom felt the dragon's grip tighten. "She has a hidey hole in the Seventh Age. I could point it out on the map… if you like."

Araqnis cast Shoebottom against a far tree. "That's better."

Shoebottom sat up, amazed the impact had not wounded him a second time. He looked back to his new master and bowed, "I am at your service."

"As it should be. Now where would her lover be?"

"You mean Jacob Lake? I didn't know they were lovers. How will I ever compete with that?"

"Shoebottom…"

"He would be with her, of course. They are inseparable, those two."

"He has the Fire Petra. The only thing I want more than the Keeper girl, is the Fire Petra. Whether it is embedded in that sword of his or not, I want that Fire Petra."

Shoebottom returned to the fire ring, brushing the dust from his silken black attire. "What has that got to do with me?"

"It has *everything* to do with you. I am going after the girl. You cryptics can never manage to take or control her. She will be mine now."

"Then what would you want of me?"

"The Keepers no longer possess the Sangrahl. I want you to go after the Sangrahl. Kill whoever has it, but bring the vessel to me."

"Very well," agreed Shoebottom. "I'll have that in my capable hands in less than sixty days. Then what?"

"These Keepers are slippery ones. Go after them. Though I have not yet located all the wellsprings that separate the Fifth and Sixth Ages, the Keepers are now permanently separated from their friends. Ride your ghost ship to the Fifth Age, take the Sangrahl, then return to the Seventh Age. Use your cunning, Shoebottom. If I cannot find them, you must."

"Your sense of smell far surpasses my ability to..."

"Use your cunning! You know them. Therefore, you, my newly ordained cryptic, may reach them first. If this is the case, you are to kill Jacob Lake and take his sword."

"And the girl?"

"Wound her this time. Sever her legs so she cannot run. Render her unable to move, but bring her flailing body back to me. You can call me simply by saying my name inside your mind."

"You know, Jacob Lake is armed with that sword and I have, but two inadequate daggers."

"Your dagger proved that a cryptic can be killed. You will find a way to get past his sword. Bring me the Sangrahl and the Fire Petra and I just might relinquish one of the other two Petras."

"Oh, give me the blue one. I think moving about the world invisible is the only way to fly."

"Very well, Shoebottom, I will give you the blue one. Bring me the girl as well and I just might let you have the green one too. You know I am a dragon of my word."

"Yes, your track record proves that."

"You have your mission, Shoebottom. The Sangrahl, then the Fire Petra and the girl, that is, in case I don't find them first. Fail me, and your life is forfeit. Do we have an accord?"

"We have an accord." Shoebottom fingered the hanging lantern to *La Constance*. The Sangrahl would be an easy nab. As to the Keepers, Shoebottom began to see eight moves ahead on the life-size chessboard.

Chapter 31
The Roman Moor Bathhouse

The Fifth Age in the Keeper's timeline journey began in 1359. Their trips to Ireland and Normandy in 1360 fell into a six-year era of peace in England's Hundred Year War with France. Whether the Treaty of Bretigny in 1360 had to do with the presence of the Sangrahl's light has yet to be established as fact.

It is because of the six-year period of peace that merchant ships like *The Rising Stargazer* could sail the English Channel from Normandy, France to Ireland without military embargoes.

While Annaquinn's crew guided her ship from the fiords of Norway to the west coast of England in 1361, the concerns of the watchmen were not regarding military incidents, but eyes to the sky for meandering flight patterns of a ghost ship or a dragon. The sailor watchmen did not sleep during that voyage for the trepidation they felt towards either possibility.

Anchoring in Scarborough, England, Tuck, Balladin, and Captain Quinn followed Angelou out of that port city. The dog guided them into the Moors north of York without incident.

Within the moors themselves was the Wheeldale Roman Road. The road and a happenchance aqueduct were reminders the ancient Romans had extended their rule across most of Great Britain.

After a half-day's trek on foot, the four of them found the place of Annaquinn's memory. Deep into a forest and tucked into a hillside canyon was an obscure Roman bathhouse ruin.

Though Angelou had undergone an exhausting ordeal with her battle with the Gévaudan, she slept during the twenty-hour voyage from Norway. The repose along with the healing power from the Sangrahl restored her back to full strength.

Once again, the Simple-Minded One was eager to remain the guide dog on a critical journey. Were it not for the dog's sixth sense, the company might not have ever found it.

"This is the place," Annaquinn said. "I recognize those gray cliffs and the broken columns. There in between is the bath meh brothers, and I took a swim in when we were children. Oh! The anger of meh father when he found out!" Annaquinn's voice had turned to sadness.

Staving off the sympathy Balladin felt hearing the sadness in Annaquinn's voice, Balladin took the lead. With both swords drawn in anticipation of anything that might oppose the delivery, he moved forward.

Tuck took the rear guard. Though he no longer bore the Tears of the Wanderer, he kept one of his few remaining arrows affixed to his bow.

With Angelou showing no sign of sensing or smelling an enemy presence, it all appeared too easy.

"We find backs against the cliffs." Balladin pointed a sword in the ruin's direction.

"So long as there is a wellspring there, we might just be all right," replied Tuck. "The question is, do we send just the Sangrahl into the water's depths or do we accompany it?"

"Annaquinn must remain in the Fifth Age. Jacobi gave us the impression the dragon was sealing off the wellsprings and we might not be able to return here."

Tuck surveyed the horizons. "Let's deliver the Lamp and get back to the ship. There is still much work to be done. We have to figure out a way to destroy that dragon."

The Roman ruin sat nestled into the dead-end canyon. Though it was not as spectacular in its architecture as the one in Bath, the hidden springs revealed a onetime haven for Roman travelers during the age of antiquity.

Ten columns in varying states of brokenness stood sentry around a rectangular pool made from large marble blocks. Three fragments of toppled column rested in the pool's bottom. Steam poured into the atmosphere, revealing that the thermal spring within was of a much warmer temperature than the autumn air that surrounded them.

"I remember this amazing place." Annaquinn said, bending to feel the water temperature. "It is like fire from the earth boiling a water kettle. It intrigued me the first time I saw it and it intrigues me still."

She set the Sangrahl box beside her and pitched off her shoes. She lifted the hem of her silk dress above her knees and dipped in her legs. Like a schoolgirl, she swished her feet through the water.

Before Tuck could make an objection to Annaquinn's abandon, Angelou too jumped into the water, swimming about in ecstatic recklessness. She avoided the far end of the pool, for it glowed blue deep within, a clear sign that indeed this was a magic wellspring.

Tuck looked in all directions, noticing the open meadows making it difficult for any enemy to approach unseen. He walked up and stood next to Balladin. "Do the women in our company have more sense than us?"

Balladin, too, was taken in by the fun Annaquinn and Angelou were having. "Or perhaps less. Tuck, the one thing we never have on these quests is recreation. Every day, we have our eyes out for the enemy."

"You have Sephus's book. Let's designate this wellspring into the record, Roman Moor Wellspring."

Balladin nodded in agreement. "I will have to write it into the margins as there are no empty pages that remain."

"Perhaps you should begin the Book of Balladin!"

Balladin smiled and nodded. "I have already begun my notetaking."

Annaquinn turned to regard her protectors. "Do yeh think we could take a swim? The water is perfect!"

Tuck, being ever the practical one, replied, "We brought no extra clothes. The air above is plenty cool."

Ignoring Tuck's logic, Annaquinn let fall her cloak, leapt from her seated position on the edge of the pool, and submerged to her shoulders. She swam over to play with Angelou, who wagged her tail atop a protruding column fragment. While Angelou barked with excitement, Annaquinn laughed with delight of the experience.

The two knights watched with wonder, and their weary minds relaxed. They approached the water's edge, each of them wondering if the springs were casting a spell to lure them within.

"Come on in!" Annaquinn said. "Oh! This is amazin'!"

A spell must have been present, for the two men could no longer withhold their desire to join her. Balladin placed his swords where he could reach them at the cliff end of the pool. He peeled off his sword belt, followed by his tunic shirt.

Tuck shook his head. "This is madness."

While Balladin slipped his body into the water, Tuck surveyed the approach to the springs along with a wary eye to the sky. He called to the others. "Watch that you don't go into the blue light, it will take you down in!"

Tuck felt like the schoolteacher having to be the adult in a group of children. He sat next to the Sangrahl and opened the box to ensure it remained within. He moved the box further along the edge. Setting down his bow and quiver, he removed his shoes, rolled up his pant legs, and allowed the warm water to invigorate his feet.

Seeing Balladin in the water, Annaquinn began flirting with him by sneaking up behind him and throwing her arms around him from behind. She attempted to pull him beneath the water's surface, casting the total weight of her body to pull him down.

Balladin could have kept his footing, but allowed the girl to win the battle.

Sitting along the edge, Tuck had to admit to himself that he felt a little jealous of the physical interaction. Setting his bag down, he had to admit, "we have our hooded cloaks to keep us warm." He set the Sangrahl apart from the wooden box to remind himself that, should anything happen, it was there and needed to be taken.

Tuck peeled off his shirt and slid into the warm water.

For Annaquinn, it was the pinnacle of her joy, something she rarely felt in her years growing up. She laughed and wallowed in the attention of two handsome men competing over her attention.

Annaquinn could never have experienced such ecstasy in the presence of her father. It made her feel a little guilty knowing that he was no longer alive to make an objection. For the first time in her life, Annaquinn was free to just be herself.

While the four of them splashed and played in the thermal springs, someone from above the cliff was watching them.

During the moonlit night, when *The Rising Stargazer* had made its overnight voyage, Shoebottom had been high above the clouds. He knew the Keeper's ship from the great distance by which he traveled and knew they would never see him so high above the sky.

"Sephus's book had given me the clues needed to know the Fifth Age Sangrahl would reach its terminus somewhere in western England…"

Shoebottom turned his eyes and backed away from his hiding place. For a moment he envied them. Never in Shoebottom's existence had he experienced such playfulness. The two men were each other's best friends. Rather than fight like dogs over the maiden, they shared in her company. This was what friendship looked like.

He froze when he noticed the dog, Angelou, watching him from the edge of the bath. When the dog did not sound her alarm against him, he drew his double swords with careful movements.

What to do? I could have killed you in the Grand Canyon alcove had you been there…

Angelou stood there without moving, her ears pricked up towards him. Even when Shoebottom took out his swords, the dog did not flinch. She sat and grinned at him with her tongue hanging out and gave a slight wag of her tail.

Shoebottom laid a sword down and scratched the back of his head. *You growled at me in La Bellaroche. Why are you amicable to me now?*

No matter. Shoebottom got up and worked his way down the hillside to the entrance to the Roman bathhouse. He peered at the three who were splashing and playing and, for a moment, thought about abandoning his cause. *Why should they be allowed a happiness that was ever denied to me in my own life? This is a happiness that will soon end.*

Angelou lopped past him and jumped back into the water. She did not show warning them, but it did not matter. Shoebottom was a cryptic, an immortal, and far as he could tell, these humans were not. Like with Dargo, there was no way that they could defeat him.

Not even Angelou's bite would make a difference, for Shoebottom did not believe from the chronicles that Angelou was a wolf. Still, it perplexed him that the dog did not become aggressive, for even Shoebottom knew dogs were sound judges of a man's character.

Tuck and Balladin together had just dunked Annaquinn beneath the surface when Balladin's eyes met those of Shoebottom. He grabbed Tuck, who turned to see their uninvited guest.

Annaquinn, sputtering and laughing when she reached the surface, squeaked when she saw what was happening. She maneuvered herself behind Balladin.

"I remember you," said Shoebottom, his eyes fixed on Balladin. "We fought each other in the wine cellar of La Bellaroche."

"Fought until I won," said Balladin.

"Only because of the added distraction from a young girl casting various objects in my direction. My memory still feels the jolt of the iron bolt that she hit me beside the head with. Care for a rematch?"

Balladin moved to the poolside and grabbed his swords. "I'll take you on a second time if that is your wish."

"Bal, let's go!" Tuck said, taking hold of his longbow and quiver. "If he is a cryptic, you cannot defeat him."

"Are you a cryptic?" Balladin said.

"Would I disclose such *personal* information? We've only just met!"

Tuck said, "He's a cryptic, Bal. I can see it in his eyes. Dargo had that same look."

"No battle?" Shoebottom clicked his tongue. "Cowardly for a trained monk."

"A fair fight I would request and nothing more," said Balladin.

"In the criminal perspective, there is no such thing as a fair fight."

Swimming out to the middle of the pool, Angelou took hold of Annaquinn's sleeve in her mouth and began pulling backwards. Following Angelou's lead, the others backed away from Shoebottom, still standing above them at the entrance edge of the pool.

"Shoebottom, I invite you to follow us," said Balladin. "The water deep inside the blue is peaceful and healing, even for someone like you."

Shoebottom smiled as the three found themselves swept under by the wellspring at the deep end of the pool. He put his double swords away.

Feeling the water's enticement, Shoebottom considered taking a swim himself, but it was not the reason for his presence there. His eyes focused on the real prize.

"Killing the indigenous man who escaped my death the first time would have been lovely," he said. "Killing the monk would have been lovelier. Who is the lovely maiden? Maybe I would have let her live. Oh, but look and see what Keeper's knights have left for me!"

Shoebottom balanced his steps on the narrow fringe of the Roman bath and skirted the left side like a boy at play until he spied what the knights had left him.

Sitting there, alone and naked, without box or bearer, was the Sangrahl.

Chapter 32
The Coiled Snake

Dragons possess a keen sense of smell that surpasses the physical body and perceives the scent of the spirit within. His olfactory receptors were especially sensitive to two smells, Keepers and wellsprings. Araqnis could sense wellsprings from faraway places. He could soar high above the earth and know their locations in air pockets. Following the currents in a downward spiral, Araqnis had little difficulty finding them.

Keepers were more of a challenge. For Araqnis to smell them, Keepers had to be in a much closer proximity. He did not know where Jacob and Marielle were present. After meeting with Shoebottom, he did have a good idea of where they would be going.

In his mind map, he sealed wellspring after wellspring until it satisfied him he had sealed them all. Even after Shoebottom had confronted Tuck and Balladin at the Roman Moor Wellspring, taken the Sangrahl, and gone on his merry way, Araqnis arrived there the following day.

He not only sealed the wellspring there for eternity, his fire caused the Roman Moor Bathhouse to capsize in on itself and the cliffs surrounding it to bury its very existence.

After Araqnis sealed this final wellspring of the Fifth Age, he moved onto the Seventh Age. It meant the long flight to the magnetic poles of the earth to span an age, but span the ages he would. Without mortality to wear him down, a dragon requires no rest.

Sealing off the wellsprings in the Fifth and Seventh Ages meant that the Keepers and their knights had to remain within whatever age they ended up. A wellspring was no longer a place by which one could flee through.

The first of two remaining wellsprings were the Havasu Falls Wellspring, which in the previous year, Tuck had utilized to meet up with Marielle in the alcove. The second remaining wellspring was the Grand Canyon Alcove Wellspring inside the escape cave where Marielle had spent three seasons.

Araqnis flew first to Havasu Falls. Seeing a dragon there sealing the wellspring put a permanent wrench in the wanderlust mechanism of the number of tourists who visited there.

By afternoon of that same day, Araqnis had reached the alcove. He knew the two lovers would attempt to go there. Shoebottom had predicted it. The alcove had been the mainstay of Marielle's concealment and the only place left for two clever Keepers to go.

After breathing fire into the Grand Canyon Alcove Wellspring to seal it, Araqnis curled himself up like a snake on the cave floor. Like a snake, he would wait—weeks if need be—for his most coveted prize, apart from the Fire Petra.

The coolness of the cave floor was a welcome touch to the dragon's reptilic skin. The cave entrance was just large enough to allow his passage and just small enough to make it a challenge snaking his body through.

This posed for the dragon a rather morbid question. "With two Keepers inside my belly, how long will I have to remain before I can snake my way out again?"
No matter. Araqnis would have two Keepers in the same meal, even if it meant being stuck inside a cave.

Chapter 33
Into the Snake Pit

Jacob and Marielle said very little to each other during their trip to the Grand Canyon's North Rim. For Marielle, it was the confusion of not knowing their future. For Jacob, it was his inability to reach out to her about what he could see in their relationship.

They drove Tuck's Humvee down the series of dirt roads in the Kiabab Forest and left the vehicle at the campsite Dargo had set up for the Keeper's abduction a year earlier. Nothing of what remained of Dargo's military equipment interested the two travelers, so they put on their same old backpacks and set off across the North Rim meadows.

For Jacob, it was beyond daunting to see the girl he loved pass by the beautiful tent site without so much as a word. He allowed the girl to walk ahead, giving her the space. The tension between them was akin to the first day after their first meeting, when Jacob brought Marielle into the wilderness for the first time.

She loves me. His thoughts brought him to this conclusion. *She has yet to speak the words which is a sign she does not speak them too rashly. If there was no love, she would not feel this way. Her heart is broken, and I have to mend it.*

Though she spoke when needed, Marielle's mind walked a different path. She felt her heart break when they passed their romantic tent site. She suppressed the tears and the realization that the day would come when Jacob and Marielle would have to say goodbye a second time forever.

They followed the same trail down into the canyon when following Angelou in their escape from Dargo de Montebank. This time, their pace was casual. No one, to their knowledge, was chasing them this day.

When they stopped, Marielle broke the silence with a question. "Jake, what are we going to do once we get to the alcove?"

"I think we should hole up there for a time. The wellspring inside the cave will be our means of escape if Araqnis should figure out where we are. I can think of no safer place."

"For how long?"

"As long as need be. We used the last of Tuck's blood money to buy the extensive provisions stored in the Humvee. We'll return to the rim to access them when needed."

Marielle sat against a large protruding boulder and drank from her red water bottle. "Everything has become so hopeless."

"Nothing is hopeless so long as there is hope."

"Jake, I see no way out of this. We're at the end of our rope. You know, when you first had that talk with me about the privilege of having a unique existence. Do you remember? As I'm thinking about it now, we don't know if our dog is alive or dead. Tuck almost died more than once, I was abducted, and you died. It just makes me not want to do this anymore. I just want to go back to my Marielle way."

Jacob hesitated to put an arm around her. He was uncertain she would accept his affection. "Marielle, no life without risks is worth living. I believe everything will turn out all right. We just have to put our faith forward, as we are still part of something big. Could it be we are among the most important people who ever lived?"

Marielle took another drink. "You know we no longer have the Sangrahl to sustain us?"

"I do. We will have to make do until we find it again."

"What if we don't?"

"One day at a time."

"I just want this to be over."

"Marielle? What was the best time of your life?"

Marielle said nothing. She did not want to face the reality of that question.

They put away their water bottles and continued the jaunt down to the bottom.

Marielle reflected on her time living in the alcove. She realized that although she was alone, it was a wonderful time of personal growth. Each day possessed the freedom to do anything she wanted. She realized she could sleep in, not get dressed for the day's work until noon, and explore the canyon labyrinths with her favorite dog.

As much as the Grand Canyon alcove, Marielle was in love with La Bellaroche. The culture, the bond of community, and the life of knights and ladies appealed to her more than everything else. She felt like she was a part of a much larger family and wished she had spent more time there.

When they got to the bottom, both of them came close to passing by the elusive entrance.

Though neither of them had spoken a word since their break, they entered the alcove with a soft step of their feet, for to them, the place had been holy ground.

The hammock hooks remained embedded in the orange sandstone rock above the grotto. Remnants of the few things left behind remained. Bare footprints along sandy patches reminded them of the seven months Marielle had spent there and the casual way in which she lived. Unless she and Angelou went exploring, there had been little need for shoes.

Marielle took hold of her backpack to release the weight of it from her back when Jacob abruptly stopped her. She turned to say, "what?" when she noticed a look of immense concern on Jacob's face.

He mouthed the words, "don't move."

Marielle froze. Whenever Jacob's senses revealed that something in their midst was not what it seemed, Marielle knew better than to question it.

He stepped back, signaling her to work her way out of the alcove without making a sound. With light footsteps, the two of them crept as if treading on the fuse of a bomb.

When they returned to the entrance and the trail leading up or down the canyon, Jacob placed his face close to Marielle's ear. "He is in there."

Marielle looked at him. Though her voice made no sound, her lips formed the word, "Who?"

"Araqnis. He is inside the cave."

Marielle's mouth dropped. "How do you know?"

"I could smell sulfur coming out. He was waiting for us."

"What do we do?"

Jacob turned and began walking on cat feet down the trail. Marielle followed in like fashion. Then they heard something attempting to snake its way out of the cave.

"He knows now we were there!" Jacob drew out his sword. "We have to run and find a place to hide."

Marielle grabbed his shoulder. "I know a place!"

"Go!"

Marielle's pace increased to a full run. She kept her steps as silent as she could without slowing down. It was a balance between breaking into a full run and remaining as quiet as she could.

Araqnis let out a trumpet like voice, letting the world know his trap had not sprung the way he had planned it. He found himself stuck for several minutes inside the mouth of the cave. Because of the nature of the rock, going in had been much easier than coming out.

He emerged out of the cave, sniffing the familiar scent of Marielle and of Jacob Lake. How well he knew them both!

He glimpsed out the western window. Not seeing any sign of the Keepers, he leapt over the entrance wall and jumped onto the trail. He sniffed up the trail and then down. Realizing they had gone down, he vanished to take up the chase. When he found a less constrained space for which to flap his wings. He took to flight.

It would be less than the passing of a minute before he would have them. Even the Grand Canyon bottom offered no permanent place to hide.

When Marielle and Jacob reached the canyon bottom, Marielle stopped at the entrance to the narrow canyon entrance to the Hanging Garden. She turned around just long enough to see Araqnis's flying figure overtaking the rock hoodoos that separated them.

Araqnis paused in mid-flight, recognized them below, and dove straight towards them. Lifting his clawed feet, he swooped to grab them. His claws came up empty.

Circling, the dragon realized the two of them had disappeared into a canyon too narrow for him to penetrate. The winding canyon was too small for a dragon's body, but not for a dragon's fiery breath!

He lighted atop the canyon walls and blew fire into the winding canyon. His ears heard the gasps and squeals of fright from deep down within, but not the gasps and squeals of a burning agony. He would scour the top impressions, find another place further in, and blow fire a second time.

"Where are you taking us?" Jacob asked as they wound through the canyon walls.

"A Firespring!"

"What? Marielle, we don't know what awaits us at the far end."

Marielle ran forward. "It cannot be worse than a dragon!"

She was right, of course. Sephus had warned in his book that a jaunt through a Firespring was dangerous and could leave one without a way to return, but it was their only option.

Out in the opening of the Hanging Garden, Marielle and Jacob ran. They stopped at the edge of the pool and removed their backpacks.

Marielle stepped out of her shoes and was about to jump into the springs when Jacob said, "Our tunics!"

Looking up into the sky and realizing that Araqnis had yet to figure out where his prey had escaped to, Jacob and Marielle scrambled into their backpacks for the Madagascar silk tunics, wishing they had kept them on their bodies all along.

Holding the tunics and cloaks in their hands, they entered the water of the Firespring. Jacob kept his sword drawn, though he had little hope it would do the dragon harm.

They swam out to the deep end looking for the red glow, but no glow welcomed them.

After blowing his second fire storm into the winding canyon, Araqnis appeared above the cliffs. After several seconds of keeping his attention inside the sandstone labyrinth, his ears perceived the splashing of water. He turned his eyes and beheld them filled with resentment and hatred. He spied the glowing Fire Petra in full brightness in the hilt of Jacob's sword. Araqnis licked his lips.

Beneath Jacob and Marielle, the pool lit up with a red glow.

Just as the dragon leapt from the cliffs toward them, the Firespring took in the two Keepers and pulled them asunder.

They knew they had no hope of returning.

Chapter 34
Stone Channels and Broken Bones

Annaquinn emerged cold and out of breath inside a cold, dark place. She flailed her arms until her hand collided with the stone cavity wall unseen by her vision. She cried out.

Balladin emerged beside her. Reaching for Annaquinn, he took her into his arms. "It is all right, Quinn, you're safe! You're safe!"

Annaquinn ceased her panic and took hold of Balladin. "Where are we?"

"In a wellspring on the far end. Tuck and I have done this many times. Come! I will show you."

Though it was still very dark inside the wellspring cave, Balladin knew just where to guide both himself and the red-haired Irish girl.

"How do you know where to go?" Annaquinn hung tight to his shoulders as he waded forward.

Balladin stopped. "By listening."

Annaquinn held her breath. She could hear the quick rhythmic panting of a canine dog. "Angelou?"

"She always knows the way!"

Angelou awaited them along the edge of an underground channel. Where Angelou stood, there was the dim light of the cave spring opening. She wagged her tail in recognition, then shook the water from her furry body a second time.

Hearing another emerge out of the water, Balladin called over his shoulder. "Tuck! We're over this way."

When the three of them followed Angelou to an opening barely large enough for a human being to squeeze through, none of them recognized their surroundings. The sunlight blinded them and the intense warmth in the air settled their cold, damp shivering.

A light, trickling waterfall cascaded over a rock opening and into a deep canyon of granite and sandstone. The sandstone varied in colors of red, orange, and brown and was smooth to the touch in some places, while rough and jagged in others.

"This is not the sandstone I am familiar with from home," Tuck said, feeling the rock with his hands. "It is much harder. See? I cannot carve into it with my fingernails."

Annaquinn squeezed the water out of the hem of her silken dress, secretly grateful to Marielle for having her make one for herself.

"That was a wellspring?" Annaquinn said.

"It was," said Tuck

"I felt like I was inside a dream."

"It heals you even if you have so much as a cold."

Annaquinn sat down on a large rock. "I have no shoes and this place looks very rough."

Tuck stood next to Balladin as the two of them surveyed the terrain. "Where do you suppose we are?"

Balladin shrugged. "This is a place we have not been to before."

"The high cliffs of salmon-colored rock darkened on the surface reminds me of walking through Zion National Park."

"Where?"

Tuck folded his arms. "I sometimes forget, you've spent very little time in the Seventh Age. Zion is... well, it looks a little like this place, only the cliffs are much higher."

Stepping off the terrace where the underground spring fed the trickling waterfall, they slid to the canyon bottom. To their right, the drainage worked its way upward into what appeared to be a barren landscape. To their left, the stream at the base of the waterfall cascaded down smooth sandstone rocks. Green foliage decorated the waterway and was the only thing growing anywhere around them.

Tuck felt the pathway at the bottom of the canyon. "Look here, Bal. This trail has been used a lot. People come up here often to access this water."

"There must not be a lot of water in this region then," said Balladin. "We had better be wary of others in the area."

"What are we to do?" Annaquinn said.

Tuck looped his longbow over his shoulder. "From where I stand, we have two choices. We can wait here until we are certain Shoebottom has gone before returning or we can explore this setting, find out if it holds any significance."

Balladin put down the satchel holding Sephus's book, took off his silken moccasins and gave them to Annaquinn to wear. "I often walk without shoes, so my feet are used to the rough ground. You are welcome to mine."

Annaquinn beamed at him as she took the shoes and slipped them to her feet. She was the same height as the Asian monk, so the shoes complemented her feet.

Balladin addressed all of them. "From my perspective, a wellspring never takes one to a place without significance. Look! Angelou, our guide, is awaiting us near the bottom."

"We will follow the dog then. Bal, let's do our usual battle formation. You, with your swords, go first, I'll take the rear."

In the year that Tuck and Balladin had become fellow knights, Balladin's swords were best in staving off a surprise attack. Tuck's rear position gave him the best position for engaging the distant enemy, especially when he and Balladin occupied the higher ground.

Not being used to the smooth surface of the silken shoe, Annaquinn's foot slid out from beneath her and she fell into the spring drainage.

Tuck grabbed her to keep her from rolling farther down.

"OH!" The girl held her left foot in both hands. Both of her legs bled from scrapes caused from her fall. She cried in pain as tears flowed from her eyes. "Oh, it hurts!"

Balladin and Tuck crouched next to her.

"You've sprained your ankle," said Tuck. He felt across her foot and ankle with his hands. "It might even be broken."

"This cannot be good," said Balladin. "Let's carry her to the water's edge. The cold water will dispel the pain and keep down the swelling."

While Angelou stood down the trail unsure of what was happening in the human world, Tuck took hold of Annaquinn's legs while Balladin wrapped his arms around her middle. Though she cried from the intense pain of her injuries, the two men brought her to the edge of the creek and submerged her swollen ankle in the cold, running water.

Balladin took out his sword and cut strips of cloth from the hem of his tunic. "If only we had the Sangrahl with us. It would…"

Annaquinn squealed, "OH! Oh no!"

The two men looked at her.

"Oh, I failed! Tuck! Balladin, I left the Sangrahl on the side of the bath!"

Tuck smiled at her.

"What?"

"Be at peace, Quinn. The Sangrahl came with us through the wellspring. You succeeded as surrogate Keeper of the Fifth Age. It is the reason we no longer have it."

Annaquinn's face did not reveal the peace that Tuck had suggested. "No! I failed as surrogate Keeper! Don't you see? I left the box resting on the stone wall. The Sangrahl was there outside of our reach when that swordsman appeared. There is no way any of us could have grabbed it before submerging the bath!"

Tuck nodded. "Balladin, Captain Quinn, there is something I need to share with you."

Balladin was on his knees, keeping Annaquinn's ankle firm in his hands beneath the water flow. He turned his gaze toward Tuck.

Tuck leaned on a rock. "When I was battling the Gévaudan, I found a mysterious wellspring not noted in Sephus's book. It took me to an oasis in the Middle East. There was a place of worship there, though I did not know from which religion. I also never found out which of the ages I had ended up. There was a stone quarry. I know you won't believe now what I tell you, but Sephus was there."

Balladin leaned back. "What? How?"

"He wasn't the old man we knew. Young and in his prime, he was energetic and healthy, but his expressions and mannerisms were identical to the one we knew."

"You don't know what age this was?"

"Neither did I find out where in the Middle East this oasis was located. Sephus would not tell me. He said it was not important that I know."

Annaquinn winced at the throbbing pain of her foot. "Tuck, what's this have to do with the Sangrahl?"

Tuck smiled a second time. He sat down next to Annaquinn. "Sephus was the stonemason who carved the original Sangrahl from the stone quarry where I found him. He was working on a mug when I discovered him. There on the shelf was a Sangrahl replica. Sephus bade me take it, and so I did. Quinn, that Sangrahl that you saw resting on the wall out of our reach, was that replica. I placed it there in case Shoebottom showed up."

Annaquinn held a hand to her mouth. "You mean…"

"Shoebottom is carrying a fake."

A collective sigh emitted from the lungs of Balladin and Annaquinn.

"Tuck, you are my hero!" Annaquinn said, and took hold of his head and kissed him along the side of his cheek. "In fact, both of you are!"

Tuck said, "Captain Quinn, you are also the hero. It takes tremendous courage to command a ship and even more to be a Keeper. Keepers have the gift of unseen valor, but you have valor that comes from only yourself."

Balladin beamed. "Do you realize, Tuck, you outsmarted the genius criminal?"

Tuck shook his head. "I never thought about that, Bal. Here, let's wrap that ankle."

Balladin lifted Annaquinn's ankle with care while Tuck went to work wrapping the strips of silk cloth tight around it. He tied off the cloth strip bandage.

While Tuck cleaned her scrapes with the Madagascar strip Balladin had provided, Balladin asked the prominent question. "Should we go back then? The wellspring will heal her of this injury."

Tuck glanced up at the cave opening. "I feel Shoebottom might stick around there longer than this. Killing us is on his bucket list, to be sure! If we need to, we can find a place to hole up for the night and then attempt the return in the morning. Besides, I want to see just where this wellspring brought us."

"Tuck, I sensed the dragon was on its way. I don't know if my instincts are correct. If that dragon came to the Roman Moor Wellspring, then there won't be any wellspring with which to return. We may be caught here... forever."

The three of them regarded each other beneath the weight of Balladin's words.

Tuck wrapped Annaquinn's ankle with a last strip of cloth and tied it tight. He rotated his quiver around to his chest, allowing Annaquinn to climb onto his back.

"I'll carry the girl, Bal, if you play bodyguard to us all. We don't know whom we may encounter here. This canyon appears to open up towards the bottom."

Angelou trotted ahead of them until the stream no longer flowed along the channel, but disappeared into the ground. Balladin took the lead while Tuck carried Annaquinn.

Balladin never carried his swords out, but kept them sheathed. He knew drawn swords signified aggression should they encounter strangers. Diplomacy always came first and besides that, Balladin could be deadly with just his hands.

The sun was arid and hot, but the canyon provided them with ample shade. Where the drainage took an abrupt drop of just a few feet, Balladin stopped to examine what he found there.

"What is it?" said Tuck.

"It appears to be an an ancient aqueduct—a small, but adequate version of what the Romans built."

"A ruin?"

"Definitely. It appears to have not been intact for centuries at least. Look, can you see how it has cracks along the edge and is destroyed farther down. By the fragments in these cliffs, I would say a massive earthquake came through here."

Tuck cast his eyes above the cliffs to the sky. "We are once again in the Middle East."

Balladin turned. "How do you come to that conclusion?"

"Search and rescue navigation training. Look, the sun is higher in the sky by its southern position, which means we are hundreds of miles south. It is later in the day than when we left England, which places us hundreds of miles east. Such a longitude and latitude places us in the Middle East. A wellspring can travel us great distances in both space and time, but the daylight changes only with our longitudinal position."

Annaquinn spoke over Tuck's shoulder. "So, what yeh are sayin' is that the wellspring always takes us to a different time?"

Tuck said, "Maybe. It could also transfer us within the same age, but into a different part of the world. The Fourth Age is closed to us and anything earlier than that. We have only the Fifth Age, or 1360, the Sixth Age, or 1690, or the Seventh Age, which we all know is 2020. 330 years separate each age."

"Yeh mean, our friend, Jacob Lake, he lived in…" Annaquinn figured in the math, "In 1030?"

"That is correct. In fact, Balladin comes from that time as well.

Balladin stopped to ponder. "Tuck, if a wellspring takes us to a place of significance, as you said, then we would have to be in the Sixth Age."

"1690?" Tuck looked around. "If this had been America, then my ancestors would still be unmolested by European conquest. The lost languages are still being spoken and many extinct peoples and customs are still alive. But as you pointed out, Balladin, the time of day shows the Middle East, not the Americas."

Balladin nodded. "You have often spoken of the desire to come back to this age to help restore the dark history of your past."

"The wellsprings have denied me access to this age until now. Here we are in a whole distinct part of the world. Balladin, if this is the Sixth Age, then we are beholden to finding the Keeper."

Annaquinn shifted her body for a better hold. "There's a Keeper in this age?"

"There is, and no one knows what's become of him. Sephus made no record of him, said he is mysterious. Dargo killed your brother Korynn before Korynn received the Sangrahl. He must have gone after the sixth Keeper, but we have no way of knowing if he succeeded. We know he attempted to find and kill Marielle and we all know how that ended up."

"Where is this Dargo now?" Annaquinn said.

"Trapped in a prison cave for eternity."

"He won't be comin' after me then?"

"No, it is worse than that."

"Oh?"

"Araqnis is coming after you!"

"OH!"

Angelou guided them north out of the canyon and into a deep, barren valley. The ground surface was flat, as Tuck had witnessed far up in the drainage.

As they emerged out onto that flat, sandy ground, the towering orange cliffs above them revealed something extraordinary. To their left, a tall, temple-like building in Greco-Roman architecture stood as if imbedded into the cliff face.

Though surrounded on top and sides with the natural, stained sandstone, the facade stood thirty feet high. On the upper left of the structure, a corner of a Greek frieze sat atop a cornice with two columns beneath it. On the upper right, a mirrored replica mimicked the left. Between the two was a rounded cornice also with two columns.

The lower half of the structure was a full triangular frieze with six columns, an entrance chamber beneath the center of the frieze, and a doorway twenty feet in height.

Even Angelou stopped to stare at the structure being unfamiliar with its design. To the others, the ancient building was awe-inspiring.

"Who would have constructed such an amazing building?" Annaquinn said.

"Not constructed, carved," said Tuck. "I know this place. I have seen documentaries about it when I was flipping through channels at home."

Balladin and Annaquinn did not know what Tuck was talking about. "What do you mean, flipping channels and what is a documentary?"

Balladin noticed that the two-leveled temple, more orange than the darkened surrounding rock, was the only sign of civilization within reach of their vision. "What do you know of this place, Tuck?"

Tuck walked up to the rock steps leading into the towering, open entrance. "Whoever lived here carved this entire piece right out of the rock at least two thousand years ago. They chipped out the columns, the friezes, the sculptured figures, all with a hammer and a chisel. The only way they could have done this without scaffolding was if they began the chiseling at the top and worked their way down."

Annaquinn couldn't take her eyes from the massive relief carving. "It must have taken them years!"

Tuck looked for other familiar confirmation of his knowledge of the place. He saw across the flat ground from the Greco-Roman carving, a split along the roadway. Straight ahead was a wide pathway between the cliffs. To the right was a tight, winding canyon.

"Balladin, you were right about us being in the Middle East. We are in the country of Jordan. This place has many names: the Lost City and the Red Rose City are two of them."

Chapter 35
A Healer in the Lost City

"The Lost City?" Balladin rubbed his chin. "You know about this place yet you have never been here?"

"It's hard to explain. To confirm my recognition of this place, that narrow channel to our right leads out into the North Arabian Desert. Straight ahead will take us into what was once one of the most glorious cities of the ancient world—a center of culture and trade. This amazing carven building to our left is the Treasury."

"An entire city? What will we find there?"

"We won't find a people. This place lost its population for several reasons. With the scarcity of water, the ancient ones had to build water pipes and aqueducts to carry water from a long distance. That spring we came out of may have been one of them. There will be temples, theaters, churches and market places. Ages in its development includes Assyrian, Byzantine, Roman, and Greek."

Annaquinn smiled. "I never thought tagging along with the two o' yeh would be such an adventure. Can we go look?"

With care, Tuck set Annaquinn down on the lower step of the Treasury. "We have to be careful. Bedouin shepherds and nomads come through here. They won't take too kindly to the site of us, especially you, Annaquinn."

"Me? What's wrong with me?"

"Your appearance to them will appear like a woman bought or sold."

"I'm no different from any woman should be."

"It is your European attire. Your red hair, too, will show your western roots."

At that moment, three Bedouin on camelback approached out of the Ain Siq, the narrow passage leading in and out of the Lost City. They wore the traditional clothes of Bedouin men, a headscarf held firm with an agal-rope. On their bodies, they wore the thoab or light, dress like garment overlaid with an over cloak—all practical for surviving the harsh sun and occasional sandstorm environment.

In each of their hands was a hooked wooden staff indicative of their craft. These three were shepherds.

At first, the trio did not recognize that the Treasury had outlanders sitting out in front like tourists, for the narrow canyon serving as its entrance was well guarded and no one suspected outsiders would penetrate the cliffs through some other way. The third man, sitting atop his camel, turned his face and noticed the intruders. He called to the other two.

They halted and looked where the third shepherd pointed. Scowling, they turned their camels and headed towards the unwelcome visitors.

"Tuck, let's stay our weapons until we know their intentions," said Balladin.

Tuck's brow furrowed. "I think we know their intensions."

The Bedouin shepherds stopped twenty feet distance from their intruders. The lead rider, an older man with a salt and pepper beard, drew out a curved scimitar and pointed at them. He yelled at them in a form of Arabic. He looked at Annaquinn and pointed his sword at her, berating her with a loud voice.

Balladin stepped forward. He spoke in his native Chinese-Indian dialect, knowing full well his enemy would not understand him. His words were gentle, and he pointed to the girl's injury.

The second nomad jumped from his camel, drew out his scimitar and approached Balladin. He was older than the other two and spoke with a deep voice of authority. When Balladin did not respond, the nomadic shepherd thrust his sword, intending to cut into Balladin's arm.

With a shift of his body, Balladin caused the sword thrust to miss. With an unexpected step, he maneuvered his hands with a quickness unseen by the others. Balladin had taken the sword from the Bedouin man's grasp and he held it behind his back.

When the first man jumped down and charged in, Balladin used the scimitar he had claimed to deflect the second man's attack and levered his attacker's force, causing him to flip head over heels into the sand. Now having disarmed them, Balladin walked up to the astonished third man, pointed the hilts of both weapons, and handed them over.

Who is this man whose body and hands move like lightning?

While the first two cursed as they got to their feet, the third man took the swords and smiled with an air of respect at Balladin. He spoke to the first two and though he was not the one in charge, he remained while the first two took back their weapons.

The two of them climbed back onto their camels, yelling at the third man and pointing their swords at the intruders. They turned their camels and rode back into the Ain Siq entrance canyon.

The third man, whose face was still young and his beard thin, motioned with his hand and body a customary Bedouin bow of respect. He looked at the girl with interest. Pointing at the girl's leg, he gestured towards the city center, speaking in words none of the others could understand. He used several hand gestures pointing to the monumental structure above them as if describing something similar.

He jumped from his camel, crouched to the ground and began drawing a map, but then stopped. Looking over his shoulder toward the entrance canyon, he stood up and signaled for them to follow.

"I don't know his words," said Balladin, "but I feel he knows someone here in the Lost City who can help Annaquinn with her injury. He pointed to the foot and tried to describe where this healer lives."

Tuck walked over to Annaquinn to help her into a piggyback ride. "Balladin, whoever he is, you impressed him by your martial arts maneuver. For now, I think we should trust this man. Be wary, though, the other two may well return with a party of warriors."

The young Bedouin shepherd took hold of the reins to his camel and gestured for them to follow.

Through the towering cliffs of three hundred feet or more, they followed the smiling shepherd who talked up a storm about the wonders of the place. Near to the Treasury, the canyon opened up to a multitude of temples and monuments honoring or perhaps worshipping figures long forgotten with time. Each of these, like the Treasury, stood hewn out of solid rock and the shepherd was eager to share what he knew of them.

The shepherd guide smiled and talked without ceasing, as if he had grown up in such a glorious setting and was showing it off for the first time. He led them into a wide avenue where the sandy ground gave way to large stone cobbles. Broken columns on each side left the impression a huge marketplace once stood there.

On both sides, the cliff faces gave way to like-carved structures with similar friezes, columns, and artisan-carven human figures. Some of the relief sculptures looked like Roman soldiers.

Other places appeared to be tombs or perhaps abandoned dwellings carved deep into the cliffs. Some temples had the same Hellenistic columns as the Treasury, while others appeared to have more Egyptian and Assyrian influences.

Towards the end of the market avenue was the pinnacle of the once majestic city, a massive and free-standing temple-like structure that may well have been the cultural center. Roman archways and Greek columns a hundred or more in number surrounded the foundations.

While the young shepherd guide talked on, he did not mind that Tuck told of all that he knew of the Lost City, its two-thousand-year history, and its abandonment in the third or fourth centuries.

"This place won't be known in the world but by these few Bedouin until the 1800s," Tuck said, feeling like a partner to their local tour guide. "In this age, where we are walking is a secret place only a small group of people know about."

"That explains why the shepherds were so defensive in the beginning," added Balladin.

When they approached the heart of the ruins, the main road curved around to the left and up into the hills. Tombs and relief structures continued wherever the cliffs walled in the valley.

The shepherd stopped amid free-standing blue marble columns. He stopped and pointed at the temple structure, gesturing them to enter.

"I recall this place from the documentary," said Tuck, bidding the young shepherd gratitude for his hospitality. "This was the old Byzantine church, the Christian influence amidst centuries of paganism."

Inside the church, the floor revealed several mosaic images, mostly of animals, but included human portraits. Their colors were still bright and unfaded by age.

At the rear of the ruin in a rectangular niche sat an elderly man. He did not notice the newcomers at first and was busy with kneading dough to make bread. He had a round face and little gray hair on top of his head. In dress and manner, he looked more like Aristotle than Trajan.

The shepherd addressed him and gave the same bow of respect he had offered Tuck and Balladin. He bowed with his body accompanied by a customary gesturing of his hands.

The old man turned, looked up at his visitors, and spoke in the same tongue as the Bedouin. Then, recognizing Annaquinn's appearance, he said in a middle eastern accent, "Are you a slave?"

"You speak English?" said Tuck. Noticing the Bedouin shepherd was backing away from the scene, Tuck imitated the same bow of respect, which made the shepherd smile.

The shepherd returned the customary exchange, got up on his camel and rode toward the Treasury.

The old man watched the shepherd go before facing his visitors. "I speak many languages. I chose English, because your woman here appears English."

Annaquinn scowled at him.

"Or perhaps Irish—one can never tell."

Annaquinn said, "Yeh must know, I am not a slave, but a part of this company."

In response, he looked at her with his mouth open. "I beg your pardon, Miss. I have never seen western travelers here, not in this place." He turned his attention to the abandoned cliffs. "The Bedouin are very protective of its borders. You must have paid them a lot to pass through."

Not awaiting their response, he turned and placed the dough onto a stone slab and slid it into a fiery brick oven.

Balladin stepped forward. "We could not speak their tongue, but the young shepherd indicated that perhaps you are some sort of healer."

The man closed the iron door. "Did he now?"

"Our woman has injured her leg. If you are a healer, could you at least look?"

The old man stood up. "That is my involuntary fate. I never thought I would spend my life as a physician, but here I am! Set her down on that slab there."

Tuck set Annaquinn on a stone slab. She winced at the pain each time she felt the change of gravity, but made no complaint.

The old man approached her, crouched down, and unwrapped the bandages about her leg. He sat back in wonder. "What brings you all the way from the western world to finding me here?"

Tuck sat next to Annaquinn. "It was all by fate or perhaps by accident. We happened upon this place though we did not know of its existence."

The healer looked at Tuck with doubt. "No one comes here by accident. My name is Aryeh, and who may you be?"

"I am Kentucky Proudfoot. My friends call me Tuck. This is Balladin and our lady here is Annaquinn."

"And the wolfdog? Does he have a name?" Aryeh bent Annaquinn's foot until she pressed her teeth and let out a squeal.

"I am impressed you recognize our dog, sir. She is Angelou, which means angelwolf."

Aryeh sat back in wonder. "You know, I dream dreams sometimes. I saw this animal in many dreams. She was leading me home on the coast of the sea."

"Annaquinn... Can you heal her?"

Aryeh raised his eyebrows towards them. "Heal her? Me? Oh, no. I am not a healer. I am not even a doctor. Oh, the Bedouin think I am, but that has never been the case. It's the reason they kept me alive. It is also the reason I am a prisoner here. They live out their lives in freedom until one of them gets sick or injured. It is then that they come to me."

Tuck folded his arms. "If you're not a healer, then how did they conclude that you are?"

Aryeh chuckled. "You know, I fled my home in Palestine out of foolery. I sought to find Aaron's tomb and the Wadi Musa finding neither and ending up here. The Bedouin have accepted my presence because, like you, they think I am a healer. They trade me food and other needs for healing."

Balladin walked to a fallen stone and sat down. "As Tuck mentioned, if you are not a healer, how is it you heal?"

Aryeh shifted his body and took hold of a dark wooden box with a familiar appearance. "I don't heal, but this certainly does."

Aryeh opened the box and took out the Sangrahl.

Chapter 36
Where Fore Art Thou Keepers?

Traveling through the orange glow of the Firespring is a much different experience than through a wellspring. While the common wellsprings and their sister Earthsprings render its travelers with the warm and calming healing of body and soul, the solitary Firespring left it travelers solemn and uncertain.

When Jacob and Marielle made the short trek through, they could feel the resentment and hatred of millions of people around the world. They could feel the sadness and brokenness of the victims who are recipients of the hatred. They came to find out that there were very few good people in the world by the end of the Seventh Age.

When they emerged out of the water, they found themselves in a time and place unrecognizable to the human senses. With only their faces above the surface of the circular-shaped water pocket, they looked about them in such wonder, the sadness within them dissipated.

The world in which they evolved was void of movement, but the colors were as vibrant as a crisp, clear mountain lake after a monsoon rain. The ground was a violet hue mixed with the vibrant greens, yellows, and oranges of the trees, grass, and other foliage that grew there. Violet and blue hills and mountains adorned the horizon. The sky was a painter's palette of clouded pastels. Colorful stars twinkled with bright intensity throughout the sheer clouds, even though the sun's warmth covered the earth.

No sound reached their ears. There were no birds singing or flies buzzing. The smell in the air was most akin to bread baking and a hint of vanilla.

Their somber moods brightened, for the air was warm and the two of them were safe. Marielle was first to lift her body from the warmth of the Firespring and into the warm summer air.

She held both of her butterfly knives sheathed in one hand. Jacob was glad she had remembered to keep them with her when they jumped into the Firespring.

Jacob placed his sword on the side of the Firespring and pulled himself from the water. With nothing to elevate his protective instincts, he looked about the world in awe. To him, the setting was very much like the island where Meeshayell brought him back to life.

As his eyes perceived the awesome beauty, they also gazed at Marielle as she wandered into the open space, for there was something just as marvelous about the girl's gracefulness as with her surroundings. The colors of the sky and the earth enhanced the beauty of her face and the skin of her hands and arms.

His heart wanted to break into a million pieces, for deep down, he never loved her more than at that moment. He was certain that she resolved to no longer love him back.

Her tunic swayed with the movements of her body as she gazed in wonder in each direction. She tousled her wet hair and for a moment, turned, and locked her eyes on Jacob.

Jacob speculated as he watched such a delicate face in sweet sorrow. How could he part from this beautiful soul? Even in her shortcomings, to him, she was perfect in every way. He knew she had loved him. She would never have become so distant and angry had she not.

He walked up to her and placed a gentle hand about her waist.

Though hesitant at first, she wrapped one arm about him and said, "Jake, where are we?"

"I remember you asked me that same question when we found ourselves in the darkness of that cavern deep in Sephus's cavern."

"This is so much better than Sephus's cavern. This is a wonder indeed. Do you think we are safe here? Sephus had warned us of the dangers of the Firespring, but I find nothing to fear here."

Jacob kept his eyes on the horizon. "I believe Sephus knew we could never go back. I don't believe the Firespring has a two-way channel. Marielle, we're alive, but we might be here for a very long time."

Jacob released his hold of Marielle and explored about their immediate surroundings. The ground beneath his feet was sandy and gentle on the feet. Patches of bright green grass adorned with small magenta blossoms adorned the ground. Trees grew along the horizon, but not in the open space about him.

"The clouds and the sky are unlike anything we've ever seen. Look at the way the stars penetrate through everything. It is like we are on a different planet altogether."

Marielle walked up beside him. "There is no sign of human habitation anywhere—or even animals. In the Fourth and Fifth Ages, we've become accustomed to not hearing traffic on some distant highway or seeing lights shining from manmade structures, but this! This is altogether different."

"The question is, can Araqnis find his own way here?"

"If so, we have nowhere to run. He was right behind us. We are lucky to be alive."

Marielle sat down crisscross on the sandy ground, her hands tucked across her lap. Her mind whirled with unanswered questions.

Jacob sat down next to her. "Marielle?"

Marielle glanced at him, but did not answer.

"It appears we have time. Can we talk?"

Marielle kept her gaze on him. She did not nod with her head, but Jacob could see she was open to listen.

"I did not address my immortality, because I did not want this to end. You and I, we've built a bond that I will never hold with any other person. Whether we can stay together for life mattered little to me. What mattered the most was this present moment. I love you from the deepest part of my soul. Whether I lied to you or to myself, I cannot say, but I feel whole and elated whenever you are near."

A tear attempted to form in Marielle's eye. She tried to hide it and turned her face away. Feeling so close while a million miles away had torn her apart inside. She held out an arm and welcomed him closer to her side.

"I know, Jake. I feel it too. We still have no answers. What are we going to do, you and I?"

Jacob welcomed Marielle's head, leaning into his shoulder. "We have this present moment. That is all that we have. Unless those answers come, I just want to be with you as long as we can."

"Everything we know, everything about our quest, has sure reached the bottom. I feel lost and without hope."

"Do you still wish you had never been a part of all of this? Do you still wish you had been a normal girl finishing high school and doing what normal people do?"

Marielle thought for a moment. "No, I suppose I don't. What disturbed me more than anything was that we had brought so little light into the world. I thought with my year-long vigil in the alcove, the world would be different. Perhaps it was. My family looked so happy without me."

"I believe it has. I noticed some things, hints of forgiveness and understanding in some people we encountered. It wasn't much, but it was there."

"Jake, I think that perhaps our cause is over. Araqnis is alive. He possesses two Petras we will never recover. Furthermore, there is no sixth Keeper to find, and who knows what became of Annaquinn's mission. Hothgarth is dead. Tuck and Angelou are likely dead. For all we know, Shoebottom turned and became a cryptic, working alongside the dragon. Everything has turned to hopelessness."

"We are still alive."

Marielle lifted her head. "Yes, we are still alive. You asked me earlier if I still regret having become a Keeper and not living a normal life. I don't. I would do it all again if given the choice. The time I spent with you, Jake, it has been the most earth-shattering of my insignificant existence in the whole of human history."

"It is the same for me. We have lost the war. For the time being, we are still alive. Like you, Marielle, I would never have traded it for anything less than what it has been."

"So, what now? Do we lay down our lives for the cause? Do we sacrifice our existence as you did with Dargo?"

Jacob shook his head, pondering her question. "We may have no other choice, but for now, at least, we still have each other. I believe we continue as we have done. When life gets you down, focus on the present moment and take each thing one step at a time."

Marielle looked up at him.

Jacob thought for a moment that she might kiss him, but her attention locked onto something far into the distance.

She leaned away from him to get a better look. "Jake? What is that over there?"

Jacob followed the direction of her gaze. Along the horizon of the foreground, a round object protruded out of the earth. Jacob got up, followed by Marielle, and the two of them walked the hundred meters to the foreign object.

Marielle had noticed it because of its inorganic shape. In a world of exclusive nature, the circular object stood out as different.

When they reached the object, they noticed it was half buried in the sand. Jacob knelt next to it. "This is a shield. Look here at this relief impression on the pewter surface."

"Look at the relief sculpture in the center of the shield. It looks like the Sangrahl!" Marielle crouched and placed delicate fingers across the surface, admiring its design.

Jacob pulled the shield from the sand. "It is finer workmanship than any shield I have ever seen. It looks so heavy, but it is actually light as a feather."

"To you, maybe, you're immortal!" Marielle got up and took hold of the shield. "Wow, it is light as a feather." She took hold of the shield and placed her hand through the loops.

"Marielle!"

Marielle looked at him. "What?"

"You're invisible!"

"What?"

"Here, give it to me and I'll show you."

Marielle's image reappeared as she took off the shield and handed it to Jacob. He slipped his own arm through the loops.

Marielle's mouth dropped open. "Is there anything left in this world that won't continue to amaze us? Whose shield does this belong to?"

Jacob set down the shield, inviting Marielle to take hold of it. It stood as higher than her hips and was perfectly round. The front revealed a shiny metal overlay around its fringe. In the center, the Sangrahl shape was in relief surrounded by artisan rays of light spraying in all directions.

Jacob secured his sword belt around his waist and took up the shield. He drew his sword and held the shield in front of him. "Take that, dragon!"

"I wonder!" said Marielle. "Could you defeat Araqnis with this shield?"

"No. My sword is not powerful enough." Jacob put his sword back into its sheath. "I believe this shield, though, belonged to Meeshayell. Sephus had written in his book of the battle with the dragon."

"Of course! It has to be! The tale tells of him dropping the shield and losing his ability to see. Jake! He became the Blind Beggar just as Sephus related." Marielle turned and looked in every direction. "This must be where the battle took place. If we can find Meeshayell and bring him your sword…"

"No, even that would not be enough. Araqnis holds two of the Petras. I saw them affixed into the golden amulet about his neck when he hunted us. It is the reason the dragon is free. Shoebottom must have given them to the dragon."

"Meeshayell is the mighty Winged Warrior. Why would he not be able to defeat Araqnis with sword and shield?"

"Meeshayell requires three petras for his restoration. Araqnis only required two. Can you think of a way to steal two Petras from a dragon?"

"Oh." Marielle shook her head in doubt. "Shoebottom helped us. He knew having the dragon free would make it impossible for us to survive. After all of that, how could Shoebottom betray us?"

"The evidence is apparent, Marielle. Whatever you said to Shoebottom confused him, at the very least. Maybe he was taken in by you. Whatever the case, his evil side must have won his internal battle."

"No, it couldn't be. Could it?" Marielle locked her eyes on Jacob.

"Leastways, we have something we did not have before, an invisibility shield. We can keep ourselves concealed if Araqnis should appear on the scene."

"You mean, one of us can remain concealed."

"No, I believe if you stand behind me like this, and I put on the shield... See? I cannot see you standing behind me. It has a power to anyone standing behind it."

"Jake, how do you know all of this?"

Jacob looked about. "Meeshayell gave me much instruction when he restored me to life, but he did not do it with words. He placed certain details into my mind, many of which I have yet to discover."

"Why couldn't we use this to sneak up on Araqnis and take the Petras while he is sleeping?"

Jacob shook his head again. "Araqnis does not sleep. He would smell us a hundred miles away. Marielle, there is just one path still left to us."

"What path is that?"

"Place our hope in the Knights of the Sangrahl and Annaquinn. If they can deliver the Sangrahl to the Fifth Age and find the Keeper of the Sixth Age..."

"You know, that is like finding a way to the moon when you have a dragon hunting you. He has been closing off the wellsprings at every turn. They may be trapped just as we are trapped."

Jacob's shoulders sank down. Marielle was right. The only path remaining required incredible luck and a tremendous span of time while running from a deity holding every advantage.

"One more fact that will dampen our spirits. We have to assume Araqnis recognizes what a Firespring is. He battled Meeshayell here, so he is likely on his way here now to find us."

Marielle swallowed the lump that formed in her throat.

Jacob's keen eyes sought the horizon for an unseen hope. The hope did not appear, but something else did.

Another object, much smaller than the shield, sat protruding out of the sand.

"Marielle, look over there! There is something else."

Marielle looked to where Jacob was pointing. She walked alongside him as they approached it.

Out of the sand was another handcrafted object, only this one was small. Its top was rounded and of polished brass, but the main part was a short, rectangular prism framed with the same polished metal, but containing small glass panels on four sides.

"It's a lantern," said Marielle, picking it up out of the sand.

"What would a lantern be doing in a place like this?" Jacob pondered. "Meeshayell never had use for a lantern."

"Oh!" Marielle's eyes peered towards nothing.

"What is it?"

"I know what this is!" said Marielle. "I've seen it before. Shoebottom had one when…"

Jacob took his eyes from the lantern and up to Marielle's searching expression. "When what?"

"When he called forth the ghost ship *La Constance*. Jake, he used a lantern just like this one. That means this lantern belongs to *The Plentitudes*."

"The what?"

"You recall from the Fire Letters in Sephus's book, the winged warriors created two time-traveling spirit vessels, or what we now refer to as ghost ships. Jake, they made them for the Keepers, but Dargo had stolen both of them in the Fourth Age! That was how he traveled time so quickly when he made his siege of La Bellaroche. Remember? Sephus did not expect to see him for a month, and there he was!"

"You mean, this is a way to time travel?"

"It is better than a wellspring, because you can control it. When Shoebottom kidnapped me, it was on the ghost ship we traveled before docking onto *Le Vin du Vie*."

"Wait a minute! Why didn't Shoebottom just take you to Ireland on the ghost ship? Why did he need to transfer you to *Le Vin du Vie?*"

"I wondered that too. I think he required a crew to outwit Bo Eskatoll, but I also think it is because ghost ships only travel on moonlit nights. By the time we reached the northern coast of France, dawn was approaching."

Jacob looked up at the sky. "That's a long time in coming, the sun is still high in the sky."

Marielle examined the sky. "You know, Jake, the sun hasn't moved since we arrived here. I wonder if we are stuck in time. Maybe nothing changes here like, ever. The air is always warm and the day is never ending."

"We cannot remain here forever, we still have a quest to complete."

Marielle jabbed him in the stomach. "What? You don't want to live here with me forever?"

Jacob smiled at the tease. He placed his arms around her and she accepted his embrace.

Marielle said, "As you suggested, we will attempt to take hold of this present moment while we still have it. Deal?"

Jacob nodded. "Deal."

"Keepers until the end?"

"That's right."

"Pinky swear?" Marielle held up her little finger.

"Let's not go that far!"

Marielle held him tight. "Jake… I know full well it will be hard for me to say goodbye. It has always been like that with us. We live in a room with no door open to forever. You and I still come from different ages, so I know that day will come when we have to say our last farewell. After that, we will never see each other again. It's always been at the back of my mind. I just didn't want to admit it. I'm selfish that way."

"Me too, Marielle, me too."

"How will I go my Marielle way without you? I cannot allow myself to even kiss you. It would make that day of departure that much more heartbreaking."

They held each other for a time until the two of them broke away, knowing they still had a mission to accomplish. They circumnavigated the area surrounding the Firespring to see if there were other objects they might have missed. The shield and the lantern were all that they found.

Marielle walked back to the Firespring to gather their silken cloaks.

"Jake, I found something else."

Jacob walked over to the Firespring. "Those look like the Tears of the Wanderer."

"They have to be! You recall the Tears would always end up here to be regathered after Tuck used them."

Jacob rubbed his chin in wonder. "I wish I could say this was a good omen."

"How is it not?"

"You hold all twenty-four gemstones.

Marielle's face became ashen when she realized what Jacob was suggesting. "Tuck would have been desperate to spend all of them."

A solemn expression poured over Jacob's face. "To lose you, Marielle, would be devastating to me. Even so, Tuck and Balladin are the best friends anyone could ever hope to have."

Marielle attempted to stave off the foregone conclusion festering inside her mind and focused on what was ahead. From all that Shoebottom had taught her on sailing *La Constance,* Marielle opened the door of the magic lantern, which caused it to light on its own. She stood up and waved the polished brass lantern even though the sun shone high in the sky.

For a short time, nothing happened. They regarded each other to see if either of them had an answer to the emptiness that surrounded them.

Jacob pointed ahead of them.

To their surprise, a mist appeared flowing towards them from the distance. With it, a large and glorious sailing ship approached. Though no sails furled on its three masts, it glided across an unperceived wind. Soon, the mist consumed the two Keepers and *The Plentitudes* lighted in front of them like a feather to the ground.

The Plentitudes, once requisitioned to Bo Eskatoll by Araqnis, had just arrived ready for service. In wonder, its two passengers climbed the welcoming rope ladder and boarded the vessel.

Marielle guided Jacob Lake up the steps to the forecastle deck and showed him the four sails. Each set rested on an elevated stage in perfect folds, each overlapping the one before it from left to right.

Marielle hesitated in touching the fabric. "Jake, you will notice the choices are in varying condition from ragged to brand new. See? This last one is in perfect condition, representing my Seventh Age. The question remains, where to from here?"

Jacob counted the sails. "We left our knights to escort Annaquinn to delivering the Sangrahl to the Fifth Age. If they were successful, their wellspring would have carried them to the Sixth Age in search of the Keeper there. The question remains, should we assist in finding the Keeper or go to the rendez-vous point in Myra in the Sixth Age?"

Marielle placed her hand over the sailcloth next to the pure white ones. "The Sixth Age. We will head back to Myra and the Table Shrine. If the Knights are successful, Sixth Age Myra may be the fastest way to putting Araqnis to an end. I say, if Tuck and Balladin are not there, then we'll go to the Fifth Age in search of them."

"As well as Angelou."

Marielle hesitated. "Yes, as well as Angelou."

Marielle touched the slightly dingy set of sails. She looked up in wonder as the gray sails disappeared from the stage and unfurled into the masts and yardarms as if a light breeze consumed them.

When they reached the helm, Marielle took hold of it. She invited Jacob to do the same in ceremonial fashion.

Marielle said, "To lay down our lives?"

Jacob took hold of one of the handles. "To lay down our lives, then. There is no greater love than to do just that. With a dragon searching both the skies and the earth, we may have to fight with everything we have."

The Plentitudes, more elegantly fashioned than *La Constance,* lifted off the ground and floated into the starry sky. It sailed out of the timeless space and into the Sixth Age. Marielle held the wheel in both hands, directing the ship towards Myra.

Chapter 37
The Battle of the Ghost Ships

The Plentitudes sailed with more gracefulness and velocity than its sister ship, *La Constance*. Both Jacob Lake and Marielle Eckenrode sat back and watched in wonder as the ship brought them from full daylight into the moonlit shadow of planet Earth.

Marielle showed Jacob how the Ghost Ship operated, as Shoebottom had shown her shortly after her abduction.

"See how the engraved handles of the helm determine direction? The top handle tells the ship which of the eight ports to go to. We can also turn the helm to guide the ship to other places. It is how Shoebottom could find us without going to a port."

"You mean, if we spy *The Stargazer* on the open sea, we can go to her?"

"Just as Shoebottom did when he brought us Sephus's book. It just depends on a moonlit night."

"What is the story behind these ships?"

"You know, during my voyage with Shoebottom as a prisoner, he passed the time by telling me the tale. Take it with a grain of salt as it was Shoebottom talking and one never knows when he is lying or telling the truth."

"What was his tale?"

"During the Renaissance, there were two lovers forbidden to be together because their families were from enemy countries. The boy was the son of the Count de Plentitudes, so named by the family's bountiful food production. The girl was from Belgium and her name was Constance. When their fathers found them in each other's arms, they killed them both before turning on each other. A year-long feud between the families followed until both families died in poverty. Because the two lovers were the only innocent ones, they became the spirit vessels, more commonly known as ghost ships."

Jacob looked out over the earth. "We are over the Mediterranean Sea now."

"Truly? We got there so fast?"

"*The Plentitudes* appears to be a fast ship. Look over there. You can see rigger ships like this one down on the sea."

"I don't think they could see us in the darkness. It would be funny, though, if they did. If we're over the Mediterranean, then we will arrive in Myra in no time. Jake, look! Over there in the clouds!"

Jacob got up from his seated position.

There, far off ahead of them, was the image of another ship seated in the clouds. It was not moving, but listed like a ship abandoned at sea.

Marielle, too, stood up. "It's the *La Constance!*"

"Are you certain?"

"I rode that ship over many hours. I can tell by its bowsprit. That is definitely *La Constance.*"

"Shoebottom's ship. Why is it stopped and sitting alone?"

"I do not know. Should we go to it?"

"Could be a trap."

"Let's approach it with that in mind."

Marielle took the helm and guided *The Plentitudes* toward *La Constance*. Both ships glowed brighter in the presence of the other. Marielle slowed down her ship and brought it alongside *La Constance.*

Jacob stood close to the gunwales. "It appears to be abandoned."

"That couldn't be. To abandon a ghost ship, one would have to jump from it."

"Suicide?"

Marielle searched her mind. "Hadrian appeared a bit on the crazy side the last time we saw him. I just cannot believe he would do something like that."

"It's also possible he's in the captain's chamber drunk out of his mind."

Marielle nodded. "That would be more like it."

Jacob returned to where Marielle stood. "I'm going to go look."

"I'm coming with you."

"One of us better keep a firm hold on this ship. If Shoebottom means to take *The Plentitudes* out from under us, he would have to go through you first. You are a knight now."

Jacob handed Marielle his sword.

Marielle looked at him with wonder. "I have my butterfly knives."

"If Shoebottom is a cryptic, your butterfly knives might only hurt him. My sword can kill him. I would rather you have it until I get back."

"What about you? What if he has an immortal weapon, too?"

"I will have the Shield of Meeshayell. He won't even know I'm there. If I carry the sword, he will see it and know where I am." Jacob took up the shield and disappeared from sight.

Marielle could hear his footsteps and knew just where he was. She remained at the helm of her ship, the hilt of Jacob's sheathed sword pointed to the ground in front of her, and kept a close watch. She knew by the opening of a cabin door that Jacob had entered the captain's chamber in search of Shoebottom.

In a flash, Marielle spied Shoebottom emerging behind the sailcloth stage on the forecastle deck. He did not even look in Marielle's direction, but set a wick aflame in a torch. It was then that Shoebottom's eyes glued to where Marielle stood. He smiled before touching the sails of *La*

Constance to the Seventh Age. Just as sails furled into the three masts and the ghost ship disappeared, Shoebottom lit the black powder sprinkled atop the remaining sails before leaping onto the main deck of *The Plentitudes.*

Marielle had no time to call out to Jacob Lake. He had entered the captain's quarters in search of Shoebottom while Shoebottom had managed a most clever act of defiance. With the three remaining sails aflame, he set the *La Constance* to an age Jacob Lake could never come back to.

Marielle was now caught in the Sixth Age with a cryptic aboard and nowhere to run.

"Oh, Jake!" she whispered. She backed away from the helm of *The Plentitudes* until the back of her thighs touched the rear railing of the ship.

On the main deck, Shoebottom leaned against the main center mast as if he had been there for hours. "You have nothing to fear of Jacob Lake's fate. He's immortal! He'll come out of this on both feet."

Marielle took hold of the rail with her free hand. "You!" She realized her folly in not making chase for the forecastle deck where she could have set the Sixth Age sails to the Seventh Age, giving Jacob Lake opportunity to return to the fray Marielle now faced.

Shoebottom walked towards the bottom of the steps like the actor he portrayed in the Myra amphitheater. "Pretty clever feat if I say so myself! Do you know that I got the idea of using this rare substance called black powder from you? I saw the burn marks around Dargo's cave when I paid him a visit. I only found a small amount of it else I would have blown his entire ship apart with him in it."

Marielle drew out Jacob Lake's sword. "So, my showing you friendship and love did little to quell your evil ways?"

"It did everything to quell my evil ways! I was so taken in by your sentiments that I completely forgot myself!

I wandered for days with you in the forefront of my thoughts. For days your shape, your face, surrounded me wherever I went. It is the very reason my minion Orface took the Petras from right underneath my nose and set that dragon free."

"Your minion did that?"

"He did."

"All because of me?"

"No, all because of me. I had lost myself in the infatuation with a girl half my age. You made such impacts on me, I was about to abandon my life's work. Your voice and your touch took me back to my mother and all the girl's I loved when growing up."

Marielle narrowed her eyes. "Then why are you doing this? Why is Jacob Lake trapped in the Seventh Age while I am stuck with the sight of you?"

"Simple. I am now a cryptic. From this point forward, now and forever, I am under the influence and will of one Araqnis, Dragon Extraordinaire, and Specter of the Well. You recall I warned you about his release. Now there is no hope for you, for the Keepers, and for any good to return to this Godforsaken world."

Marielle walked to the deck railing and pointed Jacob's sword down at him. "Why did you become a cryptic if you were so taken in by me?"

"Simple. Araqnis mortally wounded me. I was not only knocking on death's door, it was already open and inviting me into the party. In my defense, I killed Orface with Dargo's dagger, and entered the crypt for the solitary sake of survival. I am alive. It was become a cryptic or die."

"What you are saying is that because you are a cryptic, I have no more influence on you? You now cannot do good for the cause, even if it means neglecting your desire to become the world's most notorious villain?"

"That is correct."

"I don't believe it. Hadrian, you were a different man, even in the theater ruins in Myra. I think you have had a thing for me and that is tearing you apart!"

"Smitten perhaps, but far from torn apart. It is that very sword I am after now and the Fire Petra contained within. Oh! And along the way, it wouldn't hurt to have you as well. Araqnis will be very pleased when he finds I brought him the mother lode."

Shoebottom drew out his double swords from the crossed scabbards on his back.

Marielle's training played out in the back of her mind, but she felt little confidence. She had never faced mortal combat before.

"Do you recall when I warned you all about dealing with a genius criminal mind? I sat on *La Constance* attempting to think of a way to ensnare you alone without your bothersome boyfriend. That's the way I do things. I see the chessboard and attempt six or eight moves ahead."

"What did you come up with?" Marielle, in desperation, was attempting to stall Shoebottom in hopes Jacob Lake could find his way back.

"You see the queen on the board and you find ways to move her away from your target play. I sailed this ship thinking long and hard about its mechanisms. Burn the time sails and one can no longer span the ages. Clever, don't you think? I set the trap, the two of you walked into it."

When Shoebottom advanced toward the base of the wooden steps, Marielle cried out, "parley!"

Shoebottom's swords lowered. "Oh, for Pete's sake, not that again!"

"You had called parley back when we were on the *Stargazer,* now it is my turn."

"What could you possibly parley? I have you at a full disadvantage. Here, I possess two swords, while you have only one. Your opponent is a seasoned swordsman, while you are just a schoolgirl. Do not believe that the Fire Petra will assist you as you are but a mere mortal."

Marielle pondered his words. She pointed the sword at him again. "There is plenty to parley. You want this sword and I want the Shoebottom I saw in the theater."

"The Shoebottom you saw in the theater no longer exists."

"Oh no, he is still there. It is that man that I desire returned. Here is my parley. I will place Jacob Lake's sword at my feet and engage you on the main deck with another weapon of choice."

Marielle laid down Jacob's sword as she had stated, drew out the butterfly knives from her belt. She remained at the top of the steps.

Shoebottom raised his eyebrows to the short, broad blades as if attempting not to burst out laughing. "What, pray tell, are those?"

"Butterfly knives. The last immortal weapons, still capable of doing a cryptic harm."

"*Those* are butterfly knives? I have to admit, they look a little more impressive than they sound. They're still worthless against my twin swords. I think you would have a better chance with Jacob's sword. Tell me, if you are so bold, what are the stakes?"

"Winner take all. I beat you in a duel, and you are mine to command."

"And if I win?"

"You have all of me. I am yours from this day forward."

"Even unto death?"

"Even unto death. I don't fight, I don't run away."

Now Shoebottom let the laughter out. "You should know, dear girl, that in the impossible chance I lose to a schoolgirl with butter knives, I am still enslaved to the will of Araqnis. Either way, you lose."

"No, Hadrian, if I win, you are under my will and my will alone."

Shoebottom relaxed his swords to his side. "If that is your parley, I accept. Seems unfair though. You are a far more valuable a prize than I and, being a girl without battle training or experience, I am assured of the win."

Shoebottom smirked at the irony. He spat and backed away, allowing Marielle to approach him.

Marielle slipped off her silken shoes as her bare soles gave her more stability on the rough wooden surface. She descended the steps, her eyes affixed on her adversary.

While Shoebottom turned and poised himself in the center of the main deck, Marielle placed both of her feet firm on the wooded planks in the stance she learned from her master. Marielle closed her eyes envisioning the battle before opening them again. She took long, slow breaths before elevating her butterfly knives in parallel, their broad, curved edges pointed at her adversary.

Shoebottom walked in a half-arc toward one gunwale then to another like a puma surveying its impending kill.

"I will have to wound you, of course, no sense in killing you until Araqnis sees his prize. As a warning, you may lose a hand or leg in this exchange. It would be a pity to scar such a pretty face as yours."

"Are you going to spar with me with your stupid words or with your weapons?"

Shoebottom scowled, then leapt like a panther straight towards Marielle. He was certain of a quick end to the challenge. As he had done in many previous incursions, he feigned a thrust with one sword while aiming for a jab into Marielle's shoulder with the other.

To Shoebottom's utter shock, the short blades of the butterfly knives met his sword tips with a double clang. Marielle had also sidled her body in such a way that even if she had not deflected the second sword thrust, it would have met with the wooden stair rail behind her.

"Most impressive!" Shoebottom said, backing away and poising for a second assault. "That maneuver has leveled some very seasoned fighters. It does not fail often. Where did you learn to do that?"

"Oh, when will you ever shut up?" Marielle set her blades for the next assault. Her bare feet were solid to the deck, one more forward than the other. She narrowed her eyes and focused only on Shoebottom's abdomen. Shoebottom's abdomen would dictate his every intention.

Shoebottom moved in with a vigorous assault. The clanging of metal against metal rang out like church bells after an English wedding. He recognized from the start that the butterfly knives, being short and light, were quick in Marielle's hands. Though the incessant deflections of the girl's overly short weapons impressed him, he assured himself his victory would come.

He had yet to give Marielle the swordsmanship he had shown Balladin in the La Bellaroche wine cellar. He smiled when he turned towards his best maneuvering—the type he used when going straight for the kill.

You have all of me... Marielle's words turned over and over in Shoebottom's mind. After so many months, there was no prize more desirable than to have Marielle under his control. No gold or jewels, no thrill of the hunt, was more valuable than the Keeper girl who had eluded the cryptics at every turn.

Licking his lips, Shoebottom put forth his expert attack.

Chapter 38
The Return of Jacob Lake

The shadows of evening had encroached upon the Lost City when Aryeh took Annaquinn by the hands and lifted her to her feet. She stood without pain or injury.

It was during Annaquinn's healing by the water poured from the Sangrahl that Tuck and Balladin relayed their role in the Keeper's quest and how they had spanned four ages to do so. They told of Jacob's maiden journey with Marielle and all that took place since. They talked of Sephus, of Araqnis, and of Shoebottom.

Aryeh took the bread from his stone oven, set two small bowls of olive oil on the stone table before them, and offered to share his meal with them. He nodded, asking no questions during the tale.

"Do you know I was telling the truth when I said I came here from my own foolery?"

Tuck took a piece of bread and dipped it into the olive oil. He had little idea he was famished as the last time they had eaten, they were still aboard *The Rising Stargazer.*

"I had that same dream your girl Marielle had," said Aryeh. "I saw the same fate from Dargo de Montebank, just as she described it. Like her, I took flight. Unlike all the other Keepers, I saw the Masa Mabedi, the surrounding ruins, and the amphitheater in a dream. I was told in the dream that this was the place of the Sangrahl's delivery. Look around you, what do you see?"

Tuck and Balladin looked at each other. "I don't quite follow."

"You see an ancient stone church, ruins based on Hellenistic origins, and an amphitheater. Everything made from stone. Being from Palestine, I had heard of the tomb of Aaron and the spring of Wadi Musa, just five miles from here. I assured myself this would be the place I saw in my dream. This place was to be where Masa Mabedi awaited me. I found no Table Shrine here. Then the Bedouin shepherds had gotten so used to my healing practice, they won't let me leave."

Balladin said, "Did you ever light the fire?"

Aryeh looked at Balladin with a blank stare.

Balladin continued. "We uncovered something about the Sangrahl that was not clear. It is not just a vessel of healing, it bears light to the world, turns selfish souls into charitable people."

"Yes, I know all of that, but what do you mean, light the fire?"

"We found out from Sephus's book, its inner meanings, that we should light this Lamp and continuously have it atop a mountain so that it shines forth and surrounds the earth with clarity and with charity. It has its influences as it is now, but to light it..."

"You spoke of a dragon. Would lighting the Sangrahl alert his attention?"

Tuck nodded. "Balladin, he makes a good point. I believe the Keepers of the first three ages knew the secrets and lit the Sangrahl, but they did not have cryptics on the hunt for them and they certainly had no dragon."

Balladin agreed. "I can see now why Dargo did not find you. You call yourself a man of foolery, but as the three of us were discussing earlier, we are in the right time and place."

"Inside a prison with no hope of escape? How is that in a right time and place?"

"Aryeh, you came here on foot from your home. You never traveled a wellspring. That is how we reached you, so that is how we will depart."

"There is a wonderful swimming hole at the other end of the wellspring," said Annaquinn.

Aryeh stood up. "It is that or fight the Bedouin shepherds and make it to Asia Minor on foot. I don't know why someone chose me for this quest, a man of my advanced years. I don't have the stamina that the four of you have. The wellspring it is. I have never been through one and the thought of it intrigues me."

Aryeh packed up the Sangrahl and a walking stick. Through the waning sunset, he followed his companions along the Street of Facades, through the marketplace ruin, and back towards the Treasury.

As the promise of nightfall consumed the elongated shadows across the Lost City, they continued forward up the far wash where the slippery slope had laid claim to Annaquinn's ankle earlier that day.

When they reached the spring cave, Tuck peered into the depths. "Something is amiss."

Balladin came up beside him. "What do you see?"

"The spring, it has no water flowing."

Balladin felt his hand inside the opening. The cool spring water that had flowed forth from the wellspring was no longer there. Even the rock chamber was dry, as if the water had never flowed there in the first place.

"The wellspring, it's dead."

Tuck backed away from the opening. "Araqnis?"

Balladin nodded. "Sephus had written of the dragon's ability to seal a wellspring. I believe it may be his plan to trap us inside any age. It is only a matter of time now that he'll hunt for the Sixth Keeper here."

Angelou whimpered, not understanding why their course had changed.

When they returned to the bottom of the drainage, another surprise awaited them. The two Bedouin shepherds Balladin had insulted with his martial arts skill, had indeed returned with reinforcements. Twelve of the guard had returned with the two to even the score.

"I have three arrows left in my quiver," said Tuck.

"I could only take four or five before the rest would have me," said Balladin.

The shepherds pointed their scimitars at the intruders, talking in aggressive tones. As a group, they sauntered with menacing expressions towards the canyon opening.

"Light the Sangrahl," said Aryeh.

Tuck and Balladin looked at him.

"If it has such influence on the world, what do we have to lose?"

Tuck took hold of the common flint found in the canyon and sparked it against the metal of an arrow point. Lighting one of his wood-shafted arrows, he held the flame to where Aryeh held out the Sangrahl.

A flash of bright light went forth from the Sangrahl, blinding everyone, including Annaquinn and the Knights of the Sangrahl.

"I forgot about that!" said Tuck, holding his eyes with both hands.

When the shepherd assailants recovered their sight, they fell back further when they saw something approach them from far up in the night sky.

La Constance soared with Jacob Lake at the helm, though he had no control of where the ghost ship was taking him. He attempted to steer the ship by moving the helm, but the ship would not respond to Jacob's commands.

At Jacob's approach, the Sangrahl light dimmed.

The Bedouin shepherds sat up, rubbing their eyes. They had dropped their swords and looked into the canyon to where the Lamp now burned with a freestanding flame, no brighter than a torch. They regarded the Sangrahl with wonder as their aggressions softened, though none of them understood the reason.

An unforeseen mist gathered in the canyon, causing the shepherds to back away. In all of their days, they had never witnessed such a magic, and fled into the narrow Ain Siq canyon.

Aryeh looked with a newfound wonder when he saw the ghost ship descend out of the mist.

Tuck smiled in recognition of Jacob Lake aboard the upper deck of the Renaissance ship. "This, Aryeh, is the alternate form of time travel! Meet the Keeper of the Fourth Age."

Jacob wore his concerns across his face like a Mardi gras mask. He jumped down to the port side rail gate. "Marielle is in trouble. She might even be dead."

Angelou, unaware of the reality that surged through her master's mind, jumped her happy dance at Jacob's return.

Balladin, Tuck, Angelou, and Aryeh climbed aboard the ship.

"What can we do?" said Balladin.

Jacob embraced his dog. Tears ran down his face, for she was still alive. "I have no answers. What have we here?"

Tuck said, "This is Aryeh, the Keeper of the Sixth Age. His presence here in this stone city has kept him out of harm's way. As you can see, he carries the Sangrahl of the Sixth Age."

Jacob said. "Shoebottom is a cryptic. He took Marielle on the other ghost ship and sabotaged this one. Oh, this is all my fault for not foreseeing his trap! I do not think he will spare Marielle."

Tuck pondered the tale. "No, Jake, Shoebottom would spare Marielle her life, just long enough to transport her to Araqnis. Shoebottom would want her alive."

Jacob pondered Tuck's words.

Balladin nodded in agreement. "Araqnis has trapped all of us into an age in order to disallow our ability to take flight from him. Annaquinn was successful in delivering the Sangrahl of the Fifth Age. Araqnis's next target will be our sixth Keeper Aryeh."

Aryeh stepped forward. "My dream showed me the Masa Mabedi. In my mind, I perceived it to be here in the Lost City. Your knights here informed me it is in Myra in Asia Minor. That is where I am to deliver the Sangrahl."

Jacob stood up. "That's it! That's why Sephus penned in his Fire Letters, that Marielle would receive the Sangrahl, not deliver it. The Masa Mabedi is also where Marielle was to receive hers for her final year."

Balladin nodded. "We can still take *La Constance* to Myra."

"If she will still work. Shoebottom damaged this ship with fire, so I cannot promise she'll get us there."

Balladin walked towards the helm. "She got you here, Jacobi. She'll get us to Myra and to the Table Shrine. The real question is, what will await us when we get there?"

As Jacob told the tale of Shoebottom's underhanded maneuver, questions arose.

Tuck said, "If he set the sail to the Seventh Age, how did you find us in the Sixth Age?"

Balladin and Annaquinn nodded for they had wondered the same.

Chapter 39
The Battle of Masa Mabedi

17th Century Myra was little more than a graveyard of toppled stone ruins. Every house, every commercial building were only reminders of the once thriving community that dwelled there in the 5th century.

With the entire night ahead of them, *La Constance* had just enough spiritual power left in the disappearing moonlight to make it to Asia Minor and to Myra on the Mediterranean coast. Once the ship had landed, the power left her hull, and the sails vanished from her masts. *La Constance* was to be no more.

Jacob handed Tuck the Tears of the Wanderer he had found in the pool of the Firespring when he and Marielle had escaped the dragon for the last time. Myra was to be the place of the ultimate confrontation.

Tuck took the Tears of the Wanderer with a look of wonder. "These were with you in the timeless space?"

"We thought you were dead. You had spent all twenty-four, a sign you had become desperate."

"I should have been dead, Jake. Your dog and Annaquinn saved my life. In fact, they saved all our lives."

Annaquinn blushed. She had little idea she had accomplished so much.

The plans by which the Knights of the Sangrahl, Annaquinn, and Aryeh made during the brief trip to Myra, was to find the Masa Mabedi and deliver the Sangrahl post haste. Only providence would dictate what would become of them and the Sangrahl of the Seventh Age.

With Marielle no longer on the scene, Jacob would step in to become her surrogate Keeper and hope to find a way back to the Seventh Age to fulfill it. He diverted his despair and remained focus on the task ahead—even though he saw no way to fulfill the final quest.

Even Angelou walked with her tail bent low as they entered Myra in the early morning light. The city of St. Nicholas was no more welcoming than a funeral for a distant, unknown relative.

Jacob peered into the old cistern to see if the wellspring there still glowed with life. The cistern remained dark.

When they found the old church and the Table Shrine, Jacob pointed to it. "Masa Mabedi," he said to Aryeh. "If all goes well, the apparitions of the Keepers of the first three ages will appear over there. Annaquinn, you and I should stand here. You follow what I do when a Sangrahl appears in front of you."

Annaquinn nodded sheepishly. She stood in her place like a firsttime actress just before curtain call.

Jacob said, "Aryeh, take out the Sangrahl and stand on the other side of Annaquinn. We will form a circle."

Aryeh, having transformed Balladin's hooded silk cloak into a toga, took the Sangrahl from the wooden box and held it up. No light shined forth from its center. Nor did the Table Shrine come to life to welcome it. As Marielle had done in prior days, he stepped forward and set the Sangrahl on the sixth designation on the seven-section stone top, but nothing happened.

Balladin shook his head. "I believe Marielle is required to be here."

Balladin's words penetrated into all of them. The Keepers and their knights had indeed come to the end of the road. Worse still, a smell of sulfur entered the air.

"Fall back into the niche of the table," commanded Jacob.

Aryeh followed Annaquinn, Tuck, and Balladin to the rear of the apse behind the Table Shrine.

Jacob took up Meeshayell's shield. He stood in front of the group so that they, too, would become invisible.

"Everyone, huddle down low," he said. He knelt, keeping the others behind him and the shield in front of him.

As the shadow of Araqnis entered the empty streets of Myra, Jacob pressed his body against the others, clustered into a protected space surrounded by stone. He took the Sangrahl from the table and handed it back to Aryeh.

"Make no sound," he whispered to them. "Breathe slowly with your mouths open."

Annaquinn huddled between Tuck and Balladin against the back wall of the old church. For the time being, Meeshayell's shield rendered them all invisible.

Angelou was nowhere in sight.

The moment Araqnis landed along the main avenue of Myra, he vanished. Without a sound, he reappeared along the fringes of the amphitheater. His eyes sent searching beams across the empty seats of the theater. He sniffed the place where Jacob and Marielle once sat. Satisfied the scent was a few days old, the dragon disappeared again.

In several places about Myra, Araqnis appeared, searched, and then vanished. He covered the outer fringes of Myra before concentrating his efforts on the center. He knew of Masa Mabedi, but had saved it for last.

With each reappearance, the dragon sniffed through the air. Its eye beams turned toward the church wherever the air currents showed life signs. He would disappear. In a spiral pattern, the dragon drew ever nearer to his target.

Jacob fixed his eyes on the others, imploring them to keep silent.

"I still have my bow and the Tears, Jake, even if they can only distract him."

"Nothing will distract him," replied Jacob.

With only two arrows remaining, Tuck affixed a Tear regardless.

When Araqnis appeared with abruptness at the entrance to the church ruin, his sudden presence made everyone jump. The dragon turned. A broad smile materialized across his sinister face. He heaved in a breath and blew fire across the apse of the church.

Jacob Lake was certain the firestorm would incinerate them all, but the magical power of the shield staved off the attack.

Confused, Araqnis crawled in nearer. He knew there were people present, his nose never lied. *Why can I not see them?* He drew in breath, the fiery furnace at the back of his throat ignited like a smithery, and he blew into the apse a second time.

Jacob kept the shield up and his head low. He knew it was only seconds before Araqnis would feel around with his nose and use his brute strength to strip the shield from him. They would be like toasted marshmallows in little time.

"There you are, ol' chap!" came a voice from out on the street.

Araqnis took his attention away from the scent of Keepers to see what his cryptic minion had in store for him.

Shoebottom jumped from *The Plentitudes* that faded with the slow disappearance of the moonlight and the pending arrival of dawn in the eastern sky. In his right hand, he carried Jacob Lake's sword befitted with the bright-glowing Fire Petra, Araqnis's most coveted prize. In Shoebottom's left hand, he carried what appeared to be the Sangrahl.

With hands tied, blood on her arm, and looking somber, Marielle sat hunkered down along the ship's portside rail. She looked at the scene with a frightened stare.

Araqnis manifested a smile that would rival the Cheshire Cat. He left the entrance to the church to examine the accomplishments of his most sought-after cryptic,

Hadrian Shoebottom. *Had Hadrian Shoebottom actually accomplished in bringing him everything the dragon had wanted?*

"Well, I would not let you down this time, dear boy," Shoebottom said, waving Jacob's sword casually. "Which of the prizes would you like to see first, the Sangrahl, the girl Keeper, or the sword?"

Araqnis cast his gaze first on Marielle, then in full attentiveness to the Fire Petra. With such power, nothing could contain the fire cast forth from his mouth. Rocks and metal would melt from the outset. Once the Keepers were dead and the Sangrahl destroyed, Araqnis could casually hunt for the elusive Winged Warrior.

That was a hunt Araqnis could not wait to embark upon. He closed the distance between himself and Shoebottom.

"Nah! Ah-ah!" said Shoebottom like a mother hen. He held his flat palm out. "You forget Your Fiery Dragonship, we made a bargain! With all that I offer, I believe you owe me TWO Petras."

Araqnis spat. "You have no stance to bargain with me! Now all that my dragon eyes see is mine." His lightning quick paw picked up Shoebottom by the chest and held him in front of his face. Seeing that Shoebottom had dropped the Sangrahl, Araqnis peered over his shoulder and stepped on it, crushing it into the marble-laden earth.

Drawing his attention back to Shoebottom, Araqnis said, "Now, what was it you requested of me, Shoebottom? Something about a *bargain*?"

Shoebottom gathered his wits. "You don't know the half of it, dear boy! You see, I am no longer subservient to your will as a cryptic, when I lose a parley made to another."

"A parley? What do you mean?"

Araqnis's nose breath blew into Shoebottom's face with a gust.

Shoebottom gathered himself and freed one hand so that he could point and gesture like an attorney in a courtroom. "When a cryptic undergoes a double agreement, in a conflict of interest, he finds himself between two agreements and therefore must honor his own will—Book of Sephus, chapter thirteen, verse forty-five."

Araqnis cast Shoebottom's body against his snout. "What are you playing at?"

"I know you won't kill me until you have the full story, your Spidership. The Keeper girl, that's her over there, made a parley with me. We would engage in a duel with a winner-take-all accordance. No one, not even a criminal like myself, can refuse a parley. That's written in all languages since the beginnings of organized crime."

"You won the fight, did you not?"

"Not in the least! The girl beat me with skills I did not know she had. She would have severed my right arm were it not for me being a cryptic!"

"She won? I find that difficult to swallow."

"She won indeed, and that Sangrahl you just destroyed was a decoy set by Tuck at the Roman Moor Wellspring."

Araqnis squeezed his clawed palm into Shoebottom. "And what was the will of this girl now that you lost the battle?"

"That I give my life to the cause!"

"I can oblige that!"

Araqnis squeezed harder into Shoebottom's cryptic body

Gasping for air, Shoebottom's other hand thrust Jacob Lake's sword repeatedly into Araqnis's neck. The sword, even with its Petra, served no harmful effect on the dragon.

It did have a harmful effect on the amulet chain.

The first time Shoebottom had attempted to steal the Petras from Araqnis's sleeping body, he had failed to sever the chain, but did not fail to nick one link. Now, with Jacob's sword thrusting into the dragon's neck, the chain link broke with the third thrust of the sword.

While Shoebottom's body soared against the columns of Artemis's temple ruin, the amulet containing the Earth and Sky Petras fell to the earth with a resounding clank.

There, next to the amulet, was Jacob Lake's sword.

Araqnis turned, first to see if Marielle was still tied to the ship rail, then to see where he had cast away his cryptic. Shoebottom writhed in agony on the ground, but Marielle had disappeared.

Araqnis felt his neck for the amulet chain, but it was no longer there. His head swiveled to cast his eyes to the earth, but there, standing over all three Petras, was Angelou.

Just as Araqnis lifted a clawed paw to backhand the dog, Angelou lay her body over the sword and amulet. The light of the Petras surged through the dog's body, casting bright lights in all directions and blinding both human and dragon alike. The canine body glowed a brilliant gold and white.

Araqnis held its wings over its eyes to stave off the bright beams until, after seven seconds, the light had gone out.

Standing there where Angelou had stood over the Petras, stood Meeshayell, the Winged Warrior. He bent low to pick up the Fire Petra sword. In his left hand, the amulet opened and the Earth and Sky Petras magnetized into their crafted positions in the crosspiece of Jacob's sword.

Holding the sword firm in his right hand, Meeshayell cast a resolved gaze long and hard at Araqnis. He sidled to his left in order to keep the dragon from harming Marielle.

From behind a block where she had crawled to hide, Marielle stood up. The bonds that tied her arm were a ruse. The blood on her arm came not from her defeat, but from Shoebottom's.

Marielle called out, "Jake, the shield!"

Jacob Lake stood up and, with the shield, walked out to where Meeshayell stood. Jacob Lake handed the shield to him.

"So that's it?" Araqnis belched out a laugh. "You contained your spirit inside that dog this whole time? I could have had my minions kill that canine a long time ago!"

"You lose, Araqnis," called out Meeshayell, his bright wings coming to life across his armored back.

Araqnis blew fire at him, but Meeshayell brought the pewter shield with the insignia of the Sangrahl, in front of him.

Meeshayell turned into flight, casting his full assault onto the dragon.

Araqnis held clawed toes, a snapping multitude of teeth, and a whipping tail into his defense. He attempted to go after Jacob's life, he attempted to lunge after Marielle, but Meeshayell was too quick.

The Winged Warrior flashed from one place to another, keeping the dragon's offenses at bay. He persisted forward as Araqnis backed away from the church ruin.

Unlike their first battle, Meeshayell did less taunting and focused on the task at hand. In his first assault, he severed the dragon's left leg. In the second, Araqnis's tail. There was no room left for Araqnis in Meeshayell's third offense.

Meeshayell thrust Jacob Lake's sword into the dragon's chest, bursting bright red light from its wound. The dragon screamed and writhed on the earth. He flailed his wings and legs and let out a second scream. He sat up in hopes of a last-ditch effort to snap with its teeth.

In Meeshayell's final stroke, he swung the sword that took the head from the dragon. While its convulsing body burst into flame, Meeshayell turned and faced the others. The resolution to kill remained in his strained facial expression.

Jacob and Marielle ran into each other's arms while Tuck and Balladin stood in awe of what they had just seen. Aryeh and Annaquinn, too, came forth in wonder.

Meeshayell approached them. His expression softened, and he nodded at them in approval of all that they had accomplished. "I had lost hope as you have," he said. "In the end, you all remained focused on the task at hand. I will be eternally grateful to all of you."

As the sun's first rays cast beams across the ruins of Myra, Meeshayell looked to the heavens and took off in a majestic flight that left each of them breathless.

Jacob looked at Marielle with more elation than he had ever encountered with her. Marielle gazed back at him, but only for a moment. She turned and ran to where Shoebottom lay.

She placed her gentle hands about his face, not daring to touch his broken body. Tears rolled down both of her cheeks.

"You won…" Shoebottom's voice sputtered. "I cannot believe you won again. Three times now, you have beaten me… but who's counting? Is… is there anyone… who can… defeat you?"

Jacob called to Aryeh to bring the Sangrahl.

"No…" Tears flowed for the first time in Shoebottom's adult life. "I lost my third attempt to conquer this girl. If I live, I would be beholden to go for a fourth—even the score with Dargo."

Marielle cast a compassionate gaze. "We wouldn't want that now, would we?"

"Let me die. That way, you will all know, I gave my life for the cause… You, Marielle, you saved this hopeless man."

Marielle shook her head. "No, Hadrian, you did it. You will always be the world's most notorious villain."

Shoebottom made a feeble attempt to smile. While gazing up at her with the only love he had felt since his mother died, he let out his final breath.

Chapter 40
Gathering of the Seven

When delving into the sciences, a simple experiment one may observe is that light dispels the darkness, but darkness cannot dispel the light. Such is the case when Meeshayell, representing light, had ultimately overcome Araqnis, representing darkness.

Evil may win the day, but goodness will find its way in the end.

These were the thoughts that ran through Marielle's mind as she wept for Shoebottom. She was uncertain at first whether such grief came from witnessing the tragedy in death, or recognizing Shoebottom's honorable act in his final chapter. Evil as Shoebottom appeared, he also found his way in the end as a source of light against the darkness.

Jacob walked up behind Marielle and placed a gentle hand about her. She looked up at him, and while wiping away a tear, wrapped her arms around him.

"Marielle, please tell me what happened," Jacob said.

Marielle released her embrace, took a last glance at Shoebottom's lifeless body, and allowed Jacob to lead her back towards the Masa Mabedi. "Shoebottom was the genius, Jake. I think we can all recognize that. As part of his eight preconceived moves on the life-sized chessboard, he fooled both of us into thinking that the abandoned ship was for us to explore. He knew you would protect me by leaving me on *The Plentitudes.*"

"His other stroke of genius was in damaging the time sails and sent me into the Seventh Age with no hope of returning," said Jacob.

"Yet you are here in the Sixth Age, how did you accomplish that?"

"Shoebottom sent me to the Seventh Age. Bring down the pure white sails, scuff them a bit, and rub dirt into them…"

"Truly?"

"Truly. Marielle, you are correct in saying he outsmarted us all. If only we had had him on our side."

"We did, Jake, that's my point. It tore Shoebottom to pieces when he came under control of Araqnis. This man could have destroyed *La Constance,* taking away all hope of you finding Tuck and the others. Hadrian Shoebottom was one who had purpose, good or bad, in everything he did."

"You had influenced him before with an act of love. Marielle, perhaps the real genius is you."

"I am sorry, Jake, I just wanted him to feel for the first time what it was like to be held in high esteem by a friend and especially from a woman."

"From a very attractive woman."

Marielle smiled at the compliment. "I am glad you still find me so!"

They found a large rectangular stone lying on its side and sat down together.

Jacob took Marielle's hand. "So what happened after I lost you? I believed you would be dead."

"In my first encounter with Shoebottom, I conquered him with love. In the second encounter, I conquered him with steel."

"You?"

"Butterfly knives. We put everything on the line in a wager. If he won, he had full cooperation from me to take me to Araqnis as his prize. If I had him, he had to overcome the dissonance he felt within and do my bidding."

"Marielle, that was perilous!"

"You have no idea! But what choice did I have? Without the parley, Shoebottom could have killed me, taken your sword, and had his will with the whole thing despite his misgivings about serving the dragon."

"You won? How did you take down a master swordsman?"

"Jake, I know we can sit here and give my talents and training all the credit for winning a duel with a master swordsman. Even I was surprised at my abilities. Still, I don't believe Hadrian gave me his best effort. At the very least, his internal conflict distracted him, taking away his normal prowess."

"Because he loved you?"

Marielle shrugged and looked down.

"Whichever the case," Jacob said, "I am very proud of you. What was the winning stroke?"

"My butterfly knives, being short and light, are much quicker than long broadswords. Many of my blocks would pull his weapon rather than push, placing Hadrian off balance. Were he not a cryptic, I would have severed both of his hands."

"So you disarmed him?"

"And with his swords to the ground, I held a blade to his throat. He smiled at me and I told him my demands. I told him to go to Araqnis, pretending he had won. He had to sever the amulet using Jacob's sword. It was a risk of paramount proportion, as Shoebottom could have gone against my demands and handed the Fire Petra to Araqnis."

"You put your faith in him when no one else had."

"Jake, I saw no other way to victory."

Jacob embraced her and now tears flowed down his own face. "In the end, you are the genuine hero of our quest."

Tuck came up to the two of them. I sure hate to interrupt your reflections, but we have company."

Jacob and Marielle turned.

From within the distant cliff ruin, the same ghostly apparitions of three Keepers emerged in the darkened corridor. The light that glowed from their cores illuminated the apse of the church and all that surrounded the Table Shrine.

Jacob and Marielle got up and walked into the partly covered church ruin. Standing there waiting for them were Tuck, Balladin, Annaquinn, and Aryeh.

"It is time for delivery," Jacob said. "Take your places with honor alongside the legends of the past."

The Keepers of the first three ages stood with their respective Sangrahls held in their hands. When the living Keepers entered the shadows of the sanctuary, a glowing, intangible Sangrahl appeared before each of them and they could reach up and hold on to it.

Tuck gasped as he recognized the first Keeper.

Sephus regarded each of the six remaining Keepers with a smile as the Keepers took their places around the Table.

Tuck and Balladin stood side-by-side along the edge of the apse and watched in wonder at all that was about to take place. When Tuck discreetly identified Sephus to Balladin, Balladin's mouth dropped open, but no words came forth.

The first Keeper took two steps to the edge of the Table and set his Sangrahl in the triangular space in front of him. He remained with his hands on the edge of the Table while the second Keeper came up beside him, placing his Sangrahl. The third followed in kind with the second.

Three Sangrahl apparitions stood glowing on the tabletop. It was Jacob Lake's turn. He walked forward next to the third Keeper and placed his ghostly Sangrahl into its proper place. Annaquinn followed in kind and then Aryeh.

Marielle held no Sangrahl, real or intangible, and she stood there not knowing if something was still amiss as had been during her first encounter with the ghosts of the past. Everything became clear when all the Sangrahls slid to the center and merged into one. The completed Sangrahl became as real and tangible as the Sangrahl Marielle had always carried.

One by one, the ghosts backed away, turned and disappeared—all but one.

Tuck walked up between Jacob and Marielle and place his hands on each of their shoulders. "Wait for it," he said with a smile.

Jacob and Marielle regarded their friend with puzzlement.

"The first Keeper is also the last Keeper," Tuck said.

The ghost who remained was the same stone mason Tuck had encountered in the quarry. He smiled at Jacob, Tuck, Marielle, and Balladin with a knowing look.

Before the first Keeper could say a word, Marielle held hands to her mouth. "Sephus!"

The ghostly man smiled. "You have done well, my daughter. You have all done well. However! Your time is not yet up. Marielle, your vigil with the Sangrahl of the Seventh Age still requires one more year of vigilance."

Marielle held a hand toward him. "Sephus, I…"

"You need not worry about me, daughter. I am more alive now than ever before! As for you, though the forces of darkness are no longer there to thwart your efforts, your quest is not yet over. Take the one remaining Sangrahl. This ceremony signifies that this one and final Lamp of Light, is the most important for the hardened and hateful, suffering people of your Seventh Age."

Marielle took hold of the Sangrahl.

"Find a mountain that no one goes to," continued Sephus. "It does not have to be the tallest or the most majestic. You choose. Place the Sangrahl and set its light for all the world to see. Let it remain there and live your life. When the year ends on September twenty-first, return to it and extinguish the flame. Then and only then will your mission find its end."

Marielle picked up and placed the Sangrahl into the wooden box that Aryeh still held. "Receive where they deliver…"

Sephus took each of them aside to give them their counsel for their final year and honoring the good work they had done. He began with Annaquinn, who smiled at all that Sephus told her. She gazed at Tuck and Balladin, but spoke not a word of it to anyone afterward.

Sephus then spoke to Aryeh. In their conversation, Sephus did not appear stern, nor was Aryeh disheartened. Had Aryeh not found himself hidden in the high rocks of the Lost City, Dargo might have found and killed him three years prior.

He called Balladin and Tuck together and spoke them collectively.

"You two gave the Keepers all that they needed to survive. Whether this quest was to be your destiny, we will never know for certain. I believe we could not have succeeded without you. If it be your desire, your mission to defend the innocent and good will never end so long as you live."

Sephus reached and took hold of Tuck's longbow and quiver. For a moment, they glowed in Sephus's hands.

"Tuck, had you not relinquished these to me inside the quarry, you never would have found them in my cave chamber at the start of your mission. You placed your faith with me and now you may keep them forever."

Tuck noticed that his quiver was full. He bowed with Balladin and the two of them backed away.

Sephus wrapped his illuminated arms around Marielle. "You shone like the light of the sun, daughter. None of this could have happened with any other girl."

Marielle felt Sephus's shoulders and back as if he were alive. She kissed his cheek and allowed herself to back away.

Sephus turned to Jacob Lake. "I gave no knowledge to you that your dog, the Angelwolf, most commonly referred to as Angelou, was the vessel in which the disabled Meeshayell worked his magic. Jacob, I request you come with me."

The two of them disappeared into the far corner of the apse, Sephus with a ghostly glowing arm around his Fourth Keeper. They spoke in murmured tones.
When Jacob turned around, Sephus had disappeared. Jacob gazed at Marielle and then at the Sangrahl. Jacob knew something no one else did.

Chapter 41
The Immortal Mortal

A year had passed since the seven Keepers gathered in the Sixth Age to deliver the final vessel to Marielle. The Sangrahl rested in place on the top of Crystal Peak in the high desert, its light a shining anomaly to any who encountered it from far below, assuming it was a radio tower beacon with a light intended to ward off unwary aircraft.

Yet there it stood, a perpetual flame without loss of fuel or flicker.

On the steep slope of the mountain, a young woman, now nineteen years in age, scaled the vertical cliff in full climbing gear. Her hair had grown long and she had braided in down her back. Wearing blue hiking shorts, climbing shoes, and a black tank top, she stopped to reset her ropes for the final stage of her ascent.

She looked below her. Though the thousand-foot drop made her head spin, she held her composure and addressed the man below her.

"Are you coming up or did you fall asleep down there?"

"Just enjoying the view," Jacob Lake said, looking up and following the same hand and foot holds Marielle had used.

"Well, hurry up, my fellow knight. You're holding up the rear! Look, we're almost at the top."

When they reached the peak and climbed atop its rocky surface, they sat on the flat-sided pinnacle with their feet near to the edge. Sweat poured from their skin and they took ample drinks from their red water bottles. "Jake, it sure is good to see you again. I am glad you came to join me."

Jacob smiled, taking the water bottle from her in order to take his own drink. "It was painful for me, having not seen you in a year. I would never have missed it for the world."

They sat with the view of the southwestern wilderness in front of them and the Sangrahl burning bright over their shoulders. The massive valleys and hills were like ocean waves far below surrounded by tsunamis of neighboring mountains. The sun was still high in the sky, though it allowed only a brief visit to the two climbers.

Marielle capped the bottle to the water bottle and placed it back in her small pouch. "You look good," she said. "You shaved off your beard. What have you been up to these past twelve months?"

"Life is not so exciting without having some cryptic on your tail. Still, I am enjoying the peace. I've been trying to work out the rest of my life, and it has not been easy."

"Well, I have to say the same for me. I miss Angelou, of course, but I got myself another dog."

"Did you? What did you name her?"

"*Him*... He is beautiful like Angelou only he has a darker coat. I named him Myra after the Table Shrine, where everything ended. Maybe you could stay a while and meet him."

"Hmm... Myra. That's a good name. I would love to stay for a bit."

"He's back at the house. He's still a puppy, but just as wonderful as Angelou, I think. Mom thinks a dog will only get in the way of my college studies."

"You haven't had to remain in hiding. How is it with your family?"

Marielle let out a sigh. "It felt like I was a different person coming home. I was no longer that high school girl who left three years ago. Oh, they were all elated to see me, of course, but I had been through so much that they could never possibly understand, so I found myself alone a lot. Shelly had taken my room and Mom had turned Shelly's room into a home office. This past year, finishing my high school work, I was on a couch in the basement."

"You don't sound happy."

Marielle's eyes scanned the horizon for nothing in particular. "No, I guess I'm not. I was wrong about wanting to go my Marielle way. I was once a part of something big. I learned to fight. Allegedly I beat a master swordsman in a duel. It was scary going through all of that, but it was worth it."

Jacob nodded. "What would you do with your life now if you could?"

"Well, I… I guess I would do it all over again. I'm a Knight of the Sangrahl, like you. I'm medieval at heart. I fight dragons and travel the ages."

Any boyfriends?"

Marielle shook her head. "A few dates, but nothing came of them. I don't know, Jake, you go through all that you and I have been through and people have no inkling what I'm really about."

She put a hand on top of his. "They just weren't anything like you. You're still the only boy I ever kissed. I don't know if I will ever…"

Marielle placed a hand on Jacob's hand. Looking down, she noticed a patch of dark red on the side of his hand.

"Jake! Your hand—you're bleeding!"

Jacob placed his bleeding hand up to his mouth to suck on the wound. "I know, it's just a minor scrape. I bumped it against that sharp rock just before reaching the top."

Marielle's mouth dropped open as she stared at him. "Immortals don't bleed!"

Jacob took out a gauze pad from a side pouch and wrapped it tight around his hand. "No, they sure don't. Hey, do you want to have dinner with me? There might still be some money in Tuck's Humvee."

Marielle took hold of Jacob's arm with both of her hands. "Jacob Lake, you talk to me! Why are you bleeding?"

Jacob smiled at her. "Do you recall when Sephus took me aside and spoke to me and I would tell no one of our conversation?"

"Yee—yeah."

"Now I'm going to tell you what he said. He told me the way of the amaranthine is glorious. I could spend forever taking on new dragons of varying shapes and sizes. With a new sword, I could still fight this world of evil, using my power to win around every turn. This was Dargo's mistake when he killed me. He unleashed in me a forever immortal working on the side of good rather than a cryptic working on the side of bad. Tuck, Balladin, and I, we've been questing only it isn't the same without you."

"What's that got to do with why your hand was bleeding?"

"Sephus gave me an ultimatum. He said, 'Jacobi, you can do all of that as amaranthine, or you can do that as a mortal. Drink from the Sangrahl and you will return to being human.'"

Marielle narrowed her eyes. "You did this?"

"The last time we climbed this cliff to set the Lamp afire. Remember? You had a difficult time keeping up with me. We sat up here, just like this, and we drank from your water bottle. Then you marveled at the approach of a far distant storm. I poured water into the Sangrahl. I drank from it, even though you were looking right at me. You asked me to hand it to you so that we could set a fire to it."

"You're now mortal?"

"Yes."

Marielle squinted at him. "Jake, why would you do that? And why didn't you say something last year?"

"I wanted you to be with your family and sort out how you wanted to spend the rest of your life."

"You gave up immortality! For what?"

Jacob smiled at her. "For you."

Marielle's eyes lit up, and she threw her arms around Jacob. Her hands and body trembled. "So, so, that means…"

Jacob kissed Marielle on the lips and held it there as long as he could. He released the embrace and said, "Once we extinguish the Lamp and it falls to its final destination, where would you like to live the rest of your life?"

"With you?"

"If that is what you want."

She threw her arms around him again. "I don't believe this. The earth, this earth! If only it could feel the joy I am feeling right now!"

She released her hold. "Jake, all that I am and all that I imagine has you right here next to me. My heart was broken every day you were away. I know that sounds childish! I'm not supposed to give up my independent way of being."

"You don't have to give anything up. We are knights working together to better this world, are we not?"

Marielle placed her hand to her mouth as if she was suppressing too many words. "What are our options?"

Jacob turned and opened the flap of his daypack. From deep inside, he took out a lantern.

Marielle cupped hands over her mouth. *"The Plentitudes?"*

"Where would you like to go? You may recall, the ghost ship still had four working sets of sails."

Chapter 42
Return to the Dance

It remained a fact that La Bellaroche had hired an artisan sculptor to put together a figure of Jacobi du Lac to stand above the rock fountain in the mountain square. It is also still true that one cannot find La Bellaroche on a map anywhere in this age, whether searching through the eastern Alpen region of France or the western Alpen region of Switzerland.

After a thousand years of its existence, no one knows the reason for the town's disappearance, whether it came into ruin during a war or it fell on hard times, or perhaps an act of nature took it deep into the depths of the earth. Some believe the village is still here only under a different name.

So, one hoping to walk the streets of the One-Walled Fortress might only find it by the descriptions left within this tale. One may recognize a town set between two walls of a river canyon while traveling the eastern, Alpen borders of France or the western boundaries of Switzerland.

Still, a thousand years of forward history are not as important as a single moment late in the year 1032 A.D. when the village of La Bellaroche was preparing for yet another festival. This one was not a spontaneous celebration of the return of a local hero, rather the common annual harvest festival prepared and celebrated every end of September of every year in the town's illustrious history.

Two women in the du Lac home sat at the hefty wooden table placing the last-minute stitches into the new harvest fest banners that would adorn every street corner during the week-long festival.

Katherine, Jacob's mother, had lost the slinking sadness she had carried in the years following her husband's death and later after word of the death of her son, Jacobi du Lac, came to her.

Today was a different reality as Katherine spoke like a spring hen to her daughter, Isabelle, while the two women poured into the task in front of them.

Isabelle was now seventeen. She had bloomed more prominently into one of La Bellaroche's most notable beauties, though the humble maiden was in full denial of this. "So many pretty girls in our village," she would say whenever anyone complimented her.

Though many eligible men had requested permission for her courtship, the one condition Isabelle made without compromise was that she remain at the du Lac home. Because most bachelors had no desire to include a mother-in-law with the courtship, Isabelle remained single and had yet to experience so much as a kiss from any man.

When the door opened up without so much as a knock, both of the women knew right away who came to call. They stood up and wrapped their loving arms around their favorite person on earth, son and brother, Jacobi du Lac.

"It has been only a month and you came back!" Jacob's mother said with absolute elation and a tear in her eyes. "It is not like you to disappear for such a short amount of time!"

Isabelle said nothing, but had already rushed into Jacob's arms, holding him tight without mercy.

Katherine placed a loving hand on her son's shoulder. "Did you bring her?"

Jacob turned around just in time to see Marielle appear in the doorway.

The two other women enveloped Marielle's whole personage. They filled her full of questions. The most prominent question came from Isabelle.

"Jacobi said he might return with you. How long will you be able to stay this time?"

Marielle held Isabelle's arms with her own. "I thought you could use a sister. I have no other place I love in the world more than here with you—that is, when I'm not out questing with the boys!"

Three more figures appeared in the open doorway. The first two were Tuck and Balladin. "We've just been too good together to break up the Knights of the Sangrahl," Tuck said.

Isabelle looked longingly at Balladin, never forgetting the day he rescued her from Hadrian Shoebottom in the winery's basement. *Perhaps,* she thought to herself, *perhaps this one is the one I want!*

Annaquinn stood by Tuck. Having chosen him for her very own, the two of them had already had their wedding and would find a quaint, second-story home somewhere on the outreaches of La Bellaroche.

Annaquinn had no more interest in life at the sea and had sold her beloved ship, *The Rising Stargazer,* to her first mate for a very fair price. The sound of life in La Bellaroche intrigued her as much as it did Tuck. She fell in love for the second time in her life, and so did Tuck.

A fourth figure remained and was, in some opinions, the most important one in their midst.

Standing amid them all, with a silvery gray tail wagging, was Myra, the American Alsatian dog Marielle had adopted shortly after her return home. Almost a year in age and still very much a puppy, the dog would be the masthead of the life the Keepers had represented in over two thousand years.

In the populated village square, activities were buzzing to new heights. As the early autumn evening cast long shadows across the square, the town's inhabitants hung the banners, put the food fares on to roast, and lit the bonfires against the pending chill of night. Musicians tuned their instruments for the most anticipated of the activities, the dance.

The dance was a select choreography that demanded the interlocking of every hand in the village of each citizen before the dance was over. Each person moved in a weave formation symbolic of the harmony he or she shared with the others. The dance was the village's way of showing that, even with their differences; the people stood together like family, no matter what may come.

Even more important was the dance the Keepers and their knights had created through their once hopeless battle against the evils that befell every age for thousands of years. On this day, they could only hope that the light sent forth from a tiny vessel from heaven would forever change the hearts of selfish men and women throughout the ages.

This final thought was far from the minds and hearts of Tuck and Annaquinn as they joined hands together in the market square. Isabelle, Katherine, and Balladin were soon beside them just as the beat of the music began. Men's voices rang out with the words they knew well echoed in time by the women's lyrics.

Jacobi du Lac sat high on the wall overlooking the square. Next to him were Marielle and Myra, and the three watched the celebration with a joy that would fill the earth to capacity.

Marielle leaned into Jacob, placing both arms around his middle. His hand ran along her back, feeling the smooth fabric of her cream-colored dress, the same one Isabelle had given her.

"Are you happy, my love?" Jacob asked her.

"Never happier, my love. What about you, monsieur du Lac?"

"I believe that the light of the Sangrahl shines from your eyes. You bring all that is good to the world around you."

"No, Jake, this is just what it should be like for all people. May love and valor shine from them all."

The Dire Wolf Project's mission is to fill the emptiness in your life by providing everything a family needs to support a happy life for their American Alsatian dog.

To find out more or to join our email list, go to:

direwolfproject.com

Made in the USA
Las Vegas, NV
22 December 2021

39240124R00177